"A generational tale deftly written with penetrating insight, personality and feeling, *Burning of the Marriage Hat* is very highly recommended reading and would make an exceptional selection choice for women's reading groups."

—*The Midwest Book Review,*
Small Press Bookwatch

"This is a spell-binding and most poignant tale of a woman's search for the daughter she lost to adoption and the secrets she uncovers along the way."

—Joe Soll, CSW, author of
Adoption Healing…A Path to Recovery

"The denial of the existence of the problem of a pregnant teen, a theme in this book, is also a theme in life—an extremely interesting book."

—Susan Franzblau, PhD, host of
"Women's Voices, Women's Lives"
on NPR affiliate WFSS 91.9 FM

"What starts out as a novel about the author's journey back to her roots in Wyoming, turns into a catharsis as she deals with the drama of giving up her daughter for adoption in the 1960s before *Roe v. Wade*."

—Barrie-Louise Switzen, Executive Producer
"The Woman's Connection (sm)"

"This is a compelling account—both of the hardscrabble western frontier and of a modern day woman's quest for knowledge and healing. A remarkable book."

—Shelley Buck, former editor,
"Her Say News Service," San Francisco, CA

"The characters are real and the plot has a lot of 'what happens next?' The narrator Katherine comes to terms with a society which oppressed and dehumanized women by freeing the ghosts of her past."

—Jane Edwards, book reviewer, *CUB Communicator* (Concerned United Birth Parents)

"This was a wonderful book! It was beautifully written. The writer grabbed my attention by switching back and forth through time. I would recommend this book to everyone!"

—Barnes & Noble review

"A compelling novel about growing up in the 1960s in a middle class family in a small prairie town in Wyoming, *Burning of the Marriage Hat* describes the narrow-minded lifestyle one can encounter there. This book begs to be read in one sitting. Definitely a good read."

—Amazon.com review

"The book is totally engrossing. The author's mixture of the past and the present is very well done and she succeeds in portraying many characters in a truly enlightening manner. I especially appreciated her appealing descriptions of the Wyoming scenery."

—BookExpo, 2002 review

Based on the author's own account of coming of age in small town Wyoming on the cusp of the 1960s sexual revolution.

Burning

OF THE

Marriage Hat

Burning

OF THE

Marriage
Hat

A Novel of High Plains Women
Margaret Benshoof-Holler

WW
Wind Women Press
San Francisco, CA

In memory of Mother and Roger

and

for the six million

U.S. birthmothers

Let Love clasp Grief lest both be drowned,
Let darkness keep her raven gloss.
Ah, sweeter to be drunk with loss,
To dance with Death, to beat the ground.

From "In Memoriam A. H. H."
By Alfred, Lord Tennyson
(1809-1892)

Author's Note

Wyoming

Brown Rock, Wyoming and Eagle Mountain, Wyoming are fictionalized communities that portray small town life on the high plains during the 1960s and other key points in the 20th century. These towns are drawn from extensive research, travel, and the author's own upbringing in Wyoming during the 1950s and 60s. They help provide a picture of what life was like during the 60s and other eras for young girls and women in Wyoming, whose motto is the "Equality State" because that's where women first gained the right to vote and sit on juries in the U.S. The right to vote for women was granted in 1869 before Wyoming became a state. It was thought that such a law would attract more women to the state. Women in most of the rest of the country didn't gain the right to vote until the early 1920s. Wyoming's early suffrage act failed to attract many more women. Wyoming is still the most sparsely-populated state. Red Earth, Wind Peak, Fort Wind Peak, Gainesville, University of the Rocky Mountains, and Indian Mountain in Wyoming are also fictionalized places, as is Greenville, Iowa.

Medicine Lodge Creek in the Big Horn Mountains in Wyoming is an actual place, but the camping area where the narrator Katherine and daughter Cynthia and grandchildren Ben and Jeff went camping is made up. Medicine Lodge Creek is known for its Indian petroglyphs and pictographs, and for the human habitation site that was uncovered there in the late 1960s, a site that humans had continuously occupied for over 10,000 years. The Bighorn Mountains are one of many scenic and still unspoiled spots in the state. Ten Sleep, Wyoming was named by the Indians because it was "Ten Sleeps" from there to each of the main winter camps, one located near Casper, Wyoming and the other on the Clarks Fork River near Bridger, Montana.

Adoption History

Katherine, the narrator in this book, could be any of the six million birthmothers in the U.S. who have given their children up to the adoption system. Her story is similar to those of the approximately 250,000 women who each year during the 1960s relinquished their children to adoption in the U.S.

The large number of women who gave their children up for adoption began to decrease after the 60s. The number fell from 250,000 per year in the 60s to approximately 150,000 per year in the 1970s, 100,000 per year in the 1980s and 50,000 per year in the 1990s. In the year 2001, there were approximately 51,000 surrenders in the U.S. Fewer adoptions but still a great number considering the amount of money that passes hands in attorney-client adoption transactions where the approximate attorney fee runs around $30,000.

There were more adoptions in the 60s than there were in the year 2001 for a number of reasons. More teen-age girls and young women were getting pregnant 38 years ago because the birth control pill, relatively new on the market in the 60s, was not readily accessible until the mid- to late decade. Sex education classes were not part of the curriculum of most schools so girls did not know how to protect themselves. Few got abortions, which studies show are easier on a woman than giving a child up for adoption, because abortion was illegal. Before Roe v.

Wade, women basically had no choice except to get married or have the child and give it up for adoption. The societal taboo associated with being pregnant and unmarried forced women into hiding. Adoption was the logical sequence to keeping the pregnancy permanently hidden. In addition, most women were not considered adults and were not able to make legal decisions until they turned 21 since that was the legal age in most states in the 60s. Women who did marry were not able to sign for credit cards on their own or make legal decisions without the consent of their husbands.

Before the late 70s, unwed mothers were forced into hiding not only their pregnancies, but also their feelings of grief after they relinquished their children to adoption. An unwed mother went away to a maternity home, had the child one day, gave it up the next, then went back home where the subject was never brought up again in most families. The grieving process was not completed. Unlike when one loses a mother or father, sister or brother or a friend to death and there is a period of mourning, when a birthmother gives up a child to adoption, she has normally been expected to get on with her life and forget.

There has been no support system in place in the white community, as there has been in the African American community, for a single teenage girl to keep her child and raise it. Thus, few single white mothers in the United States have kept their children until more recently.

A small group of birthmothers who gave up their children for adoption started coming out of the closet in the 80s and speaking openly about what they had been through. Many found and reunited with their lost children. Many more began the searching process in the 90s. Still, even today many only talk with each other about what they went through in much the same way that veterans of World War II and Vietnam only talked afterwards with those who had gone through the same experiences. Similarly, a large number of birthmothers have suffered from a type of post-traumatic stress disorder, just like veterans of war.

Even though adoption is a more open process in the year 2002 than it was 30 or 40 years earlier, birth records are still closed in many U.S. states. This prevents adoptees from knowing their family histories and their real mothers and fathers. The closed system, in place since the Depression era, keeps birth certificates locked up tight and hidden as a way, they say, of protecting somebody somewhere. It's an antiquated system filled with a strong need to hide and keep people hidden.

Approximately one-hundred and forty million people in the U.S. have an adoption in their immediate families. Ingrained views and practices pertaining to loss, sex, out-of-wedlock pregnancies and adoption help keep many veiled and hidden. In respect to birthmothers and their children, the U.S. falls behind every other industrialized country, most of which have stopped separating the natural mother from her child after it is born except in extreme situations.

Burning

OF THE

Marriage

Hat

Prologue

1996

"Who's moving about at this ungodly hour," I wondered as I heard the floor creak outside my apartment door in San Francisco. I glanced at the clock. It said 3 a.m. Propping myself up in bed, I looked across towards the locked door. In the overstuffed chair by the head of my bed sat a red-headed woman in a rose-colored, shirt-waist cotton house dress, her hands clasped on her lap, her eyes set in a worried stare.

Terror held me strapped to the bed.

"I need your help, Katherine," the woman said.

The hair on my arms stood on end at the sound of my name. How did she know me? I looked at her again. Her body faded in and out like a television set with a short.

As I struggled to sit up, it hit me. This was a dead woman speaking to me.

Afraid that eye contact would draw me deeper into the world of the dead, I stared past her. I shivered and my heart pounded. Finally, I forced myself to look in the woman's direction. I tried to speak but the words wouldn't come as I sat frozen, caught in a strange world somewhere between reality and nightmare.

"Don't be afraid," the woman began.

"Who are you?" I finally forced the words out. My teeth chattered. Had the ghost heard my almost whispered words?

"I'm …" Then the woman's voice faded out. Static, like one might hear on a short-wave radio, rippled through the air.

She looked towards me. Was that compassion in her eyes? Her red hair fell in curls about her face. She reminded me of someone, but whom? She had red hair! Yes, that was it! She looked just like old photos of my grandmother Naomi.

I had been three or four playing around the kitchen door the first time I heard Mama and Papa mention Naomi in one of their shouting matches.

"Your father killed your mother," Mama accused Papa.

"It was an accident. I was thirteen. I remember," Papa retorted. His voice rose until I feared he might explode.

Those words stayed with me and I worried at them. Finally I asked Mama.

"What happened to my grandma?"

"She died."

"How did she die?"

"She died in a fire."

"Did someone kill her?"

"Hush! We don't talk about that," she told me and closed the subject.

From then on, I never asked, just sat back and observed Papa's volatility when the subject came up, took in the fear I felt from Mama each time he blew up. But I never forgot and the questions remained in my mind.

As I sat in my bedroom in San Francisco looking at my grandmother Naomi's ghost, I noted the intent set of her eyes and mouth.

"What do you want to tell me," I asked as I gained more courage.

Her mouth moved, but I couldn't hear her words.

I began to panic. I needed to know what the apparition wanted to tell me. But, I was losing her. Then, in between surges of magnetic electricity, I heard her say, "You... go...Wyoming..."

Did she want me to go to Wyoming? But why?

I had to strain to hear her as she continued to speak.

"It troubles me," she said. I leaned towards her to try to catch her next words. "The Lord will turn his eye again." Her voice faded then came through strongly, "on one of your broken family." The rest of her words trickled out into the night.

Did she mean that someone in my family was going to die? Who? I felt the sting of tears in my eyes.

I looked to the now empty chair.

I lay back on my bed shaken.

When I was growing up, my sisters and mother had heard and seen things that others couldn't see. Back doors slammed, lights flickered, and dog chains rattled in the middle of the night for unexplained reasons. But never when I was around. I thought that they were just afraid to be alone in the house, that they imagined it. That's what I thought each time I heard another story from some family member about a chair rocking next to their bed at night with no one in it, or a shadow passing through a hallway when all of the curtains were closed and no one else was at home.

All of that changed with the visit from the dead woman.

A week after Naomi's ghost visited me, my mother went to the doctor. When they x-rayed her lungs and found cancer, I remembered Naomi's ominous warning.

My mother was dying! A year later, I returned to Wyoming to bury her.

A year after my mother's death, I finally set out on the road to Brown Rock, Wyoming where my grandmother Naomi died. I was egged on by an apparition in a rose-colored housedress and determined to find out the truth about Naomi's burning.

Katherine

July 28, 1998
Unfinished business

$\mathcal{H}$eading east to Brown Rock on two-lane Highway 20, just off Interstate 25 in southeastern Wyoming, the wind blows dust and tumbleweeds across the highway. The car shakes.

It has been a wet year in Wyoming. Throughout the state there's been a tinge of green where there's usually gray and brown. Rain has been pouring for days up north near Riverton. The Wind River is flooding, wearing away firmly established chunks of land along its banks, revealing long-buried fossils. Down in the south just north of Cheyenne, there's wind as usual banging at windows, shaking doors, wearing away the psyches of housewives whose lives are governed by how strong the breezes that blow across Wyoming.

My shoulder blades and neck tighten painfully under the weight of the two-hundred mile trip from the western part of the state where my daughter and I just spent a week. But the journey has also given me time to think, to consider the big distance I've kept for 30 years between me and Wyoming, the most sparsely-populated U.S. state. That's where I grew up on the cusp of the sexual revolution.

Papa helped turn me into an idealist. Mama instilled good common sense among other things too numerous to mention.

The wide, open plains and high mountains of Wyoming shaped me into what folks here call a rugged individual.

The divorce of Evelyn Duran Geislingen and Leonard Geislingen, my mother and father, when I turned four forged the first craggy spots and created a large, empty space in my life.

Papa got into his pickup one day and drove away. I never saw him again until last year when I knocked on his door and he opened it to me. I had not seen him for over 40 years. He looked into my eyes and I looked back into his with the odd sensation that I was standing in front of a mirror.

"Hello Katherine," he said as he reached out and pulled me to him.

"Papa," I cried as I leaned towards him.

Puzzled and perplexed, his mouth puffed out as if he was going to cry. His eyes carried a type of sad wonder. When he stepped back and set those eyes in my direction, I felt like he could see right through me. But maybe he was just trying to decide whether I carried any of Mama in me.

He resembled the tin man from the Wizard of Oz only shorter and pudgier. He looked like his bones might creak. As far as brains, I thought of the scarecrow, not for lack of thought, but the slowness of movement that kept him from making the initial contact.

The deep brown eyes that looked into mine as I met him at the door that day stirred some deep memories. My whole life began to unfold as he took my hand and led me into the living room of his small two-bedroom tract house in Boise, Idaho.

* * *

As I drive along the highway to Brown Rock, I glance into the rearview mirror and see the same red pickup that has followed me since I turned off the Interstate now following me towards Brown Rock. A man in a cowboy hat and black glasses has eased his pickup within two car lengths of mine and stayed put for the last few miles now. I particularly note the two guns on a rack on top of the pickup.

A streak of fear puts my mind on alert. I have always appreciated the tanned muscular physiques of Wyoming's rugged male individualists. But I learned early that brawn mixed with brute is not a safe combination. Wyoming is a man's state. Too many men here have spent too much time doing masculine things like loading guns and killing deer. A lot of them have never learned how to communicate with a woman. A woman alone is an open invitation for some. I keep my eye on the cowboy hat and gun rack.

March 1953
Flashback

They moved in to the white frame house on Kerstein Avenue in Elk Mountain, Wyoming late one night while Katherine was sleeping. The next morning, a ray of sun reached in and woke her up.

"Mama! Mama! Where am I," she cried. She rubbed the sleep out of her eyes and gazed around the strange room with growing delight.

"We're in our new home," Mama said happily, coming into the small room.
Mama whisked her up and twirled her around.

"You're all sunshiny." Katherine grinned and stroked her mama's cheek.

"I'm making pancakes for breakfast," Mama said.

"Pancakes! Can I help?"

"You can sit at the table and watch."

Katherine followed Mama to the kitchen. Her three sisters—Carol, Sarah, and Linda—came running in.

"Mama! Papa! There's a ditch out in back," they cried, bouncing around the room in their excitement.

"Don't get too close!" Mama swung around and Katherine frowned as the sunshine began to fade. "How could you have moved us into a house with a ditch in back?"

"Why, it's just a small ditch." Papa shrugged as he sat down.

Carol, Sarah, and Linda skipped back outside.

"I'll have to watch those kids every minute for fear they'll drown." Mama looked out the window nervously before getting out the skillet to fry bacon.

Katherine sat on the table and watched Mama lay the strips of bacon in the skillet. She sensed, even at the age of four, that something had changed.

"You go out and watch them while I fix breakfast."

"They'll be okay. Hey, you kids," Papa yelled, "don't get too close to the ditch. Play up here by the house."

Nevertheless, he wandered outside to watch the girls. Katherine followed, keen to see this ditch for herself. It wound its way through the back yard with nothing more than a small little trail of water. To her delight a wood bridge went across the top near a fence.

"There's only a trickle of water in that ditch," Papa announced when he went back in. "Those kids aren't going to drown in a little trickle of water." He sat down at the table waiting for breakfast. "That's all that goes through there any time of year. Just a little trickle of water."

"Well, maybe it will be okay then."

Katherine watched for the sunshine to come back. After a moment she sighed and turned to the pancakes on the plate before her.

July 28, 1998
The cowboy

*W*hat's the cowboy in that red truck waiting for, I wonder, as I glance into the rearview mirror again and see him still tailing me? He's had plenty of opportunity to pass. Out for a leisurely drive? Or is he a stalker? The sight of those guns on the rack atop his pickup make me uneasy.

I hope I don't have engine trouble or a flat tire out here in the middle of nowhere. I'm not sure I'd want to open my doors or windows to him. I hit the automatic lock button just to be on the safe side.

April 1953
Flashback

Katherine played among the trees as Mama hung the clothes on the clothesline out in the back yard. She watched a red ladybug crawl across a green blade of grass. She lay on her back on the ground watching a cloud drift across the sky. As the sun traveled in the sky, a shadow fell across her face and slowly moved until Katherine was totally covered. Mama had long since gone inside.

"Katherine! Katherine! Come on in. Supper's ready."

She went inside to find the whole family already sitting around the table. Mama, Papa, Carol, Sarah, and Linda. Everybody waited as Katherine sat down on her chair. Mama chattered as she served up the mashed potatoes.

"The kids and I went to the park today."

"Oh you did? Did you kids have a good time?"

"Papa! I saw a robin!"

"A robin? Did the robin go bob-bob-bobbin?"

"What's 'bobbin'?"

"It's what robins do."

"This robin didn't bobbin. It hopped in the grass and caught a worm."

Papa lifted a cup of coffee to his lips and smiled.

"I fixed the cabinets over at the Nietson's today. They said I did such a good job they want me to come back and build all new cabinets for them."

Everyone was talking and laughing.

"I saw some wallpaper today that I thought I'd buy," Mama laughed.

"You what? Hell, we can't afford no god-damned wallpaper. I thought we already talked about this! Yer always wantin' ta buy somethin' new and ya know we can't afford it!"

Katherine covered her ears as his voice got louder.

"It was on sale! And with this new work you're doin', I thought we could afford some wallpaper." Mama raised her voice to match his.

"I don't care if it was on sale. We can't even afford to buy the kids clothes and yer out buyin' wallpaper."

Katherine tensed. Somehow this was different. Then, all of a sudden, Mama was talking about something else.

"You're treating me just like your dad did your mother."

"Hell! What do ya mean? I'm not anything like my dad!" Papa yelled. "Don't go accusing me of bein' like my dad!"

"You're just like him. And we both know what happened to your mother!"

Papa jumped up from the table, grabbed Mama and pushed her across the room and up against the wall. He knocked his fist into the wall around her head. Katherine's eyes grew round at the sight of the big holes where his fist had hit.

Mama began to cry.

"Don't hurt her! Don't hurt Mama!" Katherine cried and tears rolled down her chubby cheeks.

"Shut that kid up!" Papa yelled.

Katherine tried to stop crying but she was too frightened. Her sister Sarah picked her up and sat her down on her little chair in the living room.

Katherine sobbed and screamed until Mama finally came. She refused to be comforted. "I want Papa. I want to talk to Papa," she sobbed. Mama went back to the kitchen.

"She wants you."

"Hell, I won't talk to her while she's crying. Shut her up!"

Katherine took a deep breath and a moment later, Papa squatted down next to her.

"I hear you want to talk to me."

"I don't want to talk to you. I'm mad at you! I'm never talkin' to you again."

"I'm sorry."

Katherine hung her head in silence.

"Are ya still mad at yer papa?"

"Yeah!"

"I'm sorry, Katherine. Why don't ya come on to bed and let me tell ya a bedtime story. How about 'The Three Bears?'"

"I want 'Jack in the Beanstalk.'"

"Okay then."

The next day everything seemed just the same as it had been. Katherine ran around the yard as Mama, dressed in a red-checkered, short-sleeved dress that blew in the wind, hung the clothes. She giggled as Mama laughed and sang in the sunshine.

July 28, 1998
The cowboy

As I drive, I keep a close eye on the cowboy in the red pickup behind me. Why is he tailing me? Now he's flashing his lights at me. I have to get away from him because I don't know what he might do. Maybe he won't do anything. Maybe he's just having a little fun. Wyoming men have a tendency to go after a woman.

"Hey honey, ya sure are cute! Ya want ta come on over here and keep a lonely boy company!" That's the kind of thing I used to hear from these guys when I was growing up here. They see an attractive unattached woman and they start whistling and making cat calls. I never knew how to deal with it then. And now, it scares me.

This must be how my grandmother Naomi felt out here. Mama, too, before she died last year must have sensed that she lived in an environment hostile to women.

Man, the hunter. Woman, the hunted. I had forgotten that's how the male and female roles go out here. But, it's starting to come back to me.

1953

Muskmelon won't grow in Wyoming

"Now you kids can each choose one thing to plant in the garden this year. You let me know and I'll buy the seeds."

"I want zucchini!"

"I'll plant tomatoes."

"I like carrots."

Katherine listened as her sisters chose crops that would do quite well in the short three-month Wyoming growing season.

"I want to plant muskmelon," she told her dad.

"She can't do that," Mama said. "It won't grow here."

"If she wants to plant muskmelon, let her plant muskmelon. It never hurts to try. That's what my mom taught me. And she did pretty well with plantin' and harvestin' in her time."

So Papa went out and bought the seeds. He hoed the ground and Katherine put the seeds in.

"Muskmelon isn't known to grow in Wyoming," Papa warned her.

"Then why are we plantin' it?"

"Because ya said ya wanted muskmelon and I thought it might be worth a try."

"If I water it, will I have muskmelon, Papa?"

"Maybe. We'll see."

"Katherine's planting muskmelon!"

Carol, Sarah and Linda laughed and made fun of her after she put the seeds in the ground and covered them up. "Nothing is ever going to grow there!"

"Yes it will! Yes it will!" Katherine stomped her foot defiantly.

Her sisters' plants came up very quickly. Though Katherine watered her plot every day, she saw no sign of muskmelons. She was still waiting the night the lawyer arrived at their house.

"The lawyer's here," her oldest sister Carol whispered. "They're gittin divorced tonight."

"What's divorce?" Katherine asked.

"Well, it means that Mama's gonna leave him."

"She's gonna leave him? Where's she goin'?"

"I don't know."

"I don't want my Mama to leave!"

"Shh! She's not leavin'. Papa's the one who will go."

"Papa's leavin'? I don't want Papa to leave!"

"Shhh! They'll hear you."

Katherine struggled against the hand that suddenly clamped over her mouth.

Carol let go and they stood at the door oh so quietly and listened. Not one of them breathed.

Suddenly there was shuffling of feet in the living room.

Katherine looked at her sisters. They were no longer laughing. They looked sad and scared.

"Git the hell out of my house you god-damned lawyer, and don't ever come back," she heard Papa yell.

Then Katherine heard a door slam and it was quiet in the living room. She didn't know what they were doing or where Mama went. Katherine and her sisters listened awhile longer. Then they went to bed.

Katherine was still waiting for her muskmelons when she and Mama and her sisters moved.

Perhaps she should have listened to Mama who said, "let this be a lesson to you. In the future, don't plant muskmelon seeds unless you're sure that your dad will be there to help you harvest."

Instead, she held onto the lesson Papa learned from his mother Naomi: it never hurts to try the impossible.

July 28, 1998
The cowboy

$\mathcal{I}$ keep my eye on the rearview mirror on the way to Brown Rock. I can't go much over 65 out here on two-lane asphalt. I try to put distance between me and the red pickup but when I speed up, so does he. He's acting like a teenage kid, almost like he's playing a game of chicken.

Some guys who live out here in the middle of the Wyoming plains don't learn how to relate to a woman. Some are better off with a horse and some cows that they can rope, tackle, and tie up.

Something about the cowboy makes me think of my grandfather Sam, Naomi's husband. He must have chased after women in much the same way, making him look like a man who loved women. In reality, he was probably too emotionally isolated to know how to treat them. Just the impression I got from listening to Papa.

Another car passes him and comes between his truck and my car. A buffer of safety for awhile at least.

August 1953

Loss

"Where's Papa," Katherine asked her mom after they moved to the new house.

"He's workin'," Mama said.

"When's he comin' home?"

"I don't know. He'll be here soon."

But Papa never came.

Katherine walked up and down the street outside of their new house waiting for his pickup to come home.

"Does Papa know where we live?" she asked.

"Yes, he does," Mama answered.

"Maybe he's not able to find us. Maybe he doesn't know where we are."

"He knows where we are. I told him."

"Oh." Katherine thought about that for a moment. Her lip trembled. "I miss Papa! I miss Papa!"

"Hush. He's gone. And I want you to stop that crying and git in here and help me stir this pudding. I don't want any more talkin' about yer dad!"

Katherine wiped her tears as she stood on the chair in front of the stove and helped Mama stir.

"Can we plant muskmelon here, Mama?" Katherine asked as she stirred.

"Muskmelon doesn't grow here, Katherine."

"But Papa let me grow it!"

"I don't know what yer dad told you. But he was wrong. And we're not plantin' muskmelon. Besides, it's not time for plantin' gardens. It's practically fall."

The next summer Mama planted flowers.

And Papa never came.

July 28, 1998
Summertime on the high plains

$\mathcal{T}$he cowboy's pickup reminds me of how I used to watch every day for Papa to come back to us. Funny how after all of this time my emotions still stir, tears form in my eyes, when I say those few words. "He never came."

I glance back into the rearview mirror and see the buffer car is still there between me and the cowboy. I stick to the speed limit, hoping the car behind me will stay put. But already it's on my tail waiting for the double line to break so it can pass.

I glance out across the Wyoming landscape. I wish I had known when I was young how therapeutic driving across the plains can be. They absorb unresolved conflict like water from the surf on a beach. The perfect place to let one's mind wander since there's nothing else to do to break the tedium out here.

It's summertime now in Wyoming. The hillsides are green. If muskmelon were to grow here, it would be opening its leaves now.

The hills are alive with yellow and red flowers. If Mama were alive, her flowers would be in bloom now, too. But she's gone. Her absence makes me feel the loss of mother, father, family.

The sun bathes the Wyoming high plains and sagebrush in a golden afternoon glow just like the sunshine that used to shine from Mama's face before Papa left us.

"Papa! Papa! Papa!" The sound echoes across the land.

The shadow of a cloud passes across the prairie. I feel a sudden chill as I remember Naomi's ghost and feel her presence near me.

July 27, 1998

Ghosts

"*W*hooo! Whooo! Whooo!" The trains blew their whistles long into the night, once, then again farther down the line, then again in the distance across the Wyoming plains as I lay sleeping in the motel room. Like the ghosts of my ancestors, the train whistles seemed to speak with urgency.

"I will show you, I will show you where to go!"

The voice came to me as I lay in bed on the verge of sleep. It was a familiar voice, the voice of a woman with a rasp, with a catch—a deep voice but not too deep. I knew I had heard it before somewhere. But where?

I didn't know who the woman was when I first opened my eyes. She looked different than the woman who visited me in San Francisco. She looked a little bit like Mama—a woman who had some unresolved conflict. A lady with regrets about life's events.

Her voice came like a prelude. Though I waited for more words from the apparition as I lay in bed at the motel last night, nothing came. *I'll show you where you need to go,* she told me. I had a feeling that this wouldn't be the last time I heard her speak. What did she want me to know?

July 28, 1998
The cowboy

The buffer car catches up and passes just after I turn a curve on the way to Brown Rock. Now, the cowboy's red pickup is behind me again probably ten car lengths back.

The light ricochets off the cowboy's windshield like a flame blinding my vision for a moment as I look at it in the rearview mirror. It was a flame that killed my grandmother, I remember as I speed up to get away from the cowboy.

Brown Rock 20 miles, a sign says.

I flip on the radio.

"This is cowboy land and we're gonna give ya some good old country and western music!"

September, 1997

Papa

$\mathcal{K}$atherine sat and watched Papa light cigarette after cigarette in his living room in Boise. He belonged to the Christian Church, she knew, and they didn't believe in dancing and smoking and women flaunting themselves; but Katherine suspected he liked setting rules for other people more than following them himself.

"Do ya want some coffee?"

"Sure. I'll take some."

Once Katherine and Papa had their coffee, he began to chain smoke. He must not feel comfortable talking about his past life, she thought as she watched him.

"I finished high school two years before I married yer mom. She was only seventeen and never did git her high school education," he said. "So when I decided to divorce her, I guess it had somethin' to do with the fact that she wasn't as educated as I was."

"You divorced her?" Katherine stared at him, trying to understand the look on his face.

"Yeah." He took another puff off his cigarette.

"That's not what the divorce record says."

"Well, I don't know what the divorce record says. But yer mom lied like crazy during the divorce proceedings." His voice suddenly grew agitated and his fingers shook as he lifted his cigarette to his mouth.

"What do you mean, 'she lied'?"

"She lied about what happened."

"Could you be more specific?"

"Hell! Read the papers!"

"I did."

Those papers stated that "*on September 7, 1953, Leonard Geislingen knocked Evelyn Geislingen down because she served chicken instead of roast beef. Then he grabbed her by the throat and threw her across the room.*"

Katherine had found the divorce records in an old trunk at Mama's house just after Mama died, two months before her visit to Papa's.

"What did she say that was a lie," Katherine asked Papa.

Papa looked like someone had hit him when she asked the question. He threw his hands up in the air and left the room.

When he came back, Katherine asked again.

"It's over and done with and I'm not talkin' about it anymore."

Katherine sighed but other thoughts crowded in and demanded expression.

"When I was four years old, I used to watch for your black pickup to come. I waited by the front door every day but you never came."

"My pickup was red! I never had a black pickup!"

"I remember a black pickup."

Katherine sighed again. A word or two of understanding or sympathy would have helped heal the wounds she carried with her since she was a child. But he chose to fight about the color of the truck instead.

"I had it painted dark blue," he suddenly blurted out as if he had just realized the significance of what she had said.

Katherine just shook her head. She thought about how long she had waited for Papa to return and of all of the pickups that she had waited for since.

July 28, 1998
Strong physical magnetism

*R*oad construction begins just after Gainesville on the way to Brown Rock. I come up behind a caterpillar and slow down to a crawl and eventually a complete stop. A car coming from the other direction keeps me from passing. The cowboy pulls up behind me. He takes off his sunglasses and smiles and raises his hand in a wave. Black hair frames the kind of face that could make money in Hollywood. I'm not impressed. I ignore him.

I've never been won over by a pretty face. Well, maybe once. My first love Joe, with his dark brown eyes, dark hair, olive skin, and muscular physique, definitely fit into the category of one with strong physical magnetism.

My grandfather, too, had the type of look that attracted women, I remember Mama telling me. This reminds me of the lingering question—Why has the cowboy been following me? I glance back in the rearview mirror and have the distinct feeling I've seen him somewhere before. But, where?

September, 1997

Papa

"*M*y mom liked to work in the earth," Papa told her as they sat in his kitchen.

"Take any Oxford tomato and move it away from its native Iowa soil to a climate like Wyoming, and in three years time she'd acclimatize the plant by shortening its growing season. She could git anything to grow anywhere."

Katherine's ears perked up.

"Even muskmelon in Wyoming?"

"Well yeah. Sure. Ya remember that, do ya?"

"Sure. That's why I'm here."

He smiled as he went on with his story.

"In Wyoming, we had a big garden. Dad helped some but mom and us kids did most of the work to keep it goin'."

As she sat and listened, Katherine felt she had missed a lot by not knowing the Geislingens, Papa's family. They bonded. They went through life and death and marriage and children and birthing, sorrow and pain, love and happiness, and life's changes together. And they probably planted muskmelon.

"My mom died in the 30s. I guess she was about 45," Papa told her. "Her dying left a big void in all of our lives."

"Even your dad's?" she felt like asking, but didn't.

Her parents' divorce in the 1950s cut the family apart again, she thought as she listened. It wiped out all memory of the Geislingens for Katherine and her sisters.

"How old were you when your mom died?"

A pained look flashed across Papa's eyes as he put out his cigarette and went to the kitchen for more coffee.

When he came back to finish his story, he seemed to be slumped over and the tone of his voice had changed.

"I was thirteen when she died. But I remember an awful lot about my mom. I can tell you all about her house and how she kept her kitchen," he said.

"Was it similar to Mama's?"

"Hell, they were as different as night and day."

*   *   *

"Dirty pots and pans and dishes filled the sink and every last inch of counter space in my mom's kitchen. Flour and crumbs covered the floor. Our feet stuck to the bubbled linoleum where someone had spilled milk or juice. A crust of baked-in grease lined the pans my mom baked her bread in seven times a week. Food still sat on plates two hours after people had gotten up and left the breakfast table."

How could he remember all of those details? Katherine wondered as she listened.

"Yer mom would have had a fit if dishes were left on the table!"

Yes, she would have, thought Katherine.

"But that's how my mother did things," he continued. "When ya have twelve kids to watch after, cookin' and laundry to be done, a garden to tend to, you set priorities. Clearin' the breakfast dishes from the table wasn't at the top of her list."

The next morning Katherine took a look at the countertops in his kitchen and noted not a crumb anywhere. He must have married another woman like Mama who valued cleanliness. He must also value it to some degree if he married two women with the same cleaning habits.

In Mama's kitchen, things had been set just so, Katherine remembered. On a trip home to Wyoming a year before visiting Papa, she noticed blue mats on the kitchen table. A complementing blue rug lay on the floor. Blue Dutch windmills and birds were lined up in a white china cabinet. Mama still cooked in the old iron pots she got when she married Papa in 1940. She still baked cakes and cookies in the same pans she used in the 60s. They had no burned bottoms. Everything was spotlessly clean in Mama's kitchen.

* * *

Grandmother Naomi must have been just as strongly stubborn as Mama, Katherine thought as she sat and listened to Papa recount what he knew about his mom.

Strong and stubborn women, at least that's how most people became out on the wide, open plains. They did things their own way.

"You should put a hundred-watt bulb in your lamp sockets so you can read," Katherine remembered telling Mama on a visit home two years before she died. "That bulb is too weak and it's not good for your eyes."

"I like it this way," she'd answered.

This was how it was between Katherine and Mama. She did things one way. Katherine did them another. Whenever Katherine went to visit, Mama always made her feel that she was causing trouble.

That must have been how Papa felt, too, Katherine thought as she sat and watched Papa sip his coffee.

"How would your mother have reacted if someone had gone to her house and tried to clear the breakfast dishes from the table?" Katherine asked.

"Hell, I can almost hear her saying it now. Every time my grandmother, my dad's mom, came to visit, there would be a big row because she always tried to clear the dishes and clean up as soon as we finished eatin'. 'That's not how we do things here and we're not goin' to go changin'. We have other chores to do that are more important. We gotta git the mornin's pickin' done,' my mom would yell across the kitchen as we sat eating breakfast. 'The tomata's are gonna spoil on the vine if we don't git em in soon. N' the peas are ready ta pick. Somebody's gotta milk the cow. N' I need to git this bread in the oven. So let's git goin'.' That's what my mom used to say," he grinned. "This would send my grandmother into a tizzy. My grandma was pretty much like your mom."

Naomi probably struggled in Wyoming with the western attitude that catered to men and alienated women.

Mama, on the other hand, believed that men, like God, reigned over hearth and home. She knew how to cater to every man that walked through the front door of her house in Wyoming.

And me? Katherine wondered. Split down the middle, half flower child and half product of the wide, open spaces of Wyoming, the Equality State. I never learned to cater to men.

July 28, 1998
Fear of men

$\mathcal{G}$lancing back at the cowboy, who's now staring at me, I remember how afraid I sometimes felt growing up on the high plains of the West.

I must have absorbed Mama's fear of men, the fear that she learned being married to Papa. The fear that she never talked about as she looked after her men.

She was afraid of Papa. And Papa probably got his streak of violence from his dad, my grandfather Sam. So it must have been Sam that we've all been afraid of.

Construction work continues. The caterpillar ahead of me shows no sign of moving. I glance into the rearview mirror and see the line of traffic building up behind me. The cowboy sticks his head out the window and impatiently yells something into the wind.

Another cloud passes across the sun leaving a shadow. I shiver as the thought begins to crystalize—perhaps the cowboy is my grandfather reincarnated.

I turn the radio on to pass the time. Rush Limbaugh's voice rails out about the destruction of the American family. I quickly flip it off and allow my thoughts to drift.

September, 1997

Papa

"*L*ife wasn't easy for my mom out in Iowa before she moved to Wyoming," Papa told her. "But she never knew no different. That's just the way things was. My mom cooked over wood-burning heat, cleaned, and did all her wash on a scrub board and later in an old ringer washer. She ironed all the family's clothes with a flat iron kept hot on the stove, canned 2,000 quarts of produce a year, and made two or three loaves of bread seven times a week from a sourdough starter. Yer mom had it a lot easier. Well, maybe not in the beginning when we were struggling to make ends meet. But she had a few more conveniences than my mom."

"Did that affect your mom's outlook on life," Katherine asked.

"My mom came of age in the late 1800s. She wouldn't have approved of a lot of the things that are happenin' today."

"Like what things?"

"Oh hell, like free love, men and women livin' together without bein' married."

Did he know something about her hippy life of the 60s and early 70s, Katherine wondered? Did he know about her daughter? Maybe her sister had told him. She sat back and listened, hoping that he would reveal what he knew.

Mama was like Naomi, Katherine thought. She didn't believe in a woman taking her pants down to a man until she had a ring firmly set on her left hand finger.

She wanted to ask Papa if he and Mama had had sex before they were married. But she was afraid such a question might shove him over the edge.

"We were livin' in Iowa when we got our first crank up telephone. We got a radio when we moved ta Wyoming. It had a set of earphones that she'd plug in and listen to all kinds of things that was happening in the world. I think she only saw one movie in her whole life. My oldest brother took her to see a Charlie Chaplin movie after we moved to Wyoming."

"Other than the modern conveniences that began to trickle into our lives, things were pretty hard for my mom. She never had time for anything other than working. She took in ironing and she took in borders. This was just as the Depression was beginning."

As Katherine sat and listened, she recalled that Mama was not even 10 when the stock market crashed and a lot of people lost everything they had. It instilled a tightness that made her Mama hold onto every penny. Was Naomi like that, she wondered?

"My mom had an old coffee can in the kitchen where she put every penny. That's where she found money to buy us clothes, which didn't happen often."

"Did your mom ever get to do anything frivolous?" But Katherine knew the answer to that. So she added, "I guess church must have been the place she went to socialize."

"My mom didn't go to church regularly. But she had a much deeper reverence for things spiritual than my dad who went to church every Sunday."

Katherine sat amazed. She had him pegged as a religious fanatic. Perhaps he had a broader vision after all, she thought.

July 28, 1998
The Depression

*A*s dust blows up from the construction work on the road to Brown Rock, I remember how hard the Depression years were for Mama's family in Wyoming.

They never had a car. They usually had to walk to town to school unless they took the school bus. Her mom used to fill up an old wood tub with water heated on the stove for the whole family to take baths in on Saturday night. Mama learned from her mother to be very tight with money.

Perhaps that's why she came down so hard on me about every little thing while I was growing up. She never did understand me and my generation or how we had such an abundance of material possessions and more life choices than she had growing up.

I look out across the plains as my car idles and I wait for the construction work to finish. People out here become gnarled just like the sagebrush when the wind hits it. The cowboy? Well, some men out here remain like kids, just like my grandfather must have been.

December, 1953

The curtain falls

*E*ach afternoon Katherine played out in the yard until Papa's pickup came barreling down the street. Each day he would get out, pick Katherine up and twirl her through the air in his arms.

"How's my girl?"

"Papa! Papa! I saw a squirrel today!"

"A squirrel? And what did he say?"

"He said that spring is comin' and he wants to come inside and live with me. Is it okay Papa? Is it okay?"

"I don't know. A squirrel might have a hard time livin' inside. He's probably happier livin' out where he can find nuts and things."

"Really?"

"Yeah. But you can watch him out here."

"Okay."

But then the clouds raced across the sky to blot out the light like curtains coming down on act one. Papa left.

*   *   *

Act two of their lives found Katherine taking on an entirely different part.

"For God so loved the world that he gave his only son…"

The congregation was singing that song the day that Katherine and Mama and her sisters walked into the church and plopped themselves down on a wooden pew near the back. Katherine stood up on the pew to stare at a man near the front. He wore a khaki military uniform and stood very straight as though he had a baseball bat holding up his spine. She liked the look of him.

"That's Clark Helman, the preacher's son," the woman behind her whispered, seeing her interest.

Katherine stuck her thumb in her mouth and kept looking.

Could this be the son that God gave so freely? Was he the man they were singing about?

He was standing with the woman preacher shaking people's hands at the door when she walked out of the church.

"Are you a soldier?" she asked as he took Mama's hand.

"I was. And who are you?" he asked as he leaned down and took her hand to shake it.

She grabbed it back and stuck her thumb in her mouth and wouldn't answer.

So he stood up and started talking to Mama.

"We're havin' chicken for dinner," Katherine announced, moving close to be sure he heard her.

"Chicken!"

"Yeah. Do you want some?"

"Is that an invitation?"

She looked up at Mama who laughed and blushed.

"Yer welcome if yer not doin' anything."

So just a short time later he sat at their dining room table with Katherine on his lap making a wish as each pulled their side of the wishbone.

"We have to let it dry a bit before we make the wish," Clark told her.

Katherine waited for a whole hour after they ate before they got to make their wishes.

"Is it dry enough now," she asked him every 15 minutes.

Finally, he said "okay."

"Do ya wanna know my wish," she asked him?

"If ya want yer wish to come true, ya need to keep it secret," he told her.

So she did.

Five months later, her wish came true as Mama and this man stood in front of the church with their hands on a bible.

"Do you take this woman to be your wife, in sickness and in health till death do you part?" Clark's mother, the woman preacher, asked.

"I do," the man's response.

"I now pronounce you man and wife."

"Clark Helman weds Mrs. Geislingen," the announcement in the local paper said.

"She could have said, 'Clark Helman weds Evelyn Geislingen'. Clark's mother wrote the announcement that way from spite," was the local gossip.

July 28, 1998
Connection to God

A cool breeze blows as one lane of traffic begins to move after waiting for half an hour for a caterpillar to move a rock from one side of the road to the other. On the road to Brown Rock, I idle along at 15 miles per hour. I slowly head over the hill with the cowboy still tailing me. The Wyoming breeze blows construction dust through my open window.

I wouldn't describe Wyoming people as spiritual. I imagine most are hard workers who make a living and save every penny in much the same way as folks did during the Depression years. Any type of spirituality here gets exhibited by going to church and singing hymns on Sunday. That's the extent of it.

The Wyoming cowboy who spends most of his life outdoors probably has more connection to God than some of those who find solace on a church pew on Sundays. It was my grandfather Sam who went to church. Naomi stayed home.

I glance back into the mirror at the cowboy and try to imagine what type of cowboy he might be. The "for show" type? Or is he a serious wrangler?

1953
Flashback

She fell in love with him when he came courting Mama—his convertible, romantic air and smile. She needed a papa and he was there.

"What would you like me to call you?" Katherine had planned to call him Papa.

But, "He's not our dad. We're going to call him Clark," her sisters Carol, Sarah and Linda had told her. So she needed to be sure calling him "Papa" was okay.

"What do you want to call me?"

"Maybe it's not okay to call him Papa," she thought as she stood there in the bathroom door watching him shave. "I'll call you Clark," she told him shyly as she turned her heel back and forth on the floor. Then she ran into the other room and cried.

* * *

"Why are you and Mama holding hands," Katherine asked Clark soon after he married Mama .

"We just like to do that," he told her.

"Do you call that fucking?"

"Uh, what did you say?"

"Do you call that fucking?"

Clark laughed nervously.

"Where did you learn that word?" Mama turned white and looked very solemn.

Immediately Katherine knew that she had said something wrong.

"I don't know. I just heard it somewhere when I was out playin'."

"What kids were you playin' with?"

"I don't remember."

"Did your friend Mandy use that word?"

"I guess it was her that said it."

"When did she say it?"

"She said that she and her boyfriend Tommy had fucked. But I didn't know what it was."

"I don't want you playing with her anymore," Mama told her.

"But why? Is fucking bad?"

"I don't want you using that word! And I don't want you learnin' stuff from her that yer too young to be learnin'."

"But Mama, Mandy's the same age that I am!"

"She's too young to be doin' what she's doin'! Heaven's, I'm gonna have to call her mom and tell her," she turned to comment. "I don't want you playin' with her."

"But, Mama, there's no one else to play with!"

"You can play with yer sisters."

"They don't want me playin' with them."

"Hey you kids. You let Katherine play with you."

"Aw mom, do we have to?"

"Yes you do. And if there's any trouble, I'll hear about it."

Katherine hung her head and tried to find some new friends.

1956

On Sunday morning, Katherine sat on a stool while her older sister Sarah tried to get a comb through the tangle of knots in her hair.

"Ouch! You're hurting me," she cried.

"You need to start combin' your hair more often like your sisters," Mama said as she watched the battle.

"I don't want to," Katherine cried and ran outside.

She could feel Mama's eyes watching as she hopped on her bike and rode without hands up and down the street. When she saw Carol, Sarah, and Linda come out of the house in their felt skirts and white buck shoes, she knew it was time to go to church. Church was where they had to put up a front.

"Just as I am, oh lamb of God I come."

The final song began to play as the preacher invited "that one lost soul who needs to come to the Lord today" up to the front to be saved.

It was right at that point that Katherine began to get a knot in her stomach. Things remained incomplete in Katherine's life after Papa left. She felt alone. The church where they went every Sunday provided no comfort like the Sunday school teacher told her that Jesus did. Maybe if she went to the front of the church and got saved, the church people would accept her and give her what she lost when Papa left.

Did Carol and Sarah and Linda feel it, too?

No one in her family moved. They had to pretend like they were lily white to belong to that church. During the week, they pretty much did what they wanted. But they had to be careful when they went to a movie because someone from the church might see them.

They went home after church and sat down at the table to eat. Then out of the blue, her stepfather Clark started in on one of his stories.

"We move into the shore, get approximately 450 yards, and there's an explosion. A 500-pound bomb hits our tank. Our right front suspension is blown completely out. The tank is worthless. Three men dead."

Katherine, trying to understand, frowned. "Where were the tanks?" she asked.

"Where we were fightin'," he responded.

"Where was that?"

"The island of Wake."

"Clark. Stop making up those stories," Mama told him.

A look of hurt and confusion passed through Clark's eyes.

"I want to hear them," Katherine told him, sidling up close to him.

The next day he came home from work after they had all eaten, and Katherine went to stand in the bathroom doorway as he shaved.

"I got a good grade for reading."

"You did?"

"Yeah. Do you want to see my report card?"

"I sure do. Bring it in to the kitchen and I'll look at it while I'm eating."

But when she took it to the kitchen table, he and Mama were arguing.

"Leave the report card and I'll look at it in a bit."

Katherine stared at him for a moment. Then, with a sigh she went to her room and threw herself on her bed.

1958

"Sarah's got a boyfriend," Linda announced as the whole family was driving home from the store one night.

"Sarah's got a boyfriend?"

"No, I don't."

"Yes, you do."

"So you've got a boyfriend. Are you going to go out and let him fill you up with coke so that he can take you out in his car and squeeze it out of you?" Clark asked Sarah as he chuckled out of the side of his mouth while he drove down the street with his hat cocked on the side of his head.

"How is he going to squeeze it out of her?" Katherine wanted to know so she leaned over from the backseat to quiz him.

"Clark! Don't talk like that!" Katherine felt a shadow fall as Mama turned around on her seat.

Clark laughed. "Hey, don't you know that's what those boys do."

"How is he going to squeeze the coke out of her?" Katherine kept asking.

"Just like they all do."

"Is it like milking a cow?"

"Hush Katherine! And Clark, I told you to stop talking like that and I mean it." Mama glared at him.

Katherine sat back on the seat and absorbed what was happening. Mama thought Clark was doing something wrong. Maybe he was.

She looked at Sarah and noted that she was frowning and scrunched down on the seat. It looked like she was crying.

"He talks dirty and it makes me feel creepy," Sarah told her later.

The next time that Clark started in, Katherine noticed that Sarah left the room. So Katherine followed.

*_**

July 28, 1998
Beginning of rebellion

I don't have to wonder what Mama would think of me driving alone. She told me often enough. "I don't understand where you got your independent streak. I was never like that," she told me. Is that the gleam of a ring on his finger I see?

I came of age as the sexual revolution was beginning. It hadn't reached Wyoming yet, but the generation gap had. I was a daughter who was beginning to stand up in rebellion against her mothers' norms. As I entered adolescence, you might say I was in the pre-explosive stage where my hormones began to change but the culture that I was living in remained stagnant. Those two things slowly started working against each other until things hit a head. Then I did everything I could to shock her, to let her see that I would be following my own path. As Mama saw it, I had only one future—to get married.

If grandmother Naomi had been around at the time, things would have been different. Mama and Papa would have stayed together. I wouldn't be on the road to Brown Rock now looking for clues about what happened, wondering about the fire that killed Naomi. I push my foot down on the gas pedal eager to get to my destination and unveil the truth.

1961

Flashback

"*I* must have some rare disease," Katherine thought in panic when she first saw the blood. She wadded up some tissue and put it in her underpants to absorb the flow. Later when she took off her panties, she stuffed them into a pile of dirty clothes in the hamper to hide them from Mama. The book, *For Girls Only*, appeared on Katherine's pillow along with a sanitary belt and a box of sanitary napkins a few days after she found the blood.

The book and sanitary items raised more questions.

"What in the hell is this?" Katherine wondered as she dangled the sanitary belt in the air.

"Did you find the book?" her older sister Sarah asked her one evening after dinner.

"Yeah."

"Do you have any questions?"

"Yeah. How do I use these things?"

"Well, you use the safety pins to hook the end of the sanitary napkin to the belt," her sister explained as she turned red.

Katherine sensed her sister was embarrassed. So she asked her very little. She never heard a word from Mama.

"Wait until your wedding night," was the message she received from Mama via her older sister Sarah.

"What do you mean, 'wait until my wedding night'," she asked.

"Just save yourself until your wedding."

"Save myself? From what?"

"You don't want to do anything with a guy until you're married."

"Do? What would I do with a guy? Do you mean that I shouldn't kiss a guy until I'm married?"

"No, it's okay to kiss him. Just don't do anything more."

"Oh." Katherine nodded wisely, all the while wondering what the hell she was talking about.

July 28, 1998
Generation gap

$\mathcal{I}$glance into the rear view mirror but I don't see the cowboy's truck. Maybe he turned off somewhere; I'm relieved to be free of his persistent presence and the road construction. I want to think about my mother—and my grandmother—and remember the way things were.

The gap between Mama's world and mine expanded into a great ocean during my teenage years. It stayed that way until my stepfather died in 1993, I remember as I roll the window down to let the Wyoming wind blow through my hair. The gap narrowed some through the years, but never did come completely together.

When I turned seventeen, I remained a vulnerable young woman with hair worn in a bubble cut and a shy twist to the smile. I was seething inside, full of questions and a need to talk to some sane adult who understood an adolescent girl's mentality. But those people were few and far between in the Wyoming that I grew up in in the 60s.

If my grandmother Naomi had been alive and living nearby, perhaps she would have helped me see some of the effects that marriage can have on a woman. But she died. Papa left. Mama internalized her feelings, turning her into some kind of evil woman in my eyes. I felt alone in a hostile world with no one to talk to.

When I returned to Mama's house in Wyoming three months before I visted Papa and a month before Mama died, I sat out on the front porch listening to the bees buzz around the lilacs in the yard. The sound of a mallet hitting a croquet ball through a loop in the yard next door reminded me of when I went barefoot in the grass and felt the moisture of dew beneath my feet. The stars in the black Wyoming night reminded me of lying out under the stars with my first love Joe.

The tires of my car now race along black asphalt with a yellow line down the middle. I feel the warm Wyoming breeze blow through my hair. Will I find out what happened to my grandmother when I get there? Will knowing help heal the trauma that took hold of me the day Papa got in his truck and drove away? Will it soothe the pain that took hold of me the day that I found out that Joe wasn't going to marry me?

I glance back to the rearview mirror and see the cowboy's truck appear in my line of vision like an apparition. He's there again, but far enough back that I am not concerned.

What is it about him that makes me think of my grandfather?

September, 1997

Papa

Katherine sat at the kitchen table sipping coffee.

"Summer was different when I was growin' up out in Wyoming," Papa said. "It was nothin' like Iowa where ya could plant anything and it would grow. In Wyoming, we had to force feed it."

"People were different, too, out in Iowa. They weren't perfect. They had their prejudices just like most people. But most of them were farmers. And when people dig their hands into the soil a lot, they tend to be a little more connected to humanity. That's what I remember at least lookin' back. I was seven years old when we left."

"Out in Wyoming, I think that people were more distant," he said. "Wyoming makes you strong, but it don't necessarily make ya a warmer human being. That's what I remember from living there. I left after I divorced yer mom."

July 28, 1998
Victim

A hawk soars over the plains off to my left with blue mountains in the distance as a backdrop. The bird hones in on something down on the land, makes its drop and is back up again with what looks like maybe a prairie dog in its claws.

My eyes move back to black asphalt as, feeling like a prairie dog, I peer into the mirror at the cowboy's truck, now on my tailgate.

That must have been how my grandmother Naomi also felt out here. A victim. I feel her presence like a hand on my right shoulder. I try to shake it off. But it stays there. As my mind takes off again, I can feel her hand there guiding me.

September, 1997

Papa

"*How* did your mother die?" Katherine asked Papa as they sat drinking coffee in his living room in Boise.

"Let sleeping dogs lie," he growled.

She might have done as he asked but she had received a visit from a dead woman. A dead woman who sent her on this trip to see him. She couldn't let it go.

"But it's important. I need to know what happened."

Papa looked at her over his coffee cup with a pained look in his eyes. He took a puff of his cigarette, then answered.

"Her death kind of broke up the family. There were twelve of us in the beginning. But only two of us are alive now."

"How did your mom and dad get along? Did your dad mistreat your mom?" Katherine asked, then shrank back as Papa jumped up off his chair and started yelling.

"The past is past! You can't go back! Why do you dwell on the past?"

Katherine took a deep breath. "You told me once that anything is possible. Remember, you said that it doesn't hurt to try? Well, I'm trying! Nobody ever told me about my grandmother. I need to know her. That's what I'm trying to find out about!" Even to her own ears, Katherine's voice sounded too loud.

Oh god! Tell me what happened to her. Tell me how sorry you are for leaving! Please understand why I'm so angry! she thought as she glared at him.

He was the one who helped her plant the muskmelon seeds in the ground. He was the one who taught her how to give the impossible a shot. That's what she had been holding onto all of these years—the muskmelon seeds.

"I'm not going to dig up the god damned dirt in my family. I don't give a damn whether you like it or not. We've all let it go. Why can't you?"

"I can't let it go. Not yet. Not until I know the truth."

"I know one thing. I've got a bright future ahead of me."

"What do you mean?"

"Just that."

*   *   *

Two days before, Papa had pulled out his bible and read to her after dinner.

"For God so loved the world that he gave his only begotten son, that whosoever believeth in him shall not perish but have everlasting life."

Katherine had tried to sit patiently while he was reading. But it was an effort.

"We're living in the last days, Katherine," he warned. "The world is going to hell. But I have a bright future ahead of me."

Katherine bit back the angry words that threatened to lash out. Nothing wrong with my future either, she thought.

"God is good. God is great. And we thank him for this food. By his hand we all are fed. In Jesus' name, amen."

He prayed that prayer before every meal while Katherine was there. It stirred a memory reminding her of the day that he taught her that prayer when she must have been three or four.

"Can I say the blessing today, Papa?"

"Do you know how to say it?"

"Yeah."

"Okay. Go ahead."

Katherine bowed her head and clasped her hands together and said, "God is good, God is grapes."

"That's 'great', Katherine. Say, 'God is good. God is great."

"God is good. God is great," Katherine repeated. "And we tank him."

"And we thank him."

"And we thank him for this food. By hi sand."

"By his hand."

"By his hand we all are fed."

"In Jesus name."

"Amen."

Katherine remembered the care he took to be sure she said the right words. He had given up all vices except smoking and an occasional glass of wine or beer, as far as she could tell. He had even given up cards, his wife Mary told her. She said it was because of his religion, but Katherine suspected he had lost one too many games and refused to play any more.

"I think they ought to close the doors to all the schools and move the kids to Christian schools because public schools are just teaching them a pack of lies," Papa continued. "They're teaching them evolution and evolution is a lie."

She didn't argue with him because she knew where that would lead. Katherine learned quickly to avoid having religious discussions with Papa, a bible thumping, hell and brimstone kind of guy. Instead, she turned the subject back to his mother.

* * *

"So how did your father treat your mother?"

"I told you that I'm not digging up the dirt in my family!"

"If you think there's dirt, there's dirt."

Katherine's voice suddenly began to quiver. For a moment she thought he was going to get up and hit her. Mama must have felt like this, she thought as she braced herself.

Papa pushed himself out of his chair. Instead of reaching out to her, he stomped off into the next room. Breathing a sigh of relief, Katherine sat down to write in her notebook.

A moment later Mary stood in front of her like an apparition and held out an address book. She didn't say a word, but pointed to the name, address and phone number of Katherine's aunt Mamie. Mary kept her eye on the living room where Papa had gone as Katherine quickly wrote the information down. She whipped the book away as soon as Katherine finished.

July 28, 1998
Fear

$\mathcal{I}$ take another quick look into the rearview mirror. The cowboy is there a good distance back. I roll my shoulders a few times to get rid of the stress.

Why does he bother me so much? Mama was afraid of Papa. Any fears that I have of men I must have learned from her. Papa wasn't a cowboy. He doesn't have the weathered look of a man who has spent all of his life out on the plains like the cowboy who now follows probably does. He spent his time inside making cabinets. He had a garden in the back yard of his house.

My fear of the cowboy is different than the fear I felt when I was at Papa's standing across from him when he blew up and walked out. Papa has some type of post-traumatic stress that causes him to explode.

I suppose I soon learned anger means that someone is either going to hit you or leave.

September, 1996

Mama

"*I* never loved your father," Mama told her more than once while she was growing up.

"Why did you marry him then?"

"Oh, my mother liked him. She thought he was the greatest man she had ever met. But I couldn't stand him."

"Then you shouldn't have married him."

"When I was growing up, you did what your mother wanted you to. She wanted me to marry him. So I did and regretted it immediately."

"You should have divorced him right away." Katherine wondered if she also wished she had never had children.

"I guess I was too young to think that divorce was an option. But I was always afraid that what happened to his mother would also happen to me," she added.

"What happened to his mother?"

"That's just something we never talk about."

"Did he try to kill you?"

"No. There were just things he did that made me afraid."

"Like what?"

"Well, one time I won a washing machine in a contest. So I sold the old one. I used the money from the sale to buy wallpaper for the living room. When your dad came home and saw the wallpaper, he flew into a rage. He pushed me up against the wall and pounded holes in the new wallpaper with his fists."

Hitting his fists into the wall! The story rang a bell. Katherine remembered him doing it.

Papa said that Mama lied to get the divorce, but what Mama told her didn't sound like a lie.

September 1997

Papa

Katherine wondered if Papa would ever speak to her again. He avoided or ignored her for the rest of her visit.

He's nothing more than a sensitive, pouty little boy who has no place in his heart for forgiveness, Katherine, still shaken from the confrontation, thought as she drove away from his house.

July 28, 1998
Power

I guess the cowboy must represent Papa in some way, all of the fears that I must have felt whenever he blew up at Mama, I think as I drive down the road towards Brown Rock, Wyoming.

The cowboy, though, stirs up a different kind of fear. While Papa appears to be a sensitive, high-strung man with unresolved issues, he's not the brute or western outlaw type like the man in the cowboy hat with guns on top of his pickup back there appears. A man who carries guns around makes me think "watch out! That guy is out of touch with his inner nature." Guns give him power. But something essential is missing. You don't want to get in his way.

In my mind, the cowboy who follows me to Brown Rock fits in with the group of Wyoming boys who helped initiate me into womanhood. I glance back at his pickup in the rearview mirror. Just when I think I've left them behind and I'm going along feeling pretty strong, they come back to test me.

I used to give all of my power to a man right off. Then when the thing ended, I would feel knocked down and dragged out emotionally. It took me a long time to get back up. It still does. But now at least I know why.

I was only seventeen when my first experience of sex with a man turned into something traumatic. My values were just being set when all of a sudden men and boys were after me trying to get something. The only guy I had ever had sex with couldn't wait to turn it into locker room talk afterwards with all of the guys. The next week, my phone started ringing off the hook. I didn't realize why. At first it made me feel that I had it made. But every guy I went out with tried to have sex and when I wouldn't, one guy started calling me names.

"Hey bitch! You think I'm not good enough for you?"

"That's right! You're not," I yelled back.

I never told Mama about how I felt having so many guys chasing me like I was a piece of meat. That set some values in me early on. Sex object. That's all I was to them.

Now with this guy chasing me, it brings it all back up again.

*   *   *

The Wyoming wind blows across the plains. The lonely whine as it whips through the telephone wires makes me think of Naomi.

"Leonard! Leonard! You forgot to close the door, Leonard! Now all the fish will be ruined!"

I heard her voice in a dream I had when my daughter and I first arrived in Wyoming last week. Now on the road to Brown Rock, her voice comes back to me loud and clear as if in duet with the wind music.

Why did she say the fish would be ruined because Leonard, my father, had left the door opened?

Maybe the opened door meant that he had not dealt with the past the way he should have. Maybe she thought he should have tried harder to include me and my sisters in his family. We were his flesh and blood and he ran away from us. I'm not sure I'll ever get over that pain.

I'm not saying that Papa was a bad man. He was good at gardening, I noticed on my visit to Idaho last year. The apple tree in his back yard was strong and healthy and full of fruit. He had a large garden with green beans, beets, carrots and tomatoes.

But he couldn't give me what I needed.

Papa's people were farmers. They take great pride in the fact that they came from Iowa where they lived off the fruits of the earth.

The hard, sagebrushed, high plains of Wyoming changed all of that. Crops didn't grow as well here as they did in the deep loam soil of Iowa.

I wish I could have known my aunts and uncles, been included in the weddings and dinners where my cousins gathered. I craved the openness growing up that one finds only in extended family setups. The nuclear family I grew up in after Papa left made me feel like I was tied up.

After Mama remarried, we all thought we had attained the American dream. But I'd be lying to say that we had some type of ideal arrangement. All was not well in the state of Wyoming. There were too many ghosts from the past whose voices had not been heard.

Speaking of voices, why is that cowboy following me? Is he another apparition with an urgent message for me to listen to? His presence back there has been bringing up all sorts of past fears. Why did Naomi want me to come to Wyoming anyway? Was it to learn the truth about what happened to her? Or maybe this whole trip is some sort of divine plan that will turn my life around. Maybe the cowboy is part of that plan and was sent to escort me in. Who knows what I'll find when I get to Brown Rock.

I feel a tightening in my chest. Some old, hard feeling lodged down in there just waiting to come bubbling up and out. Some hard, old feeling like the way Papa treated me and my sisters.

I glance into the rearview mirror and note that the cowboy is now following me at two car lengths. More construction ahead. Another caterpillar crawls as we follow.

Whatever message I need to hear, perhaps I'll understand it later. For the time being, I'm going to play it safe and keep my eye on the cowboy.

*   *   *

Papa's family had a reunion near my sister Linda's town and she got up the courage to go after not having seen Papa for forty years. That was just before Papa's last two brothers died. He didn't attend the reunion.

"Nobody would speak to me," Linda told me later.

"Why wouldn't they speak to you?"

"I don't know. They went out of their way to avoid me. They treated me like I was a stranger."

"I heard he told his brothers to give her the shaft," my oldest sister Carol told me later.

"Why would he do that?"

"I guess because she's kept her distance from him for so many years."

"But he's her father! Why would a father do that to his child?" I wanted to cry as a deep pain began to take over my insides.

Now I feel a raw hot burning feeling in my chest just thinking about it. The pain of losing a father at a young age is one thing. The pain of hearing that Papa did something like that to my sister Linda makes me want to turn my back and never see him again. Why would he do that to his own children, I cry to the sky as I drive across Wyoming?!

I didn't tell Papa about the woman in the housedress who sat in the chair by my bed one night in San Francisco. Perhaps I should have. The idea of a dead woman being there might have put the fear of god in him and made him more open to my questions. Perhaps then he would have understood my driving need to know what happened to my grandmother Naomi.

I roll my window down and feel the wind blow across my arms. A shiver starts on the hairs of my arms and moves its way down to my belly.

"Leonard! You forgot to close the door, Leonard! Now all the fish will be ruined!"

Papa didn't know about the dream. But, I think he was thinking that something would be ruined when he saw that I was hell-bent on finding out about my grandmother.

The Wyoming wind shakes the car as I drive into it. I push down on the gas pedal but it won't move past thirty miles an hour. The caterpillar ahead must be going forty. As soon as I get past this construction, I need to go fast so that I can get away from the cowboy.

The wide, open plains is not a good place to be when you're a woman alone and a man in a cowboy hat with guns is following you.

I felt safer living in Europe during the late 80s just before moving to San Francisco. The United States is spread out over many miles and there is a lot of empty land out here in the middle. The open plains of the west are good for cattle and horses. They're not good for women. That's one reason why I left.

*　　*　　*

I think of the ring I found at Mama's house. A silver ring with three small diamonds. It had lain in a white box lined in blue, tucked in the back of a drawer in the dresser in Mama's bedroom until I found it while I was going through her things after she died last year.

I take a few breaths as I drive down the highway trying to unloosen the tight feeling in my chest. The summer sun shines on the gray sagebrush making it look silver.

Mama had told me she'd taken the ring back to the jewelry store when my wedding plans with Joe fell apart. But she kept it. Perhaps she hoped some day there might be another man to slip the band on my finger. That never happened. Marriage wasn't for me. If you wanted to fit in in Wyoming in the 1960s, you had to wear white to the altar. After that, well, in the recent past a man could hang for stealing a horse there. But what he did with his wife was his business.

1960s

Coming of age

*W*hen Katherine entered high school, she realized she had two options: she could remain "good" or she could be "the kind of girl who sleeps with men," as her sister Sarah once said in talking about 'fallen women' when she was ten.

At the age of ten, Katherine had been to a lot of slumber parties. She didn't see anything bad about sleeping with somebody. But she tucked that comment away for future reference. And she set off into high school sure that she would remain the type of girl who would remain "good".

But boredom and rebellion won out against the "sweet and naïve" girl that she started out as, the type that never kissed a guy on the first date. So she chose to head down the "bad girl" route and see what she might find there.

"Going all the way," though, was a concept that she didn't quite get until she turned 17. A girl she hung around with in high school explained the facts of life to her.

"Haven't you ever seen dogs do it?" she asked her when she realized Katherine had been listening to all of her stories about "doing it" but hadn't actually done it herself.

Embarrassed by her own naiveté, Katherine decided to experiment. She chose a young man at random. Her first experience was less than successful when her vagina was too tight for him to get his penis in.

"You aren't a virgin, are you?" he asked.

"No, I'm not," she told him.

"Are you sure?"

"Yeah."

Blood was mixed with her urine when she went to flush the toilet after he left that day. The next time she tried, it was easy.

July 28, 1998
Post-traumatic stress

The man in the caterpillar finally turns off the road and the traffic picks up speed. The cowboy zooms up and settles in close behind me.

"What's that guy doing?" I wonder. "Is he going to ram me or what?"

I speed up to seventy. So does he.

I feel my shoulders tense up and my heart begin to pound in my chest.

What happened to all of the cars that had been following moments earlier? I guess some passed. And when I sped up, I left the others far behind me.

What do I do now? I move to 75 then 80. At 85, I set my car in cruise. I keep my eye on the road behind me. I don't see the cowboy.

Ten minutes later with the cowboy out of sight, I try to think why this is happening. The only thing I can think about is being seventeen and in high school. This Wyoming cowboy is bringing up something like the post-traumatic stress that my stepfather Clark experienced after he fought at Wake and Guam at the age of seventeen. He relived those moments over and over for years.

1966
Flashback

A few months after Katherine lost her virginity, she and her friend rode up and down Main Street in her stepfather Clark's white pickup. A red T-Bird pulled up beside them and revved its engine.

"You want to ride around?" the dark-haired driver grinned at the girls.

"I don't know. What's yer name?" Katherine eyed him warily.

"Joe. Joe Vandorn."

"Oh yes. My sister knows you. Sure."

So Katherine parked the pickup and she and her friend Susan jumped into the T-Bird and went on a ride up to the Bison Dam.

"Do you want to go out tonight?" Joe asked Katherine when they returned to her stepfather's truck.

"Sure." Katherine smiled. She already had a date for that night but she stood up the other guy and went with Joe.

She and Joe rode around and went to a movie. Afterwards, he parked the car next to a road in the country. He didn't try to get into her pants like most guys that she had gone out with.

He held her hand and they laughed quietly.

"Why are you laughing?" Katherine demanded.

"I don't know. Why are you laughing?"

"I don't know." Then he leaned over and gently kissed her on the lips. They looked deep into each other's eyes. Then he took her home.

"This feels so right," she thought. "It feels so good to be with a guy who doesn't try to have sex with me on a first date."

Though she had already taken the "bad girl" route before she met Joe, Katherine, at seventeen, was really still just a naive high school girl. And she trusted this nineteen-year old college boy.

Soon, she and Joe were going out every night.

Mama thought she could heave a sigh of relief since Katherine was now settled down to one man instead of going out with someone different every night. But she was mistaken.

Four months later, Joe sat with her on the couch of her parents' house as they watched Bonanza on T.V. That was the day they got their blood tests and bought the rings.

July 28, 1998
The past

*A*s I glance far off across the plains, time seems to go on and on and on. The past begins in the east and moves towards the west. Each time I cross these plains, I seem to turn into someone different.

The last time I drove across here in the early 70s, my mind had not yet been diverted by an apparition in a housedress. My whole life lay before me and I was on an adventure.

This time, along with the cowboy, my mind comes back to my grandmother Naomi and what happened to her out here.

Papa was at an impressionable age when his mother died. Perhaps that why he's not able to talk about what happened to her. Perhaps that's why I'm so intent on getting to the bottom of Naomi's story.

"One time I spilled a little grape jelly I had canned and it made your father mad," Mama once told me. "He grabbed a jar and heaved it at me, barely missing my head."

What happened to Mama most likely happened to my grandmother Naomi. The link between the two of them is what hooks me into this story and drives me like a demon towards Brown Rock trying to get away from the cowboy.

September, 1997
Papa

"*M*y mother came of age at the end of the 19th century," Katherine remembered Papa telling her the day before he blew up and went stomping off. "Victorian principles were strongly ingrained in every lesson my mom ever taught me," he said.

"What do you mean," Katherine asked him.

"Well, she tried to teach me how to treat women. Things like opening doors and carrying things that might be too heavy for them. But a lot of things she tried to teach me went in one ear and out the other because I was preoccupied with what my dad was doin'."

"Why? What was he doing?"

"Well, he worked a lot." Papa got up and lit another cigarette as he was talking. I sensed he was agitated by the way his eyes squinted up and his shoulders tensed like he was trying to hold onto something. "He had a cabinet making shop. Me and my brothers helped him. I learned everything I knew from him."

"Even how to treat women?"

"Hell! That's where my dad and I parted ways. He, well let's just say, my dad always had a lot of women."

"While he was married to your mom?"

"I don't know. When I first married yer mom, I would walk into his office and he'd have a woman sittin' on his lap. I walked out and never went back again."

"Oh."

July 28, 1998
Out of touch with their feelings

Out here on the plains of Wyoming, life more closely resembles what Naomi knew than the life I now live in San Francisco. Men back in my grandmother's day were probably not that much different than this cowboy who now follows me on the way to Brown Rock.

These were men out of touch with their feelings; "he men" who could grab a bull by the horns and force it to the ground.

The isolation of Wyoming provides the perfect sanctuary for the promulgation of this type of man, whose skin is hard and leathered by the sun.

According to what Papa told me, my grandfather Sam would have probably chased a woman across Wyoming if he thought he could get in her pants. And he would have gotten away with it.

Perhaps he also got away with what happened to my grandmother.

But times have changed.

The civil rights movement and the sexual revolution of the 1960s began to bring to light secrets kept by a lot of people of my parents' generation. In the early 70s, Nixon's involvement in the Watergate break-in established the field of investigative journalism which began to uncover secrets like the cost of a burial, out-of-wedlock pregnancies, a daughter's birth record.

The 60s also imparted bruises to many of my generation who came of age in the thick of it. Most of them were not prepared to be flower children nor to participate in free love, I remember, as I look out across the plains.

1966
Beginning of the
Sexual Revolution

*K*atherine began heaving her breakfast every morning before school.

"Sick again?" Mama finally took her to a doctor.

The male doctor and woman nurse in white coats looked at Katherine intently as soon as they got her into the examination room away from Mama.

"When was yer last period?"

"The first of the month."

"Are you sure?"

"Yeah."

"So you have had a period recently?"

"Yes."

Did they know she was lying? she wondered as she sat there facing them. They didn't have her undress. They took notes of what she said in the chart. Then they had her go out in the waiting room. Mama then went in and talked to them.

Katherine was frightened. She studied Mama's face carefully as she walked back to the waiting room.

"What did they tell you?"

"They said that if you continued to be sick that I should take you back to see them."

After they left the doctor's office that day, Katherine tried to work out her options. She thought she was pregnant. But she wasn't sure. Where could she go to find out? Katherine didn't know who to talk to. She wanted to tell her sister, but she was afraid Mama would find out.

The next week she made an appointment with Dr. Derry, her family's physician.

The last time she had seen him, she was ten. He had given her a lollipop after Mama took her in to see him because she was having a lot of stomachaches.

She remembered the lollipop and thought he might be able to keep her secret. If not, well, she had no other options.

"What seems to be the problem?" the gruff gray-haired man asked.

"I haven't had my period and I've been getting sick."

"Sit up here on the table. Put yer feet in these metal stirrups and slide your rear end down here," he ordered her.

She lay on the examining table and he stuck a cold metal clamp up her vagina and opened it. Nothing had prepared her for the pain she would feel.

"Yer a month and a half pregnant," he told her as he yanked the cold metal clamp out. "Whose baby is this?"

"I don't know. My boyfriend told me he was sterile. So how could I be pregnant?"

"You're a very naïve young woman. You'd better go right home and tell your mother. And you need to tell the young man."

"Okay." she told him. But she knew it wasn't that simple. She drove round and round town thinking before finally heading home. She didn't tell Mama. Instead, she wrote a letter.

"Dear Joe,

I found out today that I'm pregnant with your child. Why did you lie to me about being sterile?

Katherine"

She sealed and mailed the letter. Then she waited.

July 28, 1998

Seventeen years old again

*A*ll of my thoughts when I left Wyoming over 30 years ago centered around Joe.

Coming back and seeing the cowboy brings up my feelings about Joe again. He was my first love. I stopped thinking about him years ago. But whenever I return to Wyoming, there he is again. I guess that means I never got over him.

The cowboy tailing me makes me feel like I'm seventeen years old again. In fact, that's the age that I usually revert to when I get into a relationship with any man. The vulnerable, passive young woman who left Wyoming returns as I look in the mirror. I thought I left her behind thirty years ago. Evidently, she's still here.

1966

Sex education

"Some girls take the pill," Katherine's friend told her.

"The pill?"

"Yeah. Haven't you heard of it?"

"No. Do you take it?"

"Are you kidding! My mom would have a fit if she found out I was taking the pill."

What do you use?"

"Usually a rubber."

Most girls either used a rubber or you took a chance, Katherine found out later.

But if you felt pregnant, there were always people ready to help.

An old boyfriend called her up one night and asked her if she wanted to go out.

"I hear you're pregnant," he said as they were riding around.

"Where'd you hear that?"

"Some people were talking."

"Oh really." Katherine didn't come right out and tell him she was pregnant. She just listened and asked questions.

"When Suzie Franz got pregnant, I helped her abort with a knitting needle. I'd be willing to help you if you wanted me to."

"Right now?"

"Not tonight. But I'd be willing to do it some other time if you wanted me to."

"Isn't that dangerous."

"It's okay. I did it with her. I know how to do it."

"I'd be afraid to do that."

"Well then, you could buy some special medicine at the drugstore," he said. "Just follow the directions on the bottle and you'll abort in a few days."

Katherine didn't do either.

A few days later Mama called Dr. Derry to make her an appointment.

"She's already been here," he told her. "She's pregnant."

"I just talked to the doctor," Mama told her as she walked into her room that night. "He told me that you're p.g. What do you want to do about it?"

Katherine hated the way Mama referred to it as "p.g." as if there was something dirty about the whole process. But she ignored it that night.

"I don't want to talk about it. I wrote to Joe," Katherine told Mama. Then she cried and cried. That's the last time she ever tried to let Mama see her real feelings.

July 28, 1998
Mama's words

The silver ring that I found in the drawer at Mama's house taunts me.

"Only bad girls get caught." I can still hear Mama's words. Though, as I drive across the Wyoming plains, they don't bother me the way they did when I was seventeen.

Mama died a year ago as I was approaching fifty. Her illness made me very aware of the fleetingness of life. She represents a period of my life that I lost somewhere.

That cowboy back there brings some of it back to me.

October, 1966
Pregnant!

"*K*atherine's pregnant. We want you to come up here this weekend!"

Joe was just reading Katherine's letter at the University of the Rocky Mountains in Windpeak, Wyoming 300 miles south of Elk Mountain the next day when he got the phone call from Mama.

"Yes, I just got Katherine's letter. I have an exam on Monday. I was planning to come next weekend," he told her.

"I don't care if you have an exam or not. We want you here this weekend." And that was that.

"I told you I'd written. Why did you have to call him," Katherine demanded when Mama said Joe was coming.

"Say, we know what we're doing," she responded. Katherine winced at the emphasis on the 'we'.

"What do you want to do," Joe asked her when he arrived at midnight two nights later and Katherine went out to sit next to him on the seat of his red T-Bird.

"I don't know," she responded as she shivered next to him.

The next morning, she and Joe sat down in the living room with her parents.

"When do you plan to marry her?" her stepfather Clark asked from the couch at the far end of the room. Katherine had to crane her neck to see him.

"I don't know. We haven't talked about it yet," Joe told him.

As Katherine sat and listened, she felt she was living someone else's life. Six years earlier this same conversation had taken place, only then it had been between her parents, her oldest sister Carol and Carol's boyfriend. Katherine had hidden in the hallway then and listened.

"You're going to have to marry her as soon as possible," Mama said to Joe, drawing Katherine back to the present. "If you get the blood tests done this weekend, you can get married next week."

"Katherine's not very mature you know," Joe said. "She's only seventeen."

"Maturity will come with time," Clark said.

The way they talked about her as if she weren't present made her feel like she didn't exist, but she knew it was pointless saying anything. They would make the decisions for her. Joe was mature, she thought; he was almost twenty and three years older than she was.

"A lot of people are young when they get married," Mama said. "We think it would be best if you got married."

"Okay," Joe nodded, but he looked to Katherine for some type of reassurance.

Katherine shook her head and smiled.

"The clinic's doing blood tests today until noon. You can get the tests done and we can have the wedding next weekend."

Ten minutes later, Joe and Katherine got in his T-bird and headed to the clinic. Half an hour later, they were sitting on a chair with needles and tubes hooked up to their arms. The nurse pulled the needle out and taped a swab of cotton on Katherine's arm.

An hour later they stood at the jewelry store counter looking at rings.

"I don't have a lot of money to spend," Joe told her.

"That's okay. My parents will probably pay for the rings."

That afternoon Mama and Katherine's sisters planned the wedding for her.

"I can buy her ten pounds of flour and a canister set," Sarah said.

"Why don't we have a shower for her," said Mama.

"I don't want a shower!" Katherine protested.

"Why not?" Joe asked.

"I just don't."

They went ahead and planned the shower anyway.

"I've got to go," Joe suddenly blurted out just after Bonanza ended later that evening.

"So early?"

"Yeah. I've got to get back. I have a test on Monday."

"Are you going to drive back tonight? Or will you wait until morning?"

"I'll probably go in the morning."

"Do you want to have breakfast here?"

"No, I'll go to sleep now and get up early and leave."

After she walked him to the front door and watched him through the window get into his red T-Bird and drive away, she walked back into the T.V. room, lay down on the couch and cried.

July 28, 1998
Good old country and western

$\mathcal{G}$etting pregnant out-of-wedlock was the reason why I left this place, the Wyoming plains remind me as I drive. I listen for my grandmother Naomi's voice riding on the wind that blows through my side window. The cowboy's truck is nowhere to be seen.

How does Naomi fit into everything that happened to me, I wonder? I sense that whatever happened to her has a connection to me. But what is it? Hopefully, I'll find out after I get to Brown Rock.

I'm on a personal quest as I listen for ghost voices to guide me. Sometimes I hear Naomi's voice in a dream. Sometimes the wind or a hawk flying across the land carries the message to me until the cowboy intrudes anyway.

I flip on the radio and listen to some good old country and western music on a radio station transmitting from Cheyenne.

November 1, 1966
Flashback

"*W*e have a lovely ballerina-length silk taffeta. Would you like to try it on?" the saleswoman in the bridal section of the store asked Katherine. It was just five days before her wedding day when she and Mama went shopping for her wedding apparel.

"Well, I don't know. I had been thinkin' of off-white wool," Katherine told the woman.

When she came out of the dressing room and saw the fitted white satin bodice and Sabrina neckline with pure white Chantilly lace, she knew that's what she wanted.

"How about a veil?"

"I don't think so."

"We have some nice ones. This bouffant finger-tip veil is nice. It has a crown of seed pearls and sequins."

"Let me try it on."

When Katherine and Mama left the store that day, she carried the dress and veil neatly folded and wrapped in white tissue paper.

The next night, the phone rang while she was watching "Wagon Train" on T.V.

"Katherine! Joe's on the phone! Get in here," Mama yelled from the living room.

She picked up the receiver and listened to Joe talking to Clark who was on the bedroom extension.

"I can't marry her," Joe told her stepfather when she began to listen in.

"Why is that?" Clark asked him.

"I called my father in Germany and he told me that if I married her, he wouldn't give me money for my education."

"It will be hard, but you can do it."

"But, Katherine's too young. And I'm not ready," she heard Joe say. "I'm sorry, I can't do it."

That's when Mama started screaming.

* ⋆ *

July 28, 1998
The omen

I can still hear Mama screaming as I drive to Brown Rock. You would have thought that I would have forgotten that by now. But there are some things that stay with you throughout life.

Mama sent back the wedding dress. I thought she had also sent back the two silver wedding bands that Joe and I bought together. But evidently Mama kept one of them.

I never walked down the aisle, wore that ring, never held a baby in my arms or suckled it at my breast. My life had turned out very differently from Mama's.

She gave birth to me and my sisters up north on the Wind River Indian Reservation.

It was a cold, dark January night when the midwife arrived at the small two-bedroom bungalow and rushed into the front bedroom of the house, my older sister Linda told me. An hour later Linda heard a baby cry. That was me being born that night. The year was 1949.

Four years later, we moved to Elk Mountain.

The new owners of the house we left behind, the house where I was born, found a dead Indian buried beneath the foundation.

"I understand the house was built on an old Indian burial ground," Mama said. "That's probably why they found the Indian there."

"That's a lie," Papa adamantly stated when I told him what Mama had said. "No Indian was buried there and that's all there is to it!"

The fire in his eyes when he told me made me wonder what misdeed he might be covering up. I didn't know.

And I couldn't find a record of a dead Indian being found there.

Whatever the case, perhaps a dead Indian buried under the house where I was born was an omen.

Ghosts roam the Wyoming plains. One only has to listen. You can't see them. But maybe I'm wrong there.

Who is this cowboy that's been tailing me as I head to Brown Rock to uncover the truth about my grandmother Naomi? Maybe he's just a ghost who will disappear after I wake up farther down the road when I arrive at my destination.

Maybe all of this is just so that I can go back and hear Mama screaming.

November, 1966

Stigmatized

*K*atherine's whole world turned black as she hung up the phone. Joe wasn't going to marry her.

Unmarried and beginning to show, she might as well have committed a felony in the Wyoming town where she and her family lived. She was shunned by small town minds that were more than happy to turn a blind eye to the escapades of their male members.

"She has a case of pregnancy," one of her classmates told a teacher when he asked what happened to her. Then the whole classroom laughed. Katherine found out about the incident from one of her friends, one of the few who were still talking to her.

She was no longer welcome in the Christian Church that she attended growing up. That was the same one that regularly sang the hymn "Just as I Am" for that one lost soul who needed to be saved by the Lord on Sunday morning.

"I'm sorry but there will be no job for Katherine here next summer," the owner of the Cattleman's Café called to tell Mama.

It was because she had gotten pregnant out-of-wedlock, though he wouldn't say it outright.

So she left Wyoming over thirty years ago, a fallen woman ostracized by the community.

July 28, 1998
Two types of women

*O*ver thirty years later as I head to Brown Rock to find out what happened to my grandmother, many things still remain to be learned.

Why is this cowboy following me, for one thing? This has not turned into a running with the wolf pack scenario. The cowboy chasing me rather resembles a predator stalking the preyed.

Naomi's voice fills my head as I drive down the highway with cowboy music playing on the radio and the wind whipping dust across the road.

Fitting in in Wyoming was not easy for me when I turned seventeen. I can't say that I ever felt I belonged here at least among the small town cliques and minds that watched every move I made.

In Wyoming there are two types of women, at least according to some people in the state.

"A good un gets married," an old-timer once told me. The other kind were called "women of ill-repute."

In small Wyoming towns where religious conservatives thrive and many of them believe that woman caused the fall of Adam, underlying attitudes often surface. That's one reason why I've never returned to live in Wyoming even though I'm a rugged individualist at heart.

There are two types of freedom, I've learned. One provides you with plenty of wide, open physical space which allows you to breathe freely. The other type gives you a place where you can just be you. I discovered the latter after I left Wyoming.

I glance into the rearview mirror at the cowboy's red pickup, which still follows me on the way to Brown Rock. It's not unusual in Wyoming to have a man following you like you might be some type of hunting trophy if he can catch you. I always felt like a piece of meat when I lived here.

Each time I have returned to the wild west from where I now live in San Francisco, I drink in Wyoming's wide open space like water on the parched lips of one dying of thirst. But I know I won't be staying.

I left Wyoming in the 60s to hide from what happened to me here. Now that I have returned, immediately I fall victim to this guy tailing me like he wants to put me in my place. And I'm letting him do it. It makes me so angry that I'm still letting this kind of thing bother me.

November, 1966
The wedding veil

Katherine took the white wedding dress out of the box, lifted it up above her head and pulled it down over her shoulders. She put on the veil and stood staring at herself in the mirror.

"Do you take this woman to be yer wife?" Katherine could almost hear the preacher say as she stood looking at her reflection.

Then she yanked the veil off her head, grabbed a pair of scissors and cut until the veil lay in shredded pieces of white on the bed. Katherine gathered them up and tossed them in the wastepaper basket. She lit a match and threw it in the basket. She watched as the flame caught hold of the netting then burned itself out.

She turned to see Mama standing at the door watching.

"What are you doing?"

"Nothing."

Mama stared a moment like she was going to say something. Then she closed the door and walked away. The next day she sent the wedding dress back to the store. "Perhaps she was afraid that I would destroy that, too." Katherine thought.

1997

Mama

Something or someone moved around Mama's house two nights after she died. Katherine shivered in her bed and thought of Mama's ghost wandering the house trying to find something she'd left behind. The soft sound of drums and chanting in the dining room kept Katherine awake for hours. Too many ghosts of the recently deceased seemed to have gathered there.

*

November 28, 1966
A fallen woman

*I*t was dark and cold with snow blowing off the ground when Katherine and her parents got up that late November morning.

As they backed out of the driveway and headed down the road, she felt a raw pain gnawing inside her. Mama felt it, too. She wouldn't let Katherine forget that she was a woman branded by a societal taboo, that this was a journey, not of fun and joy, but duty, fear, pain, letting go, leaving something behind that she would never find again.

"Don't ever tell anyone about this pregnancy," Katherine's mother told her as she turned around and looked at her from the front seat of the car as they approached Hell's Half Acre in Wyoming on the way to Denver.

"I won't," Katherine declared weakly.

July 28, 1998
A marked woman

*I*n the 1960s in Wyoming and most of the rest of the country, being pregnant and unmarried was like wearing the scarlet letter, I remember as I drive across Wyoming. It made me a marked woman. Though the sexual revolution had begun, it hadn't sunk in with most people, and hasn't totally even yet.

The cowboy back there represents all of the underlying attitudes that once put me in my place. I doubt that any man that would chase a woman across Wyoming would have a deep sensitivity for a woman who made a mistake.

I shiver as I think of how Naomi must have felt out here where a woman had to cover up her feelings like Mama after she divorced Papa. Like me when I got pregnant.

November 28, 1966
Tainted goods

They stopped on the way to Denver to see Joe in Windpeak. When they knocked on the door of his apartment, no one answered. As they were driving down the street past the University of the Rocky Mountains, they saw him. He was parking his red T-Bird. A girl was sitting next to him on the seat.

"That's him!" Katherine's mother yelled. "Park the car!"

Screech!

Clark slammed on the brakes and pulled the car over to the curb. Katherine sank down in her seat as Mama threw herself out of the car, ran back to Joe's T-bird and knocked on the window. A moment later Joe slid onto the seat next to her. She refused to look at him.

"Katherine's a much cuter girl than whoever that girl is you have in your car back there," Mama told him after she got back into the front seat and turned around to glare at him.

"She's not the reason I'm not marrying Katherine," Joe said.

"Yes, she is," Katherine's voice suddenly came from some cold, angry place down in the pit of her stomach.

"No, she's not."

"Yes, she is. I'm not going to discuss this further," Katherine announced to Joe and Mama and her stepfather Clark. "He doesn't want to marry me. He's made his decision."

Uncertain, Joe got out of the car.

Katherine refused to look at him as he walked away.

"Poor Katherine! Look at him. He can do whatever he wants. And Katherine has to go to this home in Denver," Mama lamented.

"I'm okay," Katherine told her.

"Oh, I forgot. You're a woman of the world now," Mama snapped from the front seat.

"No, I'm not."

"Yes, you are. You're the one that got yourself into this mess."

Katherine didn't respond though her words cut deep. She could feel the pain ebbing up out of her throat ready to come out. Tears began to form in her eyes.

Nobody spoke until they crossed the Wyoming-Colorado line. Then Mama began to make comments about the landscape.

"Isn't this nice. Look at the heart on the sign. A city of love! How lovely! I've never been in a town like Loveland before."

Soon they connected with Interstate 25, which carried them on into Denver in the middle of rush hour traffic.

July 28, 1998
Spooked

No cars in sight as I drive across the Wyoming plains. Only the cowboy's red pickup. I press my foot down on the gas pedal hoping to leave him far behind me.

But he's not so far behind. Just when I think I've left him, he's back again. I'm very aware of his presence each time I look in the rearview mirror.

Most women traveling alone would probably be spooked by a strange man tailing them down a highway out in the middle of nowhere. The question that lingers in my mind is "why should I be so scared?"

I haven't driven across these plains for years. I've been gone from Wyoming long enough that you would think that whatever fear I had of the men here would have dissipated. But it looks like I'm still running.

The Wyoming plains and wind also stir the ever-lingering feeling I have about Naomi's presence with me on this trip. Sometimes it seems that I can actually hear her speak to me.

Knowing who these women are who live out here helps fine-tune my ears. I know the exact turn of a phrase or almost Texas accent spoken by Wyoming people. To some, they sound uneducated. But that's just the way they speak here.

I go over and over in my mind my grandmother Naomi's daily habits, the type of woman that she was, things I heard from Papa about her.

The dust blows across the asphalt highway. I roll my window down and feel it blow through my hair. I glance back into the rearview mirror and notice that I haven't lost him. The cowboy's pickup still follows me but quite a bit farther back now.

I go on for months at a time, even years, not being worried about some man chasing me, not having to fight off unwelcome advances. I'm good at finding safe havens, getting involved in my work, keeping myself clear of entanglements. My relationships with men tend to get complicated once they pass the friendship stage and move into the arena of sexual. I haven't been able to deal with those complications. That's why I'm still single.

Yet here I am, a lone woman on the road in Wyoming being followed. Is he just a harmless local? Or could he be one of the crazies that you read about in the paper. In this country, a woman has to be especially careful.

*   *   *

Just as the Wyoming wind carries some small tinge of Naomi's voice as it blows across the prairie, it also carries a picture of Mama's house, the way it looked when I returned to Wyoming a year ago to bury her.

I remember the beige flowered teapot still set on the stove waiting for Mama to return, pour a cup of tea, and sit down at the table to read. Every nook and cranny of the house carried her presence.

I could feel her very close in the house the night that I arrived, two days before her funeral. I could almost reach out and touch her.

Now, as I drive towards Brown Rock, I think of the sound of Mama's voice.

Just as quickly, my thoughts turn to my grandmother Naomi and how I feel her at times sitting right next to me in the car. I feel her urging me on, telling me to hurry as I go to meet the truth.

I can almost catch a glimpse of her dancing across the plains. But she was tied down inside a house with twelve children. It smothered and helped kill her, I think.

I glance into the side mirror to make sure there's plenty of distance between me and the cowboy.

November, 1966
Ticket out of Wyoming

It was dark when the car pulled into the parking lot of the unwed mother's home. The lights shone brightly inside the three-story building. Nothing about the place to warm the heart, Katherine thought bitterly as her stepfather Clark parked the car in the asphalt parking lot in front of the entrance.

A home they called it. Katherine had been expecting a white two-storied, seven-gabled residence with a large open front porch, a winding oak staircase, a fireplace, a bookcase, a family place. What she saw instead looked like a hospital or an office building.

"Are you sure you want to stay here?"

Katherine could see the doubt and a trace of fear in Mama's face. She stifled her own growing fear and nodded stiffly.

The blonde secretary sitting behind the front desk as they walked in handed her parents some papers.

"Fill these out," she said. "Mrs. Blackstone will be with you soon."

Katherine stared down the long passage leading from the front office to the dining room at the back. A girl with a big belly walked out of a room at the other end. She seemed like some phantom from a previous life there to remind her that only bad girls get caught.

Mama, too, had seen the pregnant woman.

"You don't have to stay. You can come back home with us," she said.

Katherine heard the softened tone of her voice. But she couldn't believe in it. She knew that once she went back home, Mama would revert to punishing her for what she had done. She would be trapped there in Wyoming not only by Mama, but by the stigma of being pregnant and not married.

As much as she disliked what she saw around her, she knew it was no more than she deserved. She had done something bad and had to pay for it.

Some girls in the 60s went to finishing school to prepare for womanhood. Katherine went to a maternity home, her ticket out of Wyoming.

She wanted to turn around and run. She wanted to trust Mama and run back home with her. One day she was dancing the watusi at the high school prom. The next, a baby was knocking on the door of her belly. She wanted to break down the doors of the unwed mother's home and run away.

But she was one of 'them' now, the class of women with big bellies who must be hidden. She forced herself to embrace the passageway before her.

July 28, 1998
Joe's ghost

I have had to keep my eye on men since I was seventeen. I haven't fully trusted them since Joe backed out of the marriage. Maybe that's Joe's ghost back there in the pickup trying to catch my attention.

The light shining on the windshield and wind lifting up dust around the tires makes it look like a ghost vehicle. Perhaps my imagination is working overtime.

Still, I wish this guy would just leave me alone. I have enough things to think about without him causing new concerns. I'm fine without men. They always cause more trouble than they're worth. This one is intruding way too much on my mind and my space!

November, 1966

Into hiding

A tall woman with white silvery hair piled high on her head walked out of her office to greet them. She was Mrs. Blackstone, the director of the Floton unwed mother's home.

"I understand you had trouble finding us. Won't you come in."

"What do I say to this woman?" Katherine wondered as she sat down with her parents across from her.

Mrs. Blackstone glanced at some papers in front of her and made notes as she asked questions.

"When is the baby due?"

"July 1."

"Are there any strange illnesses?"

"No."

"Will she be having visitors?"

"No, I don't think so."

"Will you allow the father to see her?"

"Yes."

"You can finish high school here," Mrs. Blackstone told Katherine. "We will help you do that. Of course, most of the girls are here for only the last few months of their pregnancy. Katherine will be here for most of her pregnancy." Mrs. Blackstone looked up doubtfully.

Katherine's ears perked up. "Are there no other girls who stay so long?" she asked.

"There is one girl from Nebraska who's been here for six months. She will deliver soon."

"Oh."

"There are, of course, rules and regulations we must follow here. Each girl has a job. Katherine will be buffing the dining room floors on weekend mornings."

"But Katherine likes to cook. Isn't there a job for her in the kitchen?" Mama asked.

"Not at the moment. Maybe early next month."

"Fine. Is there some place where we can buy maternity clothes?"

"No need to go out and buy them," Mrs. Blackstone said. "We have a box in the basement filled with clothes worn by other girls who've left. She can wear those." She glanced at her sheets of paper again. "How do you plan to pay?"

"There will be a check each month from the father's family lawyer. Katherine will give it to you when it comes."

"Do you have any questions?"

"No."

"You will go by your first name here. Your last name will be kept private. We do that as a way to protect each girl's identity," Mrs. Blackstone said.

"Okay."

"I'll introduce you as Katherine. Is that okay?"

"Yes."

"Your roommate's name is Janice. She knows you're coming. I'll take you up now."

Mrs. Blackstone took Katherine's suitcase and led them to the stairs. When Mama started to follow them up to the room she was supposed to live in for the next seven months, Mrs. Blackstone stopped her.

"I'm sorry. We try to provide total confidentiality for our girls here. We don't let parents go upstairs. You might see someone you know."

Mama backed off with what Katherine saw as the beginning of tears in her eyes.

She didn't allow herself to feel anything tender. Instead she turned her back on Mama as she followed Mrs. Blackstone upstairs.

Her stepfather Clark stood somewhere in the background watching.

July 28, 1998
High school cowboy

$\mathcal{M}$y thoughts travel on the wind out across the Wyoming plains. Then just as quickly, they come back to the car again. The speedometer says 65 miles per hour.

I used to go with a cowboy when I was in high school before I met Joe. He had a letter jacket and wore a cowboy hat to school. A lot of guys did that in Wyoming.

I went with him for something to do. He was nice enough though we couldn't communicate. When he arrived to take me to a dance, he smiled as he pinned a rose on my formal and my stepfather Clark stepped back to take a picture. Once in the car, we didn't speak. Most of our dates after that were the same. Silence. We necked a lot; I let him fondle my breasts, but I never let him touch my underpants. He was my Saturday night date, my trophy to show the other girls at the junior prom, someone to sit next to as we drove up and down Main Street.

He gave me his class ring. I wadded tape around it and polished the tape with pink fingernail polish. Wearing that ring and his letter jacket gave me an identity. But I wasn't into roping calves like he was, so he began looking for someone who was. When we broke up, I only felt bad because that meant I would have to sit home on Saturday night with my parents.

I never had a strong connection to cowboys and I don't feel especially attracted to this one sitting on my tail.

November, 1966
The home

The room Katherine followed Mrs. Blackstone into was dark and cold. It held three single beds, a sink, and a closet. A black-haired girl on the far bed glanced up at their entrance.

"Katherine, this is Janice."

The girl's delivery date was a month away, Katherine remembered.

She knew Mama would think this girl was nice, but she didn't like her. She was the type of girl who probably served tea and cookies, smiled as she sat down to talk with the women. The kind of girl who knitted sweaters like any good girl would.

"Why can't you be like that," Mama would have said if she had seen her.

"I'm not the serving type," she would have responded.

Katherine left her things and walked back down the stairs. She walked out the front door of the maternity home with her parents to have dinner at the Mr. Pork Restaurant across the street. The cold of that November night stung her skin. She had never been away from home before. She shivered.

That night when she returned from dinner, her room-mate Janice invited her to meet some girls across the hall. It was out of obligation, Katherine knew. But she went.

Ten girls were sitting on beds in the room knitting sweaters and talking.

"When's your due date?" was the first thing they asked.

"July 1."

"Where's the father?"

"In Wyoming."

"Most of us were jilted. What about you," one girl asked. Then she giggled.

Too many personal questions. Katherine bit down on the lump in her throat.

"We decided not to marry," she answered.

How could she tell them he wouldn't marry her, about the rings they had bought, the blood tests, the white dress and veil, the plans, the hopes, then the phone call?

"Never tell anyone," Mama said as they were leaving Wyoming.

Katherine didn't for awhile.

The city lights and sounds of sirens frightened her as she lay in bed that night.

Her roommate Janice hated her. She didn't say it, but Katherine knew.

Two days later, the other girl who would share their room arrived from Phoenix. Katherine lay in bed pretending to sleep when they ushered her in. The girl lay down on the bed next to Katherine's. Katherine heard her crying and thought, "Maybe she's a little more like me."

The next day the girl left and her bed was empty. She went back to Phoenix, they said.

Three weeks later on Christmas day, Katherine stayed inside all day waiting for a call from home that never came. Punishment for hurting the family name, she surmised.

July 28, 1998
Discrimination

$\mathscr{I}$look back into the rearview mirror and note the cowboy still tails me as I drive towards toward Brown Rock.

"Why doesn't he pass and get it over with?" I wonder. I'm weary of his game now. In the next town I plan to stop and think about my options.

If this cowboy is a local, the police will support him. I'm sure of that. If he's a crazy, who knows what they'll do. Likely they will find something wrong with me. After all, I'm a woman.

I'm out here alone with no one to support me, just like I felt in the 60s when I had to leave.

Now the best thing for me to do is get to a town where there are people.

I glance back again at the now empty road behind me and let my thoughts return to the past.

*   *   *

"Katherine's a 19th century woman," an acquaintance piped in as some friends and I sat discussing women at a table at a bar in Denver a few years after I left the maternity home.

"I don't think so," a friend disagreed.

"Look at her, her mannerisms. She's every bit the 19th century lady."

"If I am," I remember thinking and feeling irritated at the man I hardly knew for singling me out, "it's because Mama's hand shaped me." I didn't know then how much I resembled my grandmother Naomi.

Both she and Mama were housewives who stayed at home and looked after families. This influenced who they became. I wanted to get away from that stereotype.

From the way Mama hung her cardigan sweaters and silk blouses in the closet to the way she kept her kitchen completely clean and neat, everything about her radiated from the walls of her house as I sat listening to the foundation settle the night before her burial last year. It probably radiated from me, as I left Wyoming intent on doing things differently than Mama. But, I was trapped by a system intent on punishing me.

1967
Flashback

"What ya lookin' at," Katherine's roommate wanted to know.

"I was looking at the red T-Bird driving down the street."

"Someone you know?"

"No. Just reminded me of the father of my baby."

"Hell! Are ya expectin' him to come by?"

"I doubt it. Are you expecting your boyfriend to come?"

"No. He bailed out. I never expect ta see the bastard again in my life."

Katherine didn't think of Joe as a bastard. He was the young man who looked at the stars on a dark Wyoming night and held her hand. Surely such a man would pay a visit to see how she was doing.

But he never came.

July 28, 1998
Becoming a woman

$\mathscr{I}$ lived in an institution during my senior year in high school. And I couldn't go back home, I remember as I drive through the barren landscape of southeastern Wyoming watching for the cowboy in my rearview mirror.

During the time in the unwed mother's home, I longed for the days when family gathered together in Mama's house and I was cared for and protected.

But I never saw those days again.

With my belly getting bigger every day, I used to dream about my carefree days when I dragged Main Street in my parents' car and honked at every guy I saw.

I never saw those days again either, even when I had a flat belly. By the time I left the maternity home, I had become a woman.

It took me a long time to forget the fun I had with Joe that summer. The Free Speech movement was taking off in Berkeley. But as I sat in the maternity home, I wasn't free to talk about what as happening to me.

In Wyoming, people's thoughts were on having a nicer house or car than their neighbors or the latest gossip about some local. No one thought about the race discrimination in the South or the Vietnam War.

Young people went out on Saturday nights to get drunk and live the big time, so they thought.

Mama never told me anything about what to expect when I started to become a woman. When I had my first period, I thought I had a rare disease. When I started having morning sickness before I found out I was pregnant, I thought I was going to die. I thought most women delivered their babies by Cesarean section until I arrived at the home for unwed women.

1967

Pregnant girls

"Susan broke her water last night and she delivered this morning. She ripped because she's so small."

Katherine sat in the T.V. room with the other girls and listened to the latest.

"Cindy had a C-section."

"I hear you really have to bear down to push that baby out through the vagina."

Katherine had never learned anything from Mama. Listening was the only way to acquire information, but she wasn't going to let the other girls know how little she knew. She wanted them think she was a woman of the world.

"I had my public exam today," she told them one night as they sat around the T.V. soon after she arrived.

"Your what?" the girls around the T.V. asked in unison.

Immediately Katherine knew she had made a mistake.

"It certainly is a public exam," one of the girls laughed. "It's called a 'pelvic'."

They all laughed. It wasn't malicious laughter but still Katherine wanted to crawl under a chair. They soon forgot about her, though, and the talk turned to other girls.

"Did you see the new girl? She's only 12 years old. They say it was her brother."

"Did you hear that Cindy and her boyfriend used to do it on the kitchen floor while her parents were watching T.V. in the living room?"

"Can you believe that those two are sisters? They're due the same week. They're both soshes."

"What's a sosh?"

"They're the popular people. But I stayed away from them. Those people will do almost anything," one girl told her.

"What do you mean 'anything'," Katherine asked?

"Oh, you wouldn't believe. They're just really wild!"

Katherine accumulated information that might prove useful later.

She learned that she was not the only girl from her generation who didn't know the facts of life. There were others who knew less than she did. But most of them tried to put up a front of being worldly wise women.

*   *   *

"I am so bored," Katherine thought as she lay on her bed daydreaming as Motown music blared from KIMN, Denver's rock station on the radio.

That's why she studied hard and got straight As at the school at the unwed mother's home.

She picked up a book and began writing every word from Hamlet into her notebook.

Hamlet: *Whither wilt thou lead me? Speak. I'll go no further.*

Ghost: *"Mark me."*

Hamlet: *"I will."*

"You're a very good student," the black-haired male teacher told her. "You are so much better than most of these girls. You wouldn't believe how many problems some of them have. But you pick things right up."

Katherine had never heard that in Wyoming where everyone's goal was to be a cheerleader or a football player. If you weren't one of those, then you were left out.

"I don't want any of you to think about keeping your babies," the other teacher, a blonde from Littleton, lectured them frequently. That's about all Katherine ever heard from that woman.

* * *

Katherine was watching T.V. after dinner one night when she suddenly felt the need to go to the toilet. Inside the stall, she edged herself onto the cold rim of the stool and lost some type of long stringy discharge. There was some name for it but she couldn't remember what it was called.

"You'd better go up to the hospital," one of the girls sitting around the T.V. told her.

"I want to count the contractions first. They told us not to go up there until the contractions begin to come every five minutes."

Soon after, her water broke.

When she went to bed that night, the contractions started. She lay on her bed timing them.

Her going into labor upset her latest roommate. Everything Katherine did got on her nerves, it seemed.

"Why do you wear that 'Alaskan Moomoo?'" For some reason she didn't like the blue robe Mama had sent her for Christmas. "Your slippers are making too much noise. They're keeping me awake," she complained as Katherine walked up and down the halls of the unwed mother's home alone counting the time between contractions. "Can't you take them off."

Katherine did.

She walked the cold linoleum halls barefoot at 11:00 at night. She timed the contractions until they were down to five minutes apart. Then she went upstairs to the hospital.

"How ya doin?" the nurse on duty asked her gruffly.

"Oh! The pain! The pain is so bad!"

"Sit down on the table and spread yer legs."

Katherine felt like a piece of machinery that had to be repaired.

As contractions racked her body with unbearable pain, she lay down on the cold plastic table. The nurse timed her contractions to be sure she was ready for labor. Then she put Katherine in a gown and shaved off her pubic hairs. She led her to the labor room where Katherine was to stay until she was ready to deliver.

"How's everything going?" a young intern in a white coat walked in and asked her.

"Okay. But the pain is so bad," she told him.

She would have gone through labor alone if it hadn't been for him coming by to hold her hand every half-hour.

"I want to die," she told him.

"Do you want us to give you something for the pain?" he asked as he took her hand and held it. "If we do, it might stop the labor is the only thing."

"How much longer do you think I have?"

"Not much I think. We can give you a little Demerol. It should be okay."

"All right."

Then Katherine was alone until another doctor walked in.

"Am I going to deliver now?" she asked.

"You sure are. Are you ready?"

"Yes. I am."

It was around 9:30 a.m. when they dilated her cervix, gave her a saddle block anesthesia, put her on the table, and had her spread her legs. Then they held up a mirror.

"Do you want to see your baby being born?" the nurse asked her.

Too tired and worn out from the long ordeal of labor, the mirror looked hazy. A few minutes later Katherine's vagina ripped.

Rips heal better than cuts, she had been told by other mothers.

The nurse held the baby up for her to see.

"It's a girl! Isn't she beautiful," she exclaimed as she wiped the blood off the baby's body.

Yes, she was beautiful. But Katherine knew that she had to hold her emotions aloof because she wasn't supposed to want to keep her. Why didn't they let her do the human thing — hold her baby in her arms and cradle her?

July 28, 1998
Space

*W*hy doesn't that cowboy do the gentlemanly thing and pass me and get it over with. Why doesn't he give me some space out here?

If you grow up in Wyoming, space is an important element. You don't know until you leave and live in a large city just how much you need it.

I absorb the Wyoming landscape as I drive. Up ahead, the cloud in the sky makes me think of my grandmother Naomi.

If Naomi had been alive, would she have encouraged me to keep my baby? Or would she have had the same outlook as Mama who felt I needed to hide? I feel a sudden urgency to get to my destination.

I look back to the rearview mirror and see the cowboy. I need the space to unwind from the stress of my work in San Francisco. I need to think about my life right now and where I'm going. I need to think about what I'm going to do once I get to Brown Rock.

But this guy intrudes.

July 14, 1967
Loss of innocence

"Some are very quiet when they go through labor," a big blond-haired girl told Katherine after the doctors stitched her up and wheeled her into the next room where the other mothers who had already given birth stared at her. "You screamed the whole night!"

I did? Isn't that what most of the girls did? Katherine wondered how anyone could go through that without screaming! When she stood up to go to the bathroom, blood gushed out.

"You aren't supposed to stand up," the same girl yelled at her like she was a total fool.

"Guess I goofed again," she thought.

The nurse was soon there to help her.

"I have to go to the bathroom."

"Here's a pan. Go in this."

The next day Katherine had trouble going.

"It's because of the stitches," they told her. "That'll pass."

It did. Then they began to itch. So they took her to a sitz bath.

"A new experience," Katherine thought as she sat there feeling the water ease the discomfort around the vagina and anus. "This is something I'll have to tell my sister Sarah."

Katherine was a woman of the world now. She knew the terms pelvic examinations, saddle blocks, sitz baths. Never again would anybody tell her she was naïve.

July 28, 1998
Lost opportunity

$\mathcal{M}$ama wasn't there for the birth of my daughter, I remember as I drive towards Brown Rock.

"I can't go to Denver alone," she told me. "Besides, I don't want to spend money needlessly for a motel room," she also said.

The opportunity was there for us to draw closer. Mama's fear of spending money as usual kept her away. I remembered the phone call that never came on Christmas day. So I braced myself ahead of time.

"Don't expect anything from her," I told myself. I pretended like it didn't matter.

I may not have even gone to the unwed mother's home if Joe's father hadn't paid the bill.

Mama would have probably said they didn't have the money. That's why my stepfather Clark didn't adopt me when he married Mama when I was five, they told me. I went by Katherine Helman, but the adoption didn't take place. He and Mama were just starting out and Mama had four daughters. He couldn't afford to adopt all of us, Mama said. But I knew it wasn't true. Clark was doing quite well. The Depression shaped Mama's tightness with money. She had always found an excuse not to spend it.

* * *

July 15, 1967
A name

"*H*ave you decided on a name for your baby," the nurse asked.

"What?"

"We need a name to put on your baby's birth certificate," the nurse told her the next day.

"Carmen." Katherine pulled the name from off the top of her head.

"And a middle name?"

"Lenore."

"What last name?"

Oh, god. She couldn't think. Joe's family name or hers?

"Helman," her stepfather's name, was what she finally told them.

"Did you have to use our name?" Mama was upset when she told her. "Haven't you hurt the family enough?"

*   *   *

"Are ya ready to hold your baby now?"

"Yes!"

The nurse who came looking for her two days after delivery, handed her a white gown. She put it on and followed the nurse into a room with windows. Then she brought Katherine's baby in and handed her over. She gave Katherine a bottle to feed her. Her daughter looked up at her. Their eyes met.

She, in a white layette and a pair of diapers, sucked formula from the bottle and looked up at Katherine intently.

"This is my baby," she thought with wonder. She rocked her back and forth as she stood there feeding her. The baby's eyes never left Katherine's.

"Time's up. It's time for her nap. I'll take her now," the nurse appeared at the doorway before Katherine had a chance to even feel like a mother.

"But I just got here. Can't we wait a little longer?"

"Nope. I'm afraid not."

Katherine was ushered out to the only place they let her see her baby from then on—through the window in the hallway.

July 28, 1998
Imprint

*M*others who relinquished their children to adoption had only one chance to feed and hold their babies at the Floton home in the 60s, I remember as I drive towards Brown Rock. They let you stay with your child just long enough to imprint the moment on your life forever. Then they kept you at a distance until you signed the relinquishment papers.

Death came traveling on wings. It hovered over Mama like she was Carrion. It flew round and round with its eye on her lung and the cancer. Then it made its plunge. Something similar happened with my daughter.

I deal with the loss of Mama as I think about my daughter and being alone out here on the plains with a cowboy following. An apparition urges me on, to what? I'm not yet certain.

I look out across the plains and note a rock formation off to my right. I look back to the rearview mirror and push down on the gas pedal.

July 17, 1967
Relinquishment

*T*hree days after delivery, Katherine set her hair in rollers. She pulled a blue short-sleeved v-necked top over her head then stepped into a light blue straight knit skirt. She stepped into some white high heels. She curled her eyelashes and put on massacre and light pink lipstick.

She didn't look at anyone as she walked into the dining room, though she knew everyone was looking at her. She sat down at the special table where only those who had given birth sat.

The special table for birthmothers. That's the title that she would soon be carrying for the rest of her life. Birthmother.

"You look nice this morning," the girl next to her said.

"Thank you," Katherine smiled.

Katherine was now a woman with a flat belly, at least flatter than those of the mothers who hadn't yet delivered. The women at the mother's table were the envy of all those still waiting for their babies to be born.

Little did she know that change would mean her baby would soon be gone.

Later that afternoon, she set out for a long walk. When she came back, her caseworker was waiting at the front door waving a piece of paper in the air.

"I've been looking all over for you. They're here to take your baby," she told her. "You'll have to sign these papers."

"What! You said they were coming next week! Can't they come back?"

"No, they can't. You'll have to sign now."

"And if I don't?"

"You must."

So she did. When Katherine went up to the hospital that day, her daughter Carmen was gone. The bed where she used to lie was now occupied by somebody else's baby. It would be many years before Katherine saw Carmen again.

The next week Mama and Clark arrived to take her home.

They were waiting in the hallway by the elevator when she got off with her bags.

They walked down the long passageway to the door. As they were leaving, Katherine turned and looked back.

Not a soul in sight. The sun was shining through a window leaving a pool of light near where the woman with a bulging belly had stood when she arrived seven months before.

Katherine turned her back and walked out of the Floton unwed mothers' home.

July 28, 1998
Woman of the world

"Good girl/bad girl." Those words don't mean anything to me anymore. But now there's this guy back there on the highway as I drive towards Brown Rock. Perhaps because I'm a woman alone, he thinks it's an open invitation. So I have to be careful.

But no sign of the cowboy as I approach Fort Windpeak, Wyoming.

Perhaps he pulled back because he knew we were approaching a town and was afraid I would report him.

What should I do? My apprehension about dealing with the local police holds me back from calling them. It must be some of Mama in me that doesn't want to draw attention. Or perhaps I'm just afraid they won't believe me or do anything about it. For the time being, I'll keep moving on. As long as I'm moving, I should be safe enough.

He has shown up again now that I've turned a curve in the road. What statement might he be making as he follows me without passing when he has the chance?

Twelve miles to Brown Rock, the sign says.

*   *   *

In my forties now, I have returned to Wyoming, "a woman of the world" and proud of it. The sexual revolution helped change my views of what a woman could be. It made me realize that I could live without a man. This opposed Mama's hope that I would meet a good man, find a church, and settle down.

I was always too involved in adventure and finding out who I was to commit myself to any man. Perhaps I've never really known how to relate to men because Papa wasn't there and Clark was always too busy to teach me. Or perhaps I never grieved properly when Papa left. Whatever the case, I've learned how to live without a man in my life.

When they told me that signing the relinquishment papers and giving up all rights as a mother was the best thing that I could do for my child, I believed them.

But, there were so many things I didn't know at the time.

What's done is done! There's no need expounding on it or mulling it over until the thing takes on a life of its own. I'm sure that's what Papa would have told me if I had been able to talk to him about my baby.

I have a feeling that's what my grandmother Naomi would have probably also told me if she had been there after I signed away my rights as a mother to my daughter.

I think she might have also said, "I'm so sorry honey that you had to go through that. I'm so sorry that you lost yer daughter. Our family has lost a baby girl and it will take us years to recover. But don't you worry honey. You'll be okay."

When I got back to Wyoming after giving birth to my daughter, the subject was never brought up again. When I tried to talk about it, people acted like something was wrong with me. So I kept the secret and grief hidden away.

The Wyoming wind reminds me that I found no comfort out here on the high plains after my daughter was born and given away. They turned their heads and looked away. I was expected to just get on with my life and pre-tend that it didn't happen. But I never forgot my daughter!

1971
A together woman

*F*our years after giving birth to her daughter, Katherine, with hair hanging down to her waist, sat smoking a joint in Colorado with some conscientious objectors who bowed out of the Vietnam War for religious reasons. She was working as a secretary at the time.

"Katherine is a real together woman," they said as the Moody Blues "Days of Future Past" played on her turntable and she passed the joint around.

Little did they know as she sat barefoot and cross-legged on her apartment floor writing poetry in her notebook, that there was a big empty space inside her. Easier for her to write than to talk about that part of her that was missing. She couldn't just forget and move on.

Four years after she gave away her baby, she shuffled paper and typed letters in an office and went out on dates with men on the weekend. She was committed to one man for three years. He asked her to go to Burma with him.

"I don't think I'm ready," Katherine told him as she felt herself quaking inside at the prospect.

Instead, she quit her secretarial job in Denver, gave away most of her clothes, packed up her car, and headed to the Pine Ridge area of South Dakota where, where for $40 a month she rented a farm with no running water or heat. She paid rent to a man she knew.

Her landlord, a black-haired, black-eyed dope dealer with an MBA from the University of Colorado, looked like her cousin, so she trusted him. Later she learned that he was nothing more than a businessman bucking author-ity and far from trustworthy.

"He should be paying you to stay on that farm and take care of things," a friend told her.

But Katherine hoped to gain a new perspective. So she jumped at the chance and paid the $40 rent.

She didn't tell her family where she was going. Her sister found out when she called her at work and talked to her boss.

"She's gone to live with the hippies," he said.

Her sister immediately freaked.

Two weeks after Katherine arrived at the farm, a letter arrived from Mama.

"September 17, 1970

Dear Katherine,

We're very concerned that you gave up a promising career to move to a farm. Your sister called and told me you had moved. She cried and cried. We're all very upset. We are wondering why you would do such a thing?

Love,

Mama"

"It was a dead end," she felt like saying but didn't. She didn't see how Mama could see a paper-shuffling job as promising. Being a secretary was a fine profession, but Katherine didn't want to do that forever.

None of her family ever came to visit her on the farm.

July 28, 1998
On the way to South Dakota

"*Y*our daughter is in Red Earth, Wyoming with a foster family," my older sister Sarah had told me a month and a half after I signed away my rights as a mother. Mama told her to tell me.

When I drove this way years ago on the way to South Dakota, I used to think of my daughter. I knew she'd been fostered not far from here. I think of all the wasted years and have to hold onto the anger that threatens to spill over as I glance into the mirror and see the cowboy again.

It was almost as if I were already searching for my daughter when I drove these roads back then. But, I only knew that I felt an empty space inside me hoping to fill it by living on a South Dakota farm. Perhaps I was also searching for my grandmother Naomi by living on a farm with no running water or heat, living the lifestyle that Naomi lived in the 1920s when she moved to Wyoming.

What part does Naomi play in all of this? I wonder as I push my foot down on the gas pedal and speed up to 75 to get rid of the cowboy. He keeps pace with me. I push my foot down on the brake and slow down to 60 thinking maybe I can buck him off and force him to pass. He slows down, too. Frustrated, I speed up again to 75 and put the car in cruise. I keep my eye on the mirror as I continue on.

1972

A strong woman

"*Y*ou will have a relationship with a strong woman," a clairvoyant living up Boulder Canyon had told the dark-haired Spanish man who came calling at the farm that fall. He took one look at Katherine barreling down the road towards the farm in her '62 gray Saab and decided she was that strong woman.

"Hi. I'm John," he said as she climbed out of her car. "You called and left a message that you wanted to borrow my chain saw to cut some wood."

"Oh yeah. Hi. I'm Katherine." She looked at him smiling at her from his pickup. Her heart did a flip-flop. Be careful, her head told her; but in the realm of love, Katherine's heart ruled.

She invited him inside where she wadded up some paper and threw it into the potbelly stove along with some kindling. She lit a fire, threw in a big log and filled a teapot with water.

"Are you hungry?"

"A little."

"Do you want some eggs?"

"Sure."

She took out a skillet and eggs as John pulled out a baggie of marijuana and some papers and rolled a joint. They talked while they ate and smoked.

"I'm married," John admitted.

"Oh." Now you tell me, she thought.

"We're having lots of problems. Too many things coming down. We're probably going ta separate."

"Oh. So you think that you will divorce?"

"Yeah."

She didn't know whether she believed him or not. But it was a little too late because her heart had already been caught.

After they finished eating, John looked at her and she looked at him. They fell into each other arms then headed for the bedroom. In the darkness, he whispered the words of the clairvoyant.

"What happens when he finds out I'm not as strong as he thinks," Katherine wondered as she beat herself over the head for jumping in so quickly.

She was never to find out. His wife let herself get pregnant again, most likely as a way to keep him, Katherine thought. He stayed in the marriage.

Katherine tried to get over the pain by working hard on the farm and writing songs.

Each day as she lifted the axe over her head to chop some wood, her anger ebbed up into her arms and came down hard on the man she had trusted.

July 28, 1998
Isolation and the cowboy mentality

$\mathcal{N}$ow the road to Brown Rock draws me along as the cowboy speeds up behind me. I push down on the gas pedal and the needle on the speedometer passes 75. Adrenaline begins to pump in. I get ready for a little bit of adventure, a wild chase. As the speedometer on my car reaches 80, he speeds up. Still he keeps me close. For what? I wonder.

Isolation and the cowboy mentality turn a lot of Wyoming men into thirteen-year-old boys. Similar to some of the Iranian Shiites I taught in Europe in 1987, they have trouble with communication—sitting down at a table across from a woman, looking her in the eye, and making conversation; but they do love the chase.

My grandfather Sam, Naomi's husband, also liked to chase after women, Papa said. I hope to learn more about him when I get to Brown Rock.

"My god! What's going on here?" I look into the rear view mirror and see a flame of light from the sun on his windshield just as the cowboy's truck bumps up against my back fender. "What the hell is he doing?"

Quickly I speed up to 85. I'll stop at the next town and call the police; I don't care if they are rednecks.

I look into the mirror again and notice that he has pulled his truck way back. I also notice a car coming over the hill behind him.

"He's afraid he'll get caught," I think as I speed up and put as much distance between us as I can.

1972

Nietsche?

"What do you think about Nietsche?" The blonde man with big red lips and blue eyes waved his pipe as he spoke.

"I don't know. I haven't read him." Katherine shifted uncomfortably. Roy had stood behind her and encouraged her to get it all out after the relationship with John ended, but he made her feel inadequate by asking things she didn't know.

"You haven't read *Thus Spake Zarathustra?*"

"No."

"Well, you should read him."

The next week Katherine went to the library and checked out all of his books and spent several hours a day reading. She didn't care for Nietsche, but got quickly hooked on Tolstoy and Dostoyevsky.

"Have you thought about going to college?"

"Yes, I have. But I can't afford to go right now."

"Well, you should."

"Maybe in a couple of years."

"I wouldn't wait too long. You can do it. I did it. Hell, if you decide to go, I'll support you."

"You will?"

"Sure."

Even though her heart didn't beat out of control when she was around Roy, she enjoyed his company and he was prodding her to do something different with her life.

Making love to Roy seemed to be about performing the act and getting it over with and then jumping out of bed and taking a shower really quick. Roy was a cold man. He didn't seem to really like women, but he definitely provided some intellectual stimulation in Katherine's life.

She wasn't over John the carpenter yet. So books provided the perfect outlet just as they used to do in the unwed mother's home.

July 28, 1998
Hiding

*R*est stop one mile, the sign says. I wonder if he will see me if I pull off and park behind the restrooms? I decide to chance it.

I turn off and ease my car next to some others at the back of the parking lot away from the highway.

My heart begins beating as I see the cowboy's red pickup drive by. Hopefully he didn't see me.

I settle in to wait.

1959

Secrets

"She died in a fire is what I heard."

"What kind of fire?"

"Just a fire."

"Was it a big fire?"

"I don't know. Our grandpa killed her is what I heard."

"What do you mean he killed her? I thought she died in a fire?"

"Well, it was a fire. But he set it."

"Why?"

"I don't know. Some people say it was an accident. But I don't believe them."

"Why not?"

"I just don't."

Katherine learned at an early age to keep her ears perked and to ask questions when people started talking about her grandmother. She thought her grandmother burning to death in Wyoming might have something to do with Papa leaving because Mama and Papa were always fighting about it.

"Yer darn right that's why he left," Katherine's oldest sister Carol told her. "He doesn't want to admit that his mother was murdered."

"Murdered? Who murdered her?"

"Grandpa Geislingen did!"

"Are you sure?"

"I don't know. I'm only goin' by what I heard."

Katherine never forgot those words.

July 28, 1998
Change

$\mathcal{M}$y eyes move out across the trees that line the parking lot at the rest stop. The cowboy passed ten minutes ago. I'll wait for ten more minutes before I continue on down the road.

So much has happened, I think, while I wait for it to be safe to go out on the road again. It has been a long journey.

At eighteen I lost my daughter. At twenty-three, I left the farm and returned to Colorado where I got a B.A. in journalism at the university in Colorado Springs.

In the summer of 1986, while I was finishing a master's in linguistics, I set out to find my daughter.

∩

1984

Digging

$\mathcal{I}$t was time to seek the truth, Katherine decided. She needed to know about her daughter. Afraid but determined, she rang the Floton Home.

"I can send you your medical records and any other information in your file," the nurse told her. She was the same nurse who had helped deliver her baby. "You aren't trying to find your daughter, are you?"

"No."

But as soon as Katherine got off the phone, she started making plans to head up to Wyoming to look around.

"I can put a letter in your daughter's file," the man in the Department of Social Services in Wyoming told Katherine when she went up there a week later.

Katherine's hopes began to soar; but a week later when she called him he said, "I can't find the folder."

"He changed his mind about helping me," Katherine thought, feeling dejected. The bureaucratic system seemed to be locked tight and the task of finding her daughter impossible. "Whatever made me think I could find my daughter," she asked herself after the man at the Wyoming Office of Social Services slammed the door in her face.

After a year of contacting Wyoming and getting nowhere, Katherine was about ready to give up the search.

Then one day the phone rang and she picked up the receiver.

* * *

"Have you got a piece of paper and a pencil?" the caller asked Katherine in a deep, throaty toned phonation.

"Yeah," she replied beginning to anticipate what was to come since she recognized the female caller's voice. It belonged to a woman she knew who had been helping her with her search.

"I have your daughter's name, her adoptive father's name and profession, and her adoptive mother's maiden name."

"Oh, my god! Is it really happening?" Katherine sat down and began to write.

"Daughter's name: Cynthia Jane Thompson. Adoptive father's name: John Thompson. Mother: Phyllis Jennings Thompson.

A week later, with some names in her hand, Katherine was on the road to Cheyenne to look at public records. She learned that her daughter's adoptive father was a teacher. So, she called the state department of education in Cheyenne and found out that he was working at a school in Rawlins. Then she found his name and address in the city directory.

A week later, Katherine was out on the highway again, this time driving towards the town where her daughter's adoptive father and mother lived.

When she walked into the office of the superintendent of schools there, she glanced down at the name plaque setting on the desk of the secretary she was talking to. It said "Phyllis Thompson". She looked at the woman's face and tried to keep her voice from shaking and her heart from beating out of her chest as she talked to her daughter's adoptive mother.

"Where can I find copies of old high school yearbooks?" she asked.

"They have them up at the high school."

Katherine didn't tell the woman who she was. She had decided in the beginning of the search not to tell anyone what she was doing until after she talked to her daughter. She didn't want anyone to sabotage her efforts. So she made up stories as she went along.

As she flipped through high school yearbooks in the waiting area of the high school office, she turned to the secretary.

"I just noticed in this yearbook that one of the teachers is John Thompson. My daughter has a friend named Cynthia Thompson whose father is called John. I thought they lived in Colorado, though. Maybe I was mistaken. Does this John Thompson have a daughter named Cynthia?"

"I think so. She's married, isn't she?"

"Who? Cynthia Thompson?"

"Yeah."

"No. My daughter's friend is not married. So it must be a different person."

Katherine paid for the yearbooks and went out to find a phone. Her heart was beating as she stopped and dialed the phone number of the county clerk's office.

"I'm calling from Sears. I have a young woman here applying for credit who says that her name is Cynthia Thompson; but when I try to check the name, I come up with nothing. I'm wondering whether she might have a married name. Could you check?"

"What was the last name?"

"Thompson."

"Cynthia Thompson?"

"Yeah."

"When was she married?"

"I don't have a date. Check the years between 1983 and now."

"Okay. Just a minute."

"I have a Cynthia Thompson who married a Kenneth Ore on May 19, 1983."

"May 1983?"

"Yes. That's right."

"Okay. Thank you so much. Bye." Click.

Katherine headed for the library to get a copy of the marriage announcement from the local newspaper.

Then she checked the city directory for a phone number for any "Ore".

"Hello. Is Kenneth Ore there?"

"Did you say Kenneth Ore?"

"Yes."

"He doesn't live here any more. I think they moved to Idaho."

"Kenneth Ore and his wife Cynthia moved to Idaho?"

"Yeah. I think so."

"Thanks. Bye."

When Katherine got back to Colorado, she checked the Idaho city directories and came up with the name "Kenneth Ore" in Boise. She photocopied the page with the phone number. Then she sat back and sorted out what she would say to her daughter when she called.

*   *   *

Two months later, Katherine picked up the telephone receiver and dialed her daughter's number.

"Hello."

"Is Cynthia Ore there?"

"Yes. This is she."

Then a pause as Katherine grasped for something to say. She had written down the words and memorized what she would say beforehand, but her mind went blank as soon as she heard Cynthia's voice on the phone. She began to stutter and stammer.

"I gave birth to a daughter on July 1, 1967, at the Floton Home for Unwed Mothers in Denver, Colorado," Katherine stammered. "And I've been, uh, searching for the last year, and I've recently found out that my birth daughter's name is, uh, Cynthia Thompson Ore."

Katherine felt the tears coming and didn't think she'd be able to talk after that.

Silence on the other end of the line.

"Uh, I don't know how much you know about your adoption."

"Yeah, my parents have, you know, filled me in as much as they can. Uh, could I ask you where you were from originally?"

"I was from Elk Mountain, Wyoming."

"Well, it sounds close and everything."

"Uh huh. Yeah, I'm sure that from the digging that I've been doing…" Katherine stopped to catch her breath. "It's not really likely that there's any mistake. Um, although if you're interested in finding out more, you can contact Floton in Denver, you know."

"What is it?"

"It's Floton. It's the home."

"Floton?"

"Yeah. I was in the Floton Home in Denver and, um, they still have the records, you know. And I named you Carmen Lenore when you were born."

"Oh my god!"

Katherine heard the gasp and tears in her daughter's voice when she told her the name.

"Did you know that name?"

"Yeah. My mom told me. The social worker had given her that name when they first adopted me."

The quiet sound of sobbing from both sides transferred across the telephone line for the next few moments.

"I don't want to rush you because I know that all of this could be too much. You might need some time to process things, but I'd really like to meet you."

"Yes. I want to meet you, too. You don't know how much. I've been waiting for this for a long time!"

"You have?"

"Yes. I can't begin to tell you. You wouldn't believe it."

Two weeks later, Katherine stood at Cynthia's door with a rose in her hand.

Cynthia had dark hair like her father. Hazel-eyed and tall and willowy like Katherine, she had most of her mannerisms. Yes, this was definitely her daughter, she thought as she stood there looking at her.

July 28, 1998
Skeletons in the closet

I turn the keys in the ignition and start the engine. I back away from the curb at the rest stop and head out on the highway.

Not a car or truck in sight! I let out a sigh of relief. It's been stressful having that cowboy following me.

I glance off across the plains as I drive towards Brown Rock. I'll never think about Wyoming without thinking of my daughter Cynthia as a link. I left the state thirty years ago to give birth to her. Oh yes, I've been back. But this time it's different. Now I'm returning, in part because of her.

But haunted by skeletons in Papa's family closet, I plan to do some digging to find out the truth about how my grandmother Naomi died and lay things to rest once and for all.

I glance back into the side mirror just as the cowboy's red pickup truck speeds up behind me.

What! He passed me a long time ago while I was parked at the rest stop. He must have seen me and pulled over somewhere and waited.

Well, I'll just stay put awhile unless he tries some more funny business. Maybe he'll pass me soon. Maybe I will call the police if he bothers me once I get there.

The woman who stands poised next to her husband in the 1925 photo I carry in my purse looks like she was a hard-working woman. Her brow is furrowed, her hair pulled tightly back off the face and fastened in a bun. She has the look of dirt poor, almost hillbilly. About seven years after that photo was taken, Naomi was dead at the age of forty-seven.

Did he kill her? My reason for heading to Brown Rock. I intend to find out. It could be a one-shot deal.

1997

Mama

"*How* will we know where to go when we get to the airport," Mama asked her from a morphine-induced hallucination as she lay in her bed in the nursing home as Katherine sat in a chair beside her.

"We'll know when we get there," Katherine told her. "There will be people there. We can ask."

"How will we know them?" she rasped.

Katherine took her hand and held it then said, "We'll just have to trust, Mama."

"Well, okay then."

Her eyes rolled back into her head. Then she let out a sigh of relief, lay back on the bed and went to sleep.

Katherine sensed that Mama had taken in her words like a prayer, a guiding light to lead her from life into death. Two months later, she was dead.

Mama's words stuck with her.

* ⋆ *

July 28, 1998
The birthmother

I had no idea where things would go once I met Cynthia. I suppose that I must have been living some type of fairly tale in my head. I would arrive at her house and everyone would live happily ever after. That's not exactly the way it went.

When I arrived in Cynthia's life, I must have acted like Mama, but I didn't recognize it at the time. Mama had been my only role model for motherhood.

Most women in my generation headed out into adulthood following the traditional route, like Mama. But, directions on how to be a birthmother had not yet been written up by Emily Post. I had to grope my way along.

The well-kept secret Mama told me not to tell was finally brought out of the closet and aired after I found my daughter, I remember as I drive towards Brown Rock.

"I have a daughter!" I could tell the world!

I kept forgetting in the beginning, though, that there were still people in places like Wyoming, and even in San Francisco, who viewed life much the same as they did when I got pregnant out of wedlock in the 60s. They still judged me for what happened thirty years ago.

Then there's this cowboy who probably hasn't grown out of the role that cowboys were probably playing since the turn of the century. In a lot of places, people seem to be locked in time.

*   *   *

It hasn't been easy coming out as an unwed mother, I muse as I glance in the mirror to see where the cowboy is.

"She's illegitimate," I remember overhearing some colleagues talking and laughing when I walked into the office in San Francisco. When they saw me, immediately all talk stopped. Were they talking about me, I wondered? I had never told them that my daughter had been born out of wedlock. I try to keep work and my personal life separate. But, it would have been easy enough for them to find out. One of my colleagues had been around while I was living in Colorado just after I found my daughter. I had been excited then and talked a lot. Later when I learned that there was still a stigma, I was more careful about whom I told.

"Being a birthmother is not the real thing," my own sister told me just after I found my daughter. She felt that one had to be married and raise the child to be considered a mother.

Motherhood is equivalent to sainthood in the American culture. A "saint" must be pure and white. The term "birthmother" carries a tinge of sin with it. It also gives the idea that something has been lost. Most people don't know how to deal with loss in the U.S. They are afraid to talk about it. So it gets hushed up. The same is true when one loses a child to adoption.

Even though young people today find it okay for a single woman to have a baby and not be married, the stigma still influences people's views for many different reasons. People in my own generation still carry the ideas they learned in the 60s.

I have kept my ears opened to try to assess what other attitudes society has about birthmothers. I have sensed that underlying the openness about out-of-wedlock pregnancies there still runs a judgmental current of thought that wants to keep single mothers and their children clearly identified.

Even though I became a free woman during the 60s, I wasn't the free, promiscuous woman that some people might have thought. I often went without a man for years.

After living for ten years in San Francisco, which Mama used to call the "Sodom and Gomorrah of America" because of the large gay community there, some people thought I was a lesbian because I was over forty and not married.

I'm attracted to men even though most of the eligible ones my age in San Francisco are gay. It hasn't mattered most of the time, I recall, because most of the time my mind has been engrossed in my work.

I have never been with a woman. So I guess that makes me normal, according to my family's views at least.

Living without a man has often been simpler than living with one. I have not found it easy to try to appease the white male heterosexual ego. It takes energy I could invest elsewhere.

I have never had the patience to be a good trainer of men. And I've never met a man who didn't need to be trained.

My family still lives in the age, like my classmates in high school, when you called a woman who didn't marry an "old maid." I have spent most of my life working to free myself from those types of restrictive labels.

I suspect my sister Linda has sometimes been ashamed to introduce me to her friends. She feels that a woman my age should be married. Whenever I go home, they leave me out of activities that I enjoy because they are for couples only.

In Spain where I lived for three years just after I found my daughter, things were different. There was no stigma there about being single and unmarried. People there looked on my strength and independence as exotic.

But in the U.S. in the 1990s, people in most areas are influenced by puritanical beliefs. A woman needs to be under the rule of a man. Old-fashioned perhaps, but it's still how many people in most parts of the country feel.

I glance into the rearview mirror. When my eyes move back to the highway in front of me, I think about what I might find when I arrive in Brown Rock. What clues will I uncover there that will clarify once and for all the conflicting stories in Papa's family of how my grandmother died?

1985
The birthfather

"*I*'ve discussed this with my wife. And we both feel that you shouldn't contact your daughter," Joe wrote Katherine when she told him she had been searching for and found her daughter.

Did he think she was writing for advice? Katherine wondered. She hadn't told him that she had already contacted Cynthia.

She took great satisfaction in sending him photos of their reunion and the message, "All went well."

Although he wrote to Cynthia, he made it clear that he was not welcoming her into his family.

Cynthia felt hurt and angry when she read his letter and Katherine was angry on her behalf.

"He's just repeating what he did twenty years ago when he chose not to marry me," Katherine said.

"I feel I'm intruding," Joe explained to Katherine in a letter. "She has another family, her adoptive parents whom she grew up with. I have high respect for the adoption system. And I don't want to go in and disrupt things in these people's lives."

"I'm seeing a pattern here," Katherine wrote back to him. "You didn't want her in your life twenty years ago. Why should we expect things to be different now?"

Katherine turned her mind to other things like what her daughter planned to do because Joe was afraid to tell his parents about her.

May, 1986
The adoptee

Cynthia wrote to her grandparents a couple of years after Joe's refusal. The response was immediate: "We were so glad to hear from you. If you're ever up in our area, please stop by." There was no further contact.

Several years later Cynthia wrote them again. The not so immediate reply stated: "We have health problems. You have your family. So get on with your life."

Cynthia called Katherine and told her.

"That means you can't show up at their door. But you have a right to know your grandparents. If you want to meet them, there's no law saying we can't talk to them if we see them on the street."

That was their hopeful intent when they headed to western Wyoming together. They were on an adventure not knowing what they'd meet.

July 25, 1998
The adoptive mom

"*My* adoptive mom is an alcoholic," Cynthia told Katherine.

"How long has she been drinking?"

"As long as I can remember."

"Was that hard?"

"Yeah it was. She used to get real mean when she drank. I still have problems with it."

Katherine wondered if Cynthia would follow her adoptive mother's pattern towards addiction.

"Did your mom drink while she was growing up," Katherine asked Cynthia.

"No! Her mom and dad were strict Baptists."

"So it was after she married your dad that she began."

"Yeah, I think so."

"So there must have been something missing in the marriage, an empty place she had to fill," Katherine thought out loud to Cynthia.

"My mom loved my dad! That's what she told me," Cynthia immediately began to defend her father. "Don't go blaming my dad for that!"

"Oh. Okay." Katherine could feel the strong emotion in Cynthia's voice. So she didn't bring it up again. Her feelings didn't change though about why Cynthia's adoptive mother got addicted to drink.

July 28, 1998
He passes

Five miles before Brown Rock, I look into my rearview mirror and see the cowboy. He speeds up, pulling far out into the left lane. A few minutes later, he gives me a wave as he passes. Soon he's out of sight.

"Whew!" I give a sigh of relief.

July 26, 1998
A one-shot deal

*K*atherine and Cynthia walked down the sidewalk. Cynthia remained silent, lost in her thoughts. Katherine, too, was preoccupied with wondering what to expect from Joe's father if they met him. She recalled what she knew of him.

He was an educated man, upstanding in the community. A Goldwater man in the 60s, he was probably approaching eighty now. He had lived in western Wyoming most of his life. Would he have a patronizing view towards her? she wondered. She had to force herself to let go of intimidation.

A dog barking pulled both women from their musings. They saw a tall gangly bald-headed man with a dog on a leash walking towards them.

"What a cute dog," Katherine exclaimed as she knelt down to scratch the dog behind its ears. "Is she a cocker spaniel?"

Just as she asked this, it hit her. "The Vandorn's have a yellow Labrador," one of the neighbors down the street told them when they asked for directions. This was definitely a Labrador she was petting.

She looked up from her kneeling perch beside the dog right into the probing blue eyes of Mr. Vandorn.

"Nice day for a walk," she commented as she massaged the dog's ears then stood up to meet him eye to eye.

"Yes," he said. "I thought we were in for more rain. But it looks like that front has passed."

"Oh, so you've had some rain up here?"

"Yes," he answered. "You're not from here? Where are you from?"

"I'm from California. My daughter lives in Idaho."

"Your flowers are pretty," Cynthia commented.

"Yes," he said not looking at her. "We just put them out today. You visiting family here?" he asked Katherine, almost ignoring Cynthia.

Funny you should ask, she thought, as she told him, "Yes, we are."

The time had come, she decided as she pushed back her fear and held out her hand to introduce herself and her daughter.

"My name is Katherine Helman and this is my daughter Cynthia Ore, your granddaughter."

A look of shock flashed across the eyes of this tall Dutchman. Katherine felt him pull back as though he would make a run for it.

"That's what the birth certificate says," he mumbled.

Katherine didn't let herself respond to the implied criticism.

In the Netherlands, where Mr. Vandorn's parents were born and raised, Katherine would not have been hidden away in a maternity home when she got pregnant out of wedlock, she thought angrily. She would have kept and raised her daughter with the financial support of her daughter's birthfather. No blood test would have been necessary to prove that he was the one responsible for her welfare. Protection of the child as a human being would have been the first priority there.

But Cynthia was born in the U.S. where birthfathers often back away from any responsibility with some excuse like "I'm not sure I'm the real father."

Katherine pushed down the anger and, determined not to lose this opportunity, reached out her hand.

"It's really nice to meet you."

He hesitated a moment before shaking her hand.

"How long are you up here for," he asked. He glanced at Cynthia.

"A few days."

"We've had some health problems. I have cancer," he explained. "They don't know how long I have."

"I'm sorry to hear that. How's your wife?" Katherine asked. "Is she okay?"

"Yeah, she's over in Grafton at a meeting."

As he talked, Katherine felt him edging toward the sidewalk to the house.

"Cynthia's going to the University of Idaho." She tried to keep him talking by drawing his attention from her to his granddaughter.

His eyes moved from Katherine to Cynthia.

Cynthia took off her sunglasses to let him get a good look at her face. That way he could recognize the Vandorn resemblance if he had any doubts.

The sun shining directly on her face caused her to squint.

"What are you majoring in?"

"Biology," she said.

"Biology's a good field to be in," he commented.

Exactly what his son Joe had said in one of his letters to Cynthia when she told him she was going to college, Katherine remembered. She didn't how Joe would have known since he was a stockbroker.

"When do you graduate," he asked Cynthia?

"Next June."

"Do you still have family up here?" He turned back to Katherine, still failing to acknowledge that there was a blood tie that bound him to her daughter. Shyness on his part? Or unwillingness to open up to a relationship with someone whom he was not sure was really part of him and his world? He seemed to only want to talk to Katherine. Safer perhaps?

Though he'd been in Germany in 1966 when Katherine had gotten pregnant, Mr. Vandorn had paid for her stay at the unwed mothers' home.

"My mother died," she told him.

"Yes, I saw her obituary in the paper. I was sorry to hear about that."

A few more questions and replies. Then Katherine took his hand again.

"It was very nice meeting you. You take care of yourself."

She detected a smile in the craggy stone face of this tall Dutchman. Then they said goodbye.

"Mission accomplished," she said to Cynthia as they headed down the street.

July 28, 1998
Sand in the wind

$\mathcal{I}$ miss having Cynthia here in the car with me. Such a short time out of so many years I lost with her. It was our first trip together. We learned a lot about each other in those few days that flew by like sand thrown to the wind, like childhood after it's here then gone.

Cynthia, like Mama, always felt at home in Wyoming where she grew up in Rawlins down in the southern part of the state. Cynthia married young and had a family just like Mama and my grandmother did. Family has been the center of my daughter's life, just as it had been for Mama and grandmother Naomi.

⋆⋆⋆

July 25, 1998
Misunderstanding

$\mathcal{K}$atherine sat in the passenger seat while Cynthia took her turn at the wheel as they traveled over South Pass on the way to Elk Mountain.

"Don't get too close to that truck," Katherine told her, just as Mama would have done.

"I'm not."

"Yes you are."

"Listen, I've driven these roads a lot. Can't you have some confidence in me?"

"I'm just scared about following too close since I was in a traffic accident in Hong Kong."

"Why didn't you tell me you had been in an accident? I would have understood that."

"I thought I had told you that when you asked me about Hong Kong when we first met. But maybe I didn't," Katherine told her.

They stopped in Lander on the way to Elk Mountain to chill out over a cup of tea. They sat there until they talked things through. Very different to how things were with Mama, Katherine reflected.

July 28, 1998
Almost hillbilly

I arrive in Brown Rock. As I ease my car into a space at the Super 8 Motel, I glance across the parking lot. There sits the red pickup truck with three guns on the rack on top. The man in the cowboy hat stands talking to a woman. Her red hair is pulled back into a bun. I take a second look at the woman's work-lined face, her furrowed brow, the hardened look of "almost hillbilly". The Wyoming wind whips up dust. "Naomi?"

Naomi

November, 1997
Aunt Mamie's house

*T*he light was on as Katherine and her cousin Ann stepped out of the car and traversed the stone steps that led up to the door of her aunt Mamie's simple one-story bungalow in the country south of Salt Lake City. When Katherine called Mamie after returning home from Papa's, she insisted that Katherine come for Thanksgiving. Katherine jumped at the chance to meet an unknown aunt.

Entering the house around 10:30 that night, Katherine took one look at her father's sister sitting in front of an old Singer treadle sewing machine and had the distinct feeling she knew this woman, her house and every piece of furniture in it.

Inside, the rug was worn and threadbare. The furnishings looked like they could have been lifted straight from the 1930s.

With her piercing eyes and red hair brushed off the face, Mamie, Naomi's second child, closely resembled old photos Katherine had seen of her grandmother.

Katherine took a long look at Mamie and saw that she also resembled Papa whose penetrating stare had greeted her two months earlier. She looked into Mamie's blue eyes and knew them like her daughter's as they greeted her nervously the first time they met 13 years before. Cynthia's held a lovely calm mixed with a tinge of some troubled emotion deep inside. Mamie's masked any troubled spots; but they were there, Katherine soon realized.

"I don't know what yer dad told you, but my father had a weakness for women," Mamie started telling her story without a moment's pause as soon as Katherine walked in the door. "He couldn't keep his hands off of them. He had other women from the very beginning of his marriage. It wasn't a secret."

As Katherine put her bags down and sat and absorbed the house and her aunt's words, she listened to the calm tones of Mamie's voice and thought of the dead woman who had sat in the overstuffed chair by her bed in San Francisco.

"You…go…Wyoming." Katherine remembered the dead woman's words distinctly.

Mamie's voice had a similar ring.

*   *   *

"My father had no inhibitions about parading his other women around Greenville."

"Greenville?"

"Yeah. That was the town where we were living then in Iowa." Mamie speared a piece of turkey then spooned some dressing onto her plate as they sat eating Thanksgiving dinner the next day. "He regularly flaunted them in front of all of us; but my mom, she took it. One of my father's women went so far as to send her dirty canning jars home to have my mom wash them for her."

"You've got to be kidding!" Katherine exclaimed. "Did she know who they belonged to?"

Mamie brushed a piece of hair off of her face and continued on. "Well, she knew who they belonged to all right. But she washed them anyway. She was a Christian who believed in bein' kind and all like that."

"Being kind! Why did she put up with it?"

Mamie shrugged. "We had visitors one day. My dad took the lady into the kitchen and stayed there for a long time. I was left in the living room to entertain her husband. I could hear them whispering and laughing softly at first. Then silence. When they came out, her face was flushed and long blonde hair disheveled. My dad reached over, grabbed her by the hair and ran his lips along her neck. She giggled. I looked over at the woman's husband to see his reaction."

"Was he upset?"

"No. He acted like nothing was going on; but something definitely seemed strange. I could see that something was going on between my dad and the woman. Then my mom walked in."

"Was she upset?"

"No—or if she was, she didn't show it. She always tried to be kind to company and all like that. 'Oh, I didn't know we was havin' company or I would have been home!' She would have said somethin' like that. 'Can I get ya all some cake and coffee?' That was her usual way of greeting people. But they left soon after my mom came home."

"What did you do?"

"Here I sat lookin' at what my dad was doin' to my mom. And she was takin it," Mamie said.

"Why didn't she leave him?"

"The wife just put up with things. That's how it was back then."

As Katherine reflected on her aunt's story, an image of another man who might have been her grandfather's twin began to surface from somewhere in the recesses of her past.

July 28, 1998
Chancing it

*T*he cowboy is still talking to the woman as I open my car door. I have finally arrived in the town where my grandmother died and that cowboy is not going to stop me from finding out what happened to her. I look across the lot. He doesn't appear to see me, but he'll recognize my car if he sees it.

I don't have much choice. There are only two motels in town and the other didn't look very inviting. I'll have to take a chance. As I step out of my car, I get a whiff of sugar beets.

Quickly, I open the trunk, pull out a tarp and throw it over the back of my car covering the license plates. I glance towards the cowboy who still has his back to me. Then I walk into the office of the Super 8 Motel.

"We're having a cattleman's convention in town this week. So we have only one room left. Yer lucky," the man at the reception desk tells me. "It's a double room, but I can let ya have it for $30."

"I'll take it."

After getting the key to my room, I glance out the window. The cowboy's pickup is gone. I go out and get my bag out of the trunk of my car then head to my room to take a quick nap.

As I doze off, thoughts about my grandfather, the womanizer, stir up long forgotten memories of an old flame.

1984

An old flame

$\mathcal{K}$atherine watched the people milling around her garage sale in search of some little gem. She knew they wouldn't find any. She only had the types of items that a lot of people would throw away; nothing valuable. It's like they're rummaging through my dirty underwear, she thought ruefully. Still she needed to get rid of this stuff. She noticed a very attractive blonde-haired, blue-eyed man sorting through the box of books. He seemed to have appeared out of nowwhere. She hadn't seen him drive up.

"I'd like to buy this one," he said as he handed her a book. He seemed to be almost apologizing for buying so little.

"Interesting that you're buying that one," Katherine commented as she looked at the title as she took his money. It used to belong to Mama and her grandmother before that. She opened the cover and looked one last time at her grandmother's name, "Naomi Geislingen," written on the title page. Then she handed it to him. "Any particular reason?"

"I have a garden of violets at home," he told her. But she had the feeling by the way he stood smiling as he leafed through the book that there might be another reason.

"Are you interested in a free bed?"

"I might be."

She pointed out the single frame bed her friend had asked her to give away if she could.

"Do you want it?" Katherine asked him doubtfully. She wasn't sure anyone would want it since there were blood stains all over the mattress — probably from Tina having sex with her boyfriend while she was menstruating, Katherine thought cynically.

"Sure."

"Really?"

Katherine was relieved to get rid of it so she helped him load it onto the top of his car. Then as she turned to walk away, he pulled her close to him, his hands reaching down to squeeze her buttocks.

The hug was way too intimate from a man she had just met. She had found him attractive. That was all. She was older and wiser since she had the fling with John, the carpenter in South Dakota, several years earlier. What happened with John was mutual and not some type of sleazy advance. If he had acted like this man, she would have been turned off by it then as she was now at the garage sale. She pulled herself free, drew herself up to her full height, and glared at him. That's when she glanced over and saw the woman in the passenger seat of his car watching them. With a barely repentant grin, he climbed into the car with the woman and drove away.

July 28, 1998
Dinner in Brown Rock

I had managed a thirty-minute nap, leaving me just enough time to jump in the shower before heading downtown to eat dinner.

On my way out the door, I notice a convenience store across the street. I need some toothpaste. I think I'll get some before I go eat. I look both directions before crossing what looks more like a highway than a street. No pickup with gun racks in sight. It looks like I'm safe for now, at least.

A large semi passes. Then I run across.

A truck honks. A shrill "whewt-whoo" whistles through the air, the type of whistle that I used to hear in high school. Some guy was saying that he was pleased with what he saw. A large T-bone steak would likely get the same response. I ignore it as I walk into the convenience store to buy the toothpaste. I grab a tube off the shelf, pay for it and quickly run back across the street to my car and head out to eat at the restaurant I saw earlier several blocks down the street.

There are two other people in the large dining room as I walk in and sit down at a table.

"Somethin' to drink," the middle-aged waitress asks as she hands me a menu.

"A glass of white wine. Chardonnay."

"Okay. I'll git that fer ya while ya look at the menu."

I sit back and relax, hoping that the cowboy has left town.

"Are you ready to order now." The waitress brushes back strands of bleached blonde hair and waits with pad in hand.

"Yes. I'll take the shrimp sautéed in garlic. Do I get the salad bar with that?"

"Yes, just help yourself. Would you like a potato or rice?"

"Give me rice," I tell her as I get up and head towards the salad bar. I fill my plate with lettuce leaves, cherry tomatoes, garbanzo beans, onions, croutons, and top it off with vinegar and oil. I stick my fork into a cherry tomato and pop it into my mouth. I look across the room of the Brown Rock restaurant just as the cowboy walks in.

November, 1997

Mamie

"It was my father's womanizing and lewd talk that made me get married before I finished high school," Mamie told Katherine as they sat eating Thanksgiving dinner with Mamie's daughter Ann.

"You mean profanity?"

"No."

"It's not the same as taking the name of the Lord in vain," Ann piped in. "He used words that referred to body parts and that were derogatory to women."

"Like slut and bitch?" Katherine asked.

"Yeah. And other four and five-letter words referring to body parts," Ann said.

Mamie and Ann, good Mormon women, would not want to say the words out loud.

Ann converted to Mormonism when she married a Mormon. Mamie converted later. Not typical of most Mormons Katherine had met, Mamie and Ann seemed a little too independent to be reined in by any religion. Always adamant that the rights of women come first, they probably developed that view from their experiences with men, Katherine surmised.

"Would you like some herb tea," Mamie asked as her daughter Ann cleared the plates from the table and brought out the pumpkin pie.

"Sure." Katherine really wanted a cup of coffee but assumed they probably didn't keep it around.

*   *   *

"On the day that World War I ended, our house in Greenville burned down," Mamie told the story as Ann poured hot water into their cups. "We don't know what happened, but my mother thought she kept matches by the lamps in the bedrooms upstairs where we slept. She thought maybe mice got in there or something because they liked matches."

"It sounds like you had a lot of fires around your house growing up."

"Yeah. Well, there was that one. Then one at the cabinetry shop in Greenville, Iowa. And another in Wyoming."

"Was that your mother's burning, the one in Wyoming?"

Mamie looked across at Katherine, held the gaze a moment, then answered, "No, that was a different fire."

Just a coincidence that there were so many fires, she wondered, or perhaps those fires were started on purpose?

"Do you think the fires were accidents?" she asked Mamie.

"Sure they were." Mamie handed Katherine a photo. "Here's a picture of the Christian Church in Greenville."

Closed subject, Katherine realized. Well, she could wait. Time enough to come back to it later.

"I quit going to that church when I was 14 because no one would sit beside me because I didn't have as nice a dress as they did. And I was a Geislingen and my dad was not a nice guy. And my mother had too many kids. So we were looked down on. I was baptized there."

"Really?"

"They turned a blind eye to my father, though. They even had him give sermons in church. A lot of men, even the sheriff, was havin' affairs with women."

"Your father's name and your brothers' and sisters' are in the church record, it says here," Katherine said.

"My mother's name wasn't there because she didn't go to church. My dad would be mad if there wasn't a dinner ready when we come home from church on Sunday, so my mother stayed home and cooked. But she was different, you know."

"Really? How?"

"Well, my father drank coffee and the like. But she always drank herb tea. And she never went to that church."

"What do you mean?"

"Well you know, she could have been a Mormon."

Did Mamie need those she cared about to believe the same as she did, Katherine wondered, or did she have some basis for her belief? She looked across at Mamie and recognized Papa in the way she held firmly to her convictions.

July 28, 1998
A different route

*A*s the waitress sets a plate of shrimp before me, I look across the room and notice the cowboy staring at me. I tense up. I take out my notebook and busy myself writing to take my mind off of his piercing gaze.

If I had stayed in the small town where I grew up, my family would have put pressure on me to marry. I would have probably married someone like the cowboy. But I got away.

I missed Wyoming at first. I wanted to go back home again where things were familiar — Mama, Clark, my sisters and brother Jimmy who was born the year after Mama married Clark. But I felt there was nothing there for me. People would not have forgotten. I would have still been carrying the stigma. So I stayed away.

After I left, I lived in a new environment with a different type of people than those I left. I saw women getting an education and pursuing work. I followed that model which took me on a very different road from that of my grandmother Naomi.

November, 1997

Mamie

"*I* can't begin to tell ya the toll all those women traipsin' in and out of my dad's life had on my mom. She said it didn't bother her, but she was no tough woman like a lot of people think. Ya probably never met a more sensitive soul than my mom. Yer dad was the same way. They were both of the type that could be hurt easily. But my dad took no notice of my mom's real nature."

"I'm like Papa in that respect," Katherine thought as she listened to Mamie talk. But, she didn't volunteer the information sensing that Mamie was so deeply absorbed in her story that she might not hear. Perhaps that's why Sam never listened to Naomi, why Papa didn't seem to understand the significance of my waiting for his "black" pickup. Too involved in their own problems, perhaps.

Mamie continued talking like Katherine wasn't even there.

"My dad might as well have taken a knife to my mom early on and gotten it over with. But she had to bear the burden of what a man out of control brings to a marriage. My mom looked like a worn out woman after they moved to Wyoming. But she didn't always look that way. She used ta have the smoothest skin and a kind of patrician way about her. Everybody told her that when they came visitin'. But my dad, he killed that beauty in her and turned her into the woman ya see in the photograph with her eyes all squinted up."

Katherine rubbed the back of her neck as she picked up the photo and looked at it. "Do you have a photo of your mom when she was younger?"

"Yeah, I do. I'll have to find it. But you know, my dad's mom had her part in all of the problems, treatin' him like a prince n' all. He didn't believe in workin' around the house. 'Let the woman do it,' was what he thought."

"Yes, I've met a few princes." Katherine yawned as she stood up to stretch her legs as she continued to listen to Mamie. "Fortunately I got out before they drained me dry," she thought.

"My mom practically worked herself to death takin' care of my dad and her family," Mamie continued. "Then later, Wyoming had its part in what happened to my mother."

July 28, 1998

Wyoming wind

The wind blows constantly in Wyoming. The howl, the dust, the constant shaking of house and windows by eighty-mile-an-hour winds take their toll on delicate psyches. Naomi's was strong, but still it ate away at her, at least according to my aunt Mamie.

Women who don't grow up in Wyoming sometimes have problems living here, especially with the wind, I remember Mamie telling me, as I sit eating and writing in the restaurant stopping a moment to listen to see if I can hear the wind from inside. From time to time, I look up to check on the cowboy.

Nineteen-thirty was the beginning of the dust bowl. It hit harder and lasted longer in Wyoming than in other states, Mamie had told me.

But, "we didn't have a dust bowl here," Mama said when I brought up the subject. "Not in the part of Wyoming where I was living, at least."

"I heard they did in the eastern part of the state," I told her.

"When the wind blew then, you couldn't see because dirt was everywhere," Mamie said. The full force of the dust bowl didn't hit Wyoming for two more years. Naomi had died by then.

I glance across the room at the cowboy as I take a sip of Chardonnay. He's cutting a piece of steak.

November, 1997

Mamie

"Wyoming was a major change for my mother." Aunt Mamie brushed a lock of hair off her forehead then lifted the cup of herb tea to her mouth to take a sip. She gazed into the distance, deep in thought. She shook herself and turned back to Katherine. "Inside the house day after day with no chance to get out, my mom felt the Wyoming wind's continual howl after living most of her life in Iowa's muggy green landscape."

"Did she talk about it?"

"No, but we could all hear it. I know how it affected me. And it affected my mom the same way. It whipped across that part of the state like a death rattle carrying with it a sense of foreboding. It played along the barbed wire like a piano and ran along the eaves. It was depressing. It was far different from Iowa where my mother was born and raised."

1885

Naomi

The snow lay in drifts around the farm near Greenville, Iowa. The stars shone bright and clear. A sleigh pulled by two brown dapper horses arrived. A woman jumped out and hurried into the house.

"How's Emma?" she asked the man holding the door.

"The pains are gittin' worse. She's lyin' on the bed."

"Git me some hot water. Then ya watch after the young un." The midwife walked straight to the bedroom.

Within an hour, the cry of a baby replaced the screams and moans of a woman contracted in labor. When the man and his son entered the room, Emma lay cuddling the baby.

"I'll call her Naomi from the book of Ruth in the Bible," said Emma as she rocked her back and forth on the bed.

In 1885, the year that Naomi was born in Iowa, Sitting Bull joined Buffalo Bill's wild west show, Ulysses S. Grant died of cancer, and the Washington Monument was dedicated.

Just nine years before her birth, Alexander Graham Bell patented the telephone and Custer's army was wiped out in the Battle at the Little Big Horn.

1893

Naomi's hands were numb from the cold winter storm that hit Iowa during the winter of 1893.

"Come on, Daisy. Give me just a few more drops of milk," Naomi urged as she pulled the cow's teats.

"Naomi, ain't ya through with that cow yet. Ma's got breakfast on the table. Come on," her older brother Ron called.

"I'm comin'. I'm tryin' ta git jist a couple more drops. Okay, Daisy. That's it fer today."

Naomi picked up the pail and headed for the house. The cold winter storm whipped at her face as she edged her way from the barn.

"Where's yer sister? Ain't she finished with that milkin' yet?" Emma looked at the door as she dished up the oatmeal and laid out a dish of homemade bread on the table.

"She said she was comin'" Ron yelled from the foyer where he was taking off his boots and gloves.

Suddenly the door opened and the wind blew in snow as Naomi edged her way with the pail of milk.

"Naomi, put that pail over by the sink. And ya'd better rub those hands n' cheeks a little. What happened ta yer gloves?"

"I can't milk with gloves on. The pail's hard ta catch hold of with 'em on, too. So I left 'em in the barn."

"Well, git yerself over here and eat while the food's hot. And ya'd better hurry. It's gonna be hard walkin' with that snow blowin'. I've a mind ta keep ya home. I could use some help around here. I don't see how ya can git ta school with this storm."

"Oh, Ma! No! I'm supposed ta give a speech taday. I worked hard on it. Please let me go."

"Well I don't know. George, what da ya think. Do ya think she kin make it in this snow."

"I think ya'd better stay home and help yer ma make the cheese. Ron's not goin' ta school today. He's stayin' home, too, n' helpin' me.

"Oh, Ma, please let me go!"

"Naomi. It's fer yer own good. The storm's jist too bad."

By the time Naomi reached the third grade, money was scarce.

"We need more money ta make ends meet," George said. Hail had destroyed a promising crop of corn the summer before and the money her father had counted on to get the family through the winter was gone. "We're gonna haf ta pull Naomi from school."

"I always wanted my daughter to git an education like I never got. She's doin' so well. She's smart as a whip, and so good at public speakin'. Isn't there another way we kin git the money?" Emma considered the problem.

"No, it's the only way. I could pull Ron from school. But I hate to do that, him bein' the oldest boy n' all."

"No! Please let me stay in school. I'll do anything if you let me stay. Please, Mom! Please!" Naomi cried when she heard the decision.

"Yer dad's decided. If it was up ta me, I'd let ya stay. I can't go against yer dad, him bein' so touchy about finances n' all."

"Can't ya talk ta him, ma. I could work at night. Anything!"

"What's she yellin' about," her father looked over at Naomi as he walked in the door.

"Please, Dad! Let me stay in school! Oh please!"

"Ya git out n' do yer chores. There's gonna be no talkin' about this. I've made my decision! Ya say more n' I'll have to git the whip!"

Naomi cried for two days.

November, 1997

Mamie

"*Two* days after my mom left school, her dad took her to the neighboring Dominick farm where she was to work as a servant," Mamie said as they finished up the last crumbs of pumpkin pie on Thanksgiving. "Her salary of $2 a week was sent home to her father."

"So your mom only had a third grade education?" Katherine asked thinking about her mother who quit school at 17.

"Yes. That was very common back then for girls to leave school to work so they could bring extra money in. But, my mom's education didn't end when she left school at the age of ten," said Mamie. "She learned to make do with very little. She watched the sun and moon and stars, knew when to plant and when to reap. That's a lot more than most kids today know. Any book she found lying around she'd read by kerosene lamp before she went to bed at night. But, of course, the Bible was her main source of reading."

"She must not have had too much free time, working hard as a servant," Katherine commented as she rolled her shoulders back and forth as she listened.

"Working at the Dominick farm was the first time my mom came in touch with the finer things in life like a daughter being sent off to college to study teaching, new clothes bought at Sears Roebuck, bustling skirts and big feathered hats."

1898

Naomi

"I sure like that hat yer wearin," Naomi commented as Mrs. Dominick prepared to leave for Renton to do some shopping.

"Why, Naomi, thank ya. It's new ya know."

"Where'd ya git it?" Naomi asked.

"Montgomery Ward."

"It's real purty."

"We'll be in town til supper. Could ya see that the good linen is put on fer dinner. Doc Marshall and his wife are comin' for dinner. We're havin' roast beef. That's yer favorite, ain't it?"

"It sure is. Here, let me help ya with that coat. Ya sure have the nicest clothes."

"Some day I'm gonna have me a hat just like Mrs. Dominick's," Naomi wrote home to her younger sister after she'd been working as a servant for five years. "I'm gonna dress fine like she does."

November, 1997

Mamie

"*M*y mom always appreciated nice things even though she so seldom got them after she married my dad," Mamie told Katherine. "She shouldn't have married him. But that's so much water under the bridge. She wanted ta go ta college n' become a teacher; but as things were, she didn't get to. Second best was becomin' some man's wife. I guess she thought of it as a way ta get ahead."

"But she didn't get ahead, did she?" Katherine thought of Mama who, when she married Papa, wanted some of the same things as grandmother Naomi. But, she didn't get them until she left him.

"No. She never had fine clothes. She spent all of her time slaving away and having babies."

"How did you feel about that growing up? Did you think that you were going to do things differently?"

Mamie pushed aside the pack of cards she'd pulled out of a long-forgotten corner of the cupboard and glanced at Katherine a moment before continuing on. "When my mother died, it was a very hard time for me and my family. Remembering it all again is not easy. Here, I'll get you some coffee."

"You have coffee?"

"Oh yeah. I keep it in the cupboard for company."

Katherine noted the quiver in Mamie's voice and the unsteadiness in her hands as she spooned the instant coffee then poured water into her cup. Katherine sensed that she had the same longing for the coffee and those cards that an ex-smoker has for a quick nicotine fix.

"Are you sure it's okay for me to drink the coffee here since you don't drink it?" Katherine asked.

"Oh sure. You go ahead." Mamie sat and watched her nervously.

"We can talk about this later if you like," Katherine said, even though she was keen to find out more.

"It's okay. It's just that last night I didn't sleep so well. Too many memories are flooding in. A lot of things I had forgotten. Now I'm remembering them again."

Mamie stared at the card pack. Finally, she took a deep breath and looked up.

"My father had a violent streak and temper that he passed on to his sons. One year he cut down our apple tree because he got mad. Another time he cut the grapevine down. If he didn't hit her, he'd do that instead," she said.

A pressure cooker ready to explode—that's the feeling Katherine had gotten from her father when she asked him about Naomi.

Katherine's uncle Peter spent five years working on a family genealogy that went out of its way to avoid mention of how his mother died. He was dead now or she'd be asking him questions, too. He would have probably told her the same thing that her father told her.

"Her death was an accident," everyone always said.

Katherine was convinced they must have banded together and agreed on a public story.

As Ann cleared the dessert dishes away, Katherine sat back and absorbed the room—the china hutch, the cobwebs hanging over teapots. As she watched Mamie, she had a sense that she was sitting at her grandmother Naomi's table. Suddenly she saw a shadow move across the hallway that led from the dining room to the bed-rooms.

"What was that?"

"Just ghosts," Mamie told her.

The bond between mother and daughter is strong. The daughter learns from her mother even if the mother isn't there. Naomi, though dead, was still very close to Mamie, Katherine felt.

As Katherine listened to Mamie talk, she knew that shadow belonged to Naomi. She felt a deep cool breeze blow across her soul.

July 28, 1998
Cowboy

*T*he cowboy takes his hat off and hooks it on the back of his chair. He and the people he sits with are talking and laughing. One of the children jumps on his lap.

I lift the glass of wine to my lips as I watch them. Looking at the cowboy holding the child reminds me that if I had stayed in Wyoming, children and families would probably have been part of my life. But I left.

He must like children, I think. I feel a twinge remembering that I've always been attracted to men who have a way with kids. I think of Robert, the man who resembled my grandfather.

1984

Robert

*K*atherine was sitting in a restaurant waiting for a friend when she felt a cool, gentle, healing breeze touch something deep inside of her. She looked up to see who or what had stirred her, but all she could see was the back of a man heading towards the front of the restaurant as though he were looking for somebody.

"There's something familiar about that back," she thought as she looked at the blonde hair. But it was the feeling she had as he walked by that intrigued her. The phantom man, she thought as he approached her on his way back to his table. She stopped him.

"How do I know you?" Katherine asked him.

He looked shocked. She sensed him trying to grope for power as he responded.

"Maybe you've been a patient in my office."

"In your office? What office do you work in?"

"I'm a gynecologist."

"Oh." Why did the thought that he was a gynecologist make her feel like he had just stripped her? As she sat there groping for something to say, she remembered. "No, that's not it. You're the man who bought the book on violets at my garage sale."

"Oh yeah." He looked a little uneasy. "What's your name?"

"Katherine."

"Hi. Mine is Robert Smith. Do you live in Colorado Springs?"

"Yeah."

"Do you have a phone number?"

"Yeah." Katherine thought for a moment remembering her first impression of this man and the woman sitting in the car watching them as his hands groped her buttocks. But she remembered the cool breeze that hit her moments earlier when he walked by her. Something about him made her feel that she had known him for centuries. She needed to know why he had stirred her so. So she jotted down her phone number on a piece of paper and handed it to him.

"Thanks. I'll give you a call." Then he was gone.

Katherine's heart beat wildly as she watched him leave.

"Be careful," her mind said. But she didn't listen.

He called her on the phone two days later.

* * *

Katherine's heart immediately began a flip-flop at the sound of his voice as if it came from some deep dark past that both of them had experienced together. She was immediately captured.

"How are you?"

"Great. I've been busy," she said.

"Doing what?"

"Searching for my daughter."

"Searching? Where is she?"

"I gave her up for adoption when I was eighteen."

She had never been able to talk about the loss of her daughter without her voice choking up. So she rarely told people. She surprised herself by talking so freely to Robert. There she was talking to a man she barely knew and one whom she had some reservations about, telling him her life's secrets. She didn't know why she was telling him. She could have lied. It would have been easier.

"You must find your daughter," he replied immediately.

"Well, that's the plan." Katherine tried to keep the irritation out of her voice. "That's why I'm searching." Quickly she changed the subject. "Do you have any children?"

"Yes, three. They live with their mom and not with me."

"Do you get to see them?"

"Once a month. I couldn't live without seeing them. I really hope that you find your daughter."

Katherine, still feeling slightly irritated by his trying to take control of the situation that she thought that she already had control of, let it go as he continued talking. She recognized how much he seemed to care for his own children. That must be why he came on so strong concerning her search for her daughter.

"Hey, let's get together some time," he said.

"Okay."

"I'll call you later in the week."

She was tempted to turn him down when she remembered the woman sitting in his car at the garage sale that day, but she was caught by his spirit that stirred something deep in her soul. Who was this man, she wondered? "Where have I met him before?" She found herself saying yes before she had a chance to think.

November, 1997

Mamie

"*How* did you feel about your dad?" Katherine asked.

"I never got too close to him." Mamie scratched her chin thoughtfully. "I respected him for awhile. Then I didn't. I resented him when he made my mother cry. Whatever my dad wanted, he got—like other women."

"But you were close for awhile?"

Mamie shrugged. "There are some family matters you just don't talk about."

"Sometimes it's good to talk about those things," Katherine said, wondering how far she could push. "Were they big problems?"

Mamie looked at her a moment in silence then continued on as if Katherine hadn't even asked the question.

"My mom was nineteen years old the day she first laid eyes on my father. She was buying flour at the market in Greenville one Saturday for the Dominick family. On the way out of the store, she dropped her bag just as he was walking up the sidewalk."

January, 1905

Naomi

"*May* I help ya with that?" Sam Geislingen asked as he leaned down to pick up the package.

"Thank ya," Naomi blushed as she looked up into his big brown eyes.

He picked up the bag and walked beside her.

"Ya don't have to carry that. I kin do it," she told him.

"No, I want to." So he did.

From then on he set out to do everything he wanted with her.

Sam, a dashing young man who dressed in snappy clothes, seemed to have it made in the small farming community of Greenville. He had just graduated from high school. And every girl in town had her eye on the budding ladies' man.

Naomi thought he was the most handsome man she ever met. Soon they were seeing each other regularly. She would slip out at night after she finished her chores and they would walk for miles when the moon was full.

*　*　*

"Look Sam! There's the big dipper! And look over there. There's Venus."

"It's all so immense, Naomi. It makes me feel like such a small part of somethin' so great. Our lives are nothin' compared to it."

"But I feel my life is somethin', at least when I'm with you. Ya make things so beautiful and real ta me."

"Really? Do I, Naomi?"

"Yes. Yer so alive. And ya got so many ideas."

"I feel the same way about you. Yes. I feel it, too." Sam's hand tightened on Naomi's as they walked along the country road looking up at the sky.

* * *

"Come up here. The hay is soft n' it's warm," he told her as he drew her up to the loft.

"I don't know if we should." She held back.

"Come on. It's okay." He drew her up the ladder.

"Sam, I don't think we should be up here."

That cold February night when the stars were bright, Sam drew Naomi up into the loft of the barn on the farm where she worked.

"Come on, Naomi. Nobody knows we're here. It's dark. N' ya feel so good." He began to touch her breasts.

"Don't do that! Come on. Let's go."

"We'll just stay a little while." He pulled her to him. His tongue began to probe.

They kissed. He pawed. She resisted then gave in to his advances.

* * *

"I let him take advantage of me. Look at the way he looks at those other girls," Naomi thought a few days after she made love to Sam in the loft that night.

"Yer late," she told him after she'd waited for an hour in the barn for their date the next week.

"I had some things to do in town."

"Who were ya with this time? I heard yer also seein' Susan Smith."

"Yer wrong. Yer the only one I'm with," he stated as he drew her down in the hay.

A month later, Naomi told him her period was late.

"Are ya sure?" Sam asked. "Maybe we kin find someone to help ya git rid of it."

"No, I won't," Naomi cried. "If ya don't want to do the right thing by me, then I'll just have it on my own."

Despite his mother's protests, Sam took Naomi across the Iowa/Nebraska line to get married in Omaha before the justice of the peace.

July 28, 1998
Doubts

$\mathcal{I}$look down at my notepad as I finish eating dinner and realize that I've been staring off into space thinking and forgotten the cowboy. I glance across the restaurant to check on him.

A lot of men out in Wyoming don't know what slot to fit a woman into if she isn't married.

"Why ain't a good lookin woman like you married?" That's the kind of thing that I would expect the cowboy across the room to ask.

And if he did, what could I say?

I've long since said goodbye to my "bad girl" side. I'm very careful about how I present myself here in the "equality state." In a lot of places in the U.S., Americans just plain have a problem with sex. They've been that way since the Salem witch-hunt when Nathaniel Hawthorne wrote *The Scarlet Letter*. Puritanism is still strongly ingrained in the American culture.

But Puritan ethics were far from my mind when I met Robert in Colorado Springs.

1984

Robert

*H*e came like a phantom from some previous life carrying with him a strong current of magnetic electricity. He also helped provide a counterbalance to her life as she searched for her daughter. That and the still vivid memory of the woman sitting in his car looking on as he made a sexual overture towards Katherine the first time she saw him at her garage sale helped her keep him at arm's length for several months as far as sex was concerned. Then one night he leaned over and touched Katherine's shoulder. He brushed his lips gently along her neck.

Meeting no resistance, he undid the buttons on her blouse and moved his hands up and down her spine until she began to tingle.

"No, don't. I don't want to. I'm not ready."

"Okay," he said but his hands continued to cause tingling feelings along her spine. "Some day we will get in bed together," he told her.

They continued on that night until finally she found herself losing all ability to say no to him. They had their clothes off and their legs intertwined as they lay on the rug in front of the fire.

A romance made in heaven on the couch that night? Perhaps. But hell had its part in it, Katherine soon found out.

*   *   *

"Hi Robert."

There was a moment of silence on the other end of the line when she called him one night two or three months after their sexual encounter.

"Uh, hi."

"I'm sorry. Am I interrupting something?" Katherine frowned.

"No, that's okay. Just a minute. I have to get something," he told her.

Katherine heard a woman's voice in the background.

"Oh. You've got company?"

"No. No one's here but me."

"But I just heard a woman talking to you."

"You're imagining things."

"I certainly wasn't imagining anything. I heard a woman and you answering."

"You're entirely too paranoid about my having other women."

"No, I'm not. I just want a straight answer."

"There's no woman here."

"Fine. I've got to go, Robert. I'll talk to you later," she told him as she hung up.

November, 1997
Mamie

"*My* grandmother used to tell me what a gallant young man her son was before he married my mother. She wouldn't let any of us forget it. She insinuated that he became something else after he was married. She blamed my mother for holding him back," Mamie told Katherine as they looked at her parents' wedding pictures.

"Why would she blame your mother?"

"That's just the way she was. My dad could do no wrong according to his mother. Any problems in that marriage were my mother's fault. I guess she forgot that it takes two to tango," Mamie rolled her eyes and laughed as she told Katherine. "One look from my dad's flashing dark brown eyes and any woman, no matter what age, would find her face getting warm and her hands clammy. My dad, even as a young man, knew he had the power to seduce. And he used it to melt every woman in Greenville."

"How did you know?"

"I saw him doin' it all the time while I was growing up. My dad could have any woman he wanted. And he did, even before he was married," Mamie said.

*　*　*

Mamie brought out the photos on Thanksgiving night. Sam looked like a young steed in a black suit and white collared shirt ready for an adventure, Katherine thought. "My mom was a red-headed beauty full of life with a pale Irish complexion—red lips, white skin, rosy cheeks and flashing blue eyes," Mamie told Katherine as she looked at the black and white photo. In her wedding picture, Naomi wore a high Victorian lace collar and a large feathered hat.

"My mother bought that wedding hat herself. Every week she kept back a few pennies from her wage and put them in an old canning jar beneath her bed," Mamie said. "Whenever she did something extra around the house, Mrs. Dominick would give her a little extra. She didn't tell her dad. Instead, she tucked it away for a special occasion. Her wedding was pretty special. At night when she went up to her room, she would take the hat down off the shelf and finger it before she placed it on her head in front of the mirror. My mom used to tell me how special that hat was to her."

The young woman with the curvaceous hips and full breasts was every bit as dashing as the man she was about to marry, Katherine thought.

"She was the town belle," said Mamie. "My mom was prettier than any woman in town with money. That's what one of my aunts said. She and my dad were married on April 18, 1906, the day of the great San Francisco earthquake. Eight years later, by the time Margaret Sanger coined the term "birth control," my mom had given birth to her first eight children."

July 28, 1998
A bad family?

The penetrating stare of the cowboy's eyes on my face draws me back to the restaurant. I continue writing in my notebook, trying to ignore him as I sip the rest of my wine.

I think about Naomi as I finish eating dinner. Both excitement and fear push me on in this search for the truth. What will I find tomorrow when I start to dig around?

My grandmother Naomi came from a different station in life, a cousin once told me. "Hers was a bad family," he said.

I glance around at the people in the restaurant. What was a bad family? What would that mean to these people sitting here eating dinner? I wonder what it meant to Naomi.

The cowboy, his dark fiery eyes fixed on me, stands by the salad bar. I find it hard not to stare at his tight blue jeans. I force my eyes up and note the top buttons of his western shirt are undone and I can see smooth bare skin and hair. Something warm stirs deep inside me and I feel moisture between my legs. Quickly I look away.

I turn my mind back to Naomi and families.

Genealogies in this culture are linear along the male line. The female loses her family name when she marries and takes her husband's. It's more difficult to trace the matriarchal line than it is the man's. That's why most men want a son to carry on the family name.

Class lines are also strong in most American small towns where snobbery abounds. In Wyoming, those lines are solidly set.

The cowboy stands beside my table with a plate of salad in his hand. He looks like he's going to speak, but I look down at my writing and he walks away.

⋆

November, 1997

Mamie

"*M*y mother's family wasn't so bad," Mamie told Katherine. "Outside of the fact that my mom's dad was Jewish and coverin' it up, they were pretty honest people."

So they were covering something up, Katherine thought as she sat and listened. Just like what Mamie seems to be doing by keeping silent about what happened between her and her dad.

"Sure they were poor, but so were a lot of people back then. They scraped by. So what was the big deal?"

That's what Katherine was wondering as she sat and listened. It must have been money that determined good and bad families, but she wondered whether their being Jewish might be the real reason for her cousin's earlier remark. Racism runs rampant against African American, Mexican, Asian, and any person of color in most places in the U.S. So it would have made sense.

"They weren't no better or no worse than my dad's family," Mamie said. "At least my mom never talked to anybody the way my dad's mom talked to her. Mom was nice to my dad's family even with the way they treated her."

"My grandmother believed my mom trapped my dad into marriage," Mamie admitted. "I suspect my mom marrying her son had a lot to do with any stories about my mom's family that got passed around among the Geislingen's."

"How did your mom deal with it?"

"Oh, she took it because she believed in being kind and all; but it got to her after awhile."

1906

Naomi

"*W*here's that wife o' yours?" Sam's mother Isabel demanded when Sam walked into the house alone.

"She had to check the stove. She's comin'." Sam hung up his hat.

"She married ya for yer money. Ya know that, don't ya. She's nothin' but a whore n' she's gonna take ya fer everythin' ya got."

"That's not true," Sam answered. "If ya don't have nothin' good to say, please don't say nothin'."

"And she's a horrible housekeeper! I don't see how you can stand it!"

They looked towards the door at the sound of a quiet knock.

"Come in!" Isabel yelled towards the door.

Sam looked up with a gleam in his eyes as his young bride with a bulging belly walked in.

"How ya all doin' today?" Naomi smiled at everyone.

"We're doin' just fine. How ya doin'," Isabel inquired.

"Just fine," Naomi answered. Isabel quickly headed to the kitchen.

"Git me some more coffee while yer out there," Sam's father Howard yelled after her. "Be sure ta put some sugar in it! N' make it quick. How's yer dad doin' down there on that farm, Naomi?"

"Strugglin'. But I think he'll make it."

"Well, he need any help, ya jist let me know."

"That's mighty nice of ya. I will." Naomi got up and headed to the kitchen.

"Hell, woman! Where's that coffee," Howard yelled at Isabel as Naomi walked out.

"Kin I help ya out here with the dinner," Naomi asked.

"No, I'm doin' just fine."

"Let me take the coffee in ta the men."

"Howard likes two teaspoons of sugar."

Naomi poured the coffee and carried it in to the living room. As she handed it to him, some spilled out the top.

"Hell. Be more careful with that coffee! Ya want ta burn me ta death or somethin'?"

"I'm sorry." Naomi used a napkin to wipe his arm off. She knew that Howard had a way of ordering women around, but it bothered her. She was trying to get Sam to help out at home so he wouldn't turn into his dad, but she wasn't having much luck with him either. Just grin and bear it, she kept telling herself as she headed back to the kitchen.

"Let me cut those carrots fer ya."

"Okay. But be sure to wash yer hands first. N' don't use that knife."

"What about this knife?" Naomi asked as she headed toward the sink.

"Yeah. That's okay. But be sure you wash your hands."

Naomi didn't say a word as she walked to the sink and washed her hands off. She had become used to her mother-in-law's cutting comments. She tried to keep up a front when she went to Isabel's house, but it ate away at her.

"Where'd ya git that dress?" Isabel critically appraised Naomi from top to bottom.

"Oh, don't ya like it? Mrs. Smith gave it to me. It belonged to her daughter when she was pregnant with her first child. I thought it was rather pretty myself."

"I always made my clothes. Never in my life did I depend on welfare. Of course, I finished twelve grades like most of us did in our family."

Naomi flinched. "Ma mom taught me how to sew when I was seven. Actually I got a prize once at the fair fer one of ma dresses."

Sam walked into the kitchen and put his arms around Naomi. "Ya look so beautiful in that dress, don't she, Mom?"

Silence.

"Git me a knife n' I'll help ya cut those carrots."

Sam and Naomi laughed and joked as they finished cutting. Isabel didn't say a word.

"Git me some more coffee!" Howard banged his cup on the table in the living room.

Isabel ran out the kitchen door to get the cup.

Sam gave Naomi a hug.

*   *   *

The moon was full the night that Naomi gave birth to her daughter Ruth. Sam was working late. So Naomi walked next door to ask the neighbor lady to fetch him.

"Could ya go down to Sam's shop n' tell 'im I'm in labor n' need 'im? And could ya stop at the midwife's along the way," she asked the woman.

"Well, I suppose I kin, though I'm awfully busy," the blonde-haired woman said as she chomped on a wad of gum and filed her nails.

"I'd appreciate it." Naomi clamped her teeth as labor pains racked her body. She went home and lay down on the bed to wait.

"Naomi. Naomi, are ya there," her sister Samantha's voice called through the open front door.

"I'm back here," Naomi moaned. "Kin ya help me? The baby's comin'."

"Where's Sam," Samantha asked as she helped Naomi undress. She then laid her back on the bed with her legs spread.

"I told the neighbor lady to go git 'im n' to tell the midwife. That was an hour ago. He should a bin here by now."

"Never mind. This baby's comin'. Bear down. Push. Push. It's comin'. It's comin'."

Soon Samantha held the baby in the air, gave it a swat on the behind to get it breathing. "It's a girl!"

When Sam walked in the house two hours later, Naomi was sitting in bed holding the baby.

"Why didn't ya send someone to git me?"

"I told the woman next door. Didn't she come n' tell ya?"

Sam reddened. "She came by the store, but she didn't tell me ya were havin' the baby."

"She didn't? I guess that's why the midwife didn't come. That's the last time I ask fer her help. That's some neighbor lady."

"I had some work ta do down at the store. Otherwise I'd a been home sooner. I'm sorry."

"Isn't she cute, Sam? Do ya want ta hold her?"

Sam walked over to the bed and took the baby. "That's my baby girl." He smiled as he held her in his arms and gently rocked her back and forth.

"I thought we'd call her Ruth, ya know, after Ruth in the bible," Naomi said.

November, 1997

Mamie

*M*amie reached over and picked up Katherine's cup of coffee as Katherine looked through the book of photos.

"Mmm! This smells good."

Katherine looked up at Mamie. "Is it too tempting to have the coffee around?" she asked.

"I'm not supposed to drink it, but they say that coffee can be good for the digestion. So I think I'll have a cup."

"Really?"

"Yeah. Coffee is okay in the Mormon Church if you drink it for health reasons. My sister Ruth was the only one of us girls who had a biblical name, ya know. *The Book of Ruth* in the Old Testament was my mom's favorite book in the bible. I guess that must have been the Jewish connection. 'Whither thou goest, I will go. Thy people shall be my people.' My mom used to recite those words from Ruth. I think that's part of what kept her in her marriage."

1908

Naomi

Naomi fed baby Ruth and put her to bed. Sam was going to be late getting home, she knew, but she decided to surprise him by taking his dinner to him. The baby was sleeping and should stay that way for at least an hour. "No harm in leavin' her alone a few minutes," she thought. The shop was just a couple of blocks away.

Naomi put Sam's dinner in a large basket and carried it to his cabinetry shop. The store was dark when she opened the front door. She walked to the back office and lit the lamp. Sam was lying naked on a rug with the blonde neighbor woman.

Naomi stared at the man she loved in the arms of a woman who slighted her at every chance.

"Naomi," Sam pulled on his shorts as he got up. "I kin explain."

"Don't bother," Naomi retorted. "I got eyes in my head ta see! So this was why ya didn't come home n' help me when I was birthin' our child! Ya were with her!" She blew out the lamp and slammed the door as she left.

Naomi kicked him out of the house the next day, but soon she began to miss him and went to his shop.

"Hello, Sam."

"How ya doin', Naomi?" Sam looked up as she walked in.

"I jist stopped by to invite ya to dinner this evenin'. The Mexican family down the street gave me a chicken. Thought I'd make dumplin's n' remembered it was yer favorite."

"What time ya eatin'," he asked.

"About six. I thought I'd put the baby down early."

"Okay. I'll be there."

Naomi fixed the dinner and carefully set the table with a candle in the middle and made sure the baby was asleep. Then she put on the only good dress she owned, the red silk dress she got married in. To that she added a dash of cologne, a wedding present from her mom that she kept hidden away in a drawer.

When he arrived at the house she drew him to the table. As they ate she enticed him with her succulent roast chicken and fluffy dumplings and seductive looks. Sam was clearly smitten.

"Ya look awful nice in that red silk," Sam said.

"D'ya think so," Naomi asked as she looked into his eyes and held him there.

He reached across the table and took her hand. "Course, I'd like it better if ya took it off."

Without letting her eyes move from his, her hands began to undo the buttons on the front bodice of her dress. No words passed as they stared into each other eyes.

She saw him put his hands between his legs as he shifted position on his chair.

Pulling the sleeves down from her dress and undoing the corset, letting them hang at her waist, she sat with her bare upper body bathed in candlelight. She reached up and undid the bun holding back her thick red hair. It poured down over her shoulders and breasts.

She saw Sam's smile, heard him say, "Take it all off," as his hand began to finger the hard place at his crotch.

Naomi stood and pulled her dress down over her hips. Then she released her petticoat.

"Come let me touch ya."

As she drew near he stood, fumbled with the belt that held his pants, then yanked off his shirt. He reached and pulled her hips to his and they made love on the kitchen floor that night.

Sam moved back home the next day.

* * *

A month later, Naomi began to heave her breakfast.

"Oh my god! Not again!" She leaned over the toilet hole in the outhouse nauseated by the fecal smell and sickened by the eggs she had just eaten.

Her belly began to swell with child. And soon Sam no longer found her attractive.

"Workin' late?" she asked Sam when he left for work.

"Yeah. It's the busy season. I've got two cabinets ta make. Keep dinner warm for me."

He was out getting his needs met elsewhere. Naomi knew it.

Eight months later she was saddled with another newborn baby. And he was out with another woman.

Once again, she kicked him out. Once again she invited him back to her bedroom. Soon she carried a third child.

This story repeated itself twelve times.

July 28, 1998
Running

My meal is finished. Time to go back to my room. I look up and notice the cowboy watching me. I put my notebook away and go up to the cashier to pay.

"Somebody has already paid your bill," the cashier tells me.

"Who paid it?" I feel my face redden as I ask.

The cashier nods towards the cowboy.

"I don't know him," I tell her. "I can't accept that."

I hand her a ten-dollar bill. She gives me my change.

I check to see that the cowboy's not following me as I leave the restaurant. He's out of his chair and heading my way.

*   *   *

I move quickly down the corridor towards the parking lot. When I look back, I see the cowboy in pursuit and getting closer.

I begin to run across the pavement to my car. I hear footsteps running behind me.

I fumble for my keys, yank the car door open, get in and lock it. I sit there a moment trying to catch my breath.

A man streaks out of the space between the two cars in front of me as I start the car.

I turn the headlights on. Quickly I pull out of the parking spot.

I almost run over the cowboy as I drive away.

November, 1997

Mamie

"*My* mother would never have gotten an abortion like a lot of women do today," Mamie insisted. "She valued family above everything."

Did she value it as much as Mamie thought? Katherine wondered as she listened. Or was Naomi trapped because birth control and probably abortions were inaccessible? She didn't volunteer her opinion because she had the feeling that her view on this topic might be very different than Mamie's.

Clearly Naomi used sex to keep her husband, but Katherine wondered if she didn't also enjoy it. There was probably no other source of joy in her marriage outside of the bed where she at least got to share some intimate moments with the man she married. That was one scenario that Katherine played back and forth in her mind.

The other pictured her grandmother as a victim of a womanizing man who didn't know how to touch nor to communicate with a woman. Maybe it was a kind of sickness with him, a power trip over women. Maybe he never learned how to respect a woman.

*　*　*

"My mom never stopped loving my dad even when she found out about his other women. She loved him even though it was a knock-down drag-out situation before they moved to Wyoming," Mamie, holding a cup of coffee in her hand, told Katherine. "I learned that from my mother's sister."

"How could she love him if he was abusing her?" Katherine remembered that Mama had told her once that "I never loved yer dad." Katherine felt that the physical abuse she suffered living with him made her feel that way.

"I guess she thought that was what a marriage was about. Her own mom had had troubles with her husband. And my mom, as a child, had probably seen it. So she must have thought the abusive relationship with my dad was normal. But my mother paid the price. He would fly off the handle at the smallest thing and hit her."

1908

Naomi

"*H*ell! Do you expect me to eat this crap," Sam yelled as he took the plate of potatoes that Naomi had set down in front of him and threw it into the trash.

Naomi, surprised by his sudden move, tried to get out of his way.

But Sam pushed her down on a chair and hit her.

"Don't hit me, Sam! It will hurt the baby!"

Sam backed off and stormed out of the house as Naomi sat at the table crying.

"I'm sorry if I did anything to hurt ya." Sam tried to make amends when he walked back in a few minutes later.

"I'm so hurt. So hurt." Naomi continued crying.

Sam stood at the kitchen door turning the knob back and forth.

"I know ya don't love me."

"Yeah I do."

"I don't think ya do."

"I told ya I do."

"I don't think ya would have hit me if ya loved me."

"Okay. So maybe I don't love ya."

"What do ya mean?"

"Maybe I don't love ya."

"Ya don't love me?"

"No, I don't."

"I knew it." Naomi began to cry some more. Then she blew her nose and began to wash the dishes.

November, 1997
Mamie

"*The* day that baby Sally died, my dad was out with another woman. My mom was at home canning fruit and making jelly. Me and my sister Ruth were helping her in the kitchen," Mamie remembered.

"My sisters and I used to also help my mom make jelly. It's one of my most vivid memories of growing up," Katherine volunteered the information as she listened.

"You did?" Mamie looked over at Katherine and smiled. Then, without a moment's pause, continued on with her story.

"From time to time I went to check on Sally who was sick in bed in the other room. She was running a fever and couldn't keep any food down, so my mom put her to bed. The last time I went in to check on her, she was turning blue. I became frantic. I ran into the kitchen and grabbed my mother's skirt. My mom was pregnant at the time, of course." Mamie smiled ruefully.

"'Ma! Ma! Sally's not breathin! She's not breathin'!', I screamed. Mom dropped what she was doing, laid the pot of wax back on the stove, and ran to the bedroom. She leaned over Sally and began to blow into her mouth trying to get her to breathe. Ruth ran for a doctor. He and my dad arrived at the same time. The doctor was too late to save the baby. My mom was distraught."

Mamie took a deep breath. Even after all this time it still hurt her, Katherine thought.

1915

Naomi

$\mathcal{I}$t's all yer fault," Sam yelled. "If ya hadn't had so many kids, ya would've had time ta take care of this one properly. Ya don't even have dinner ready fer me when I come home." He walked over to the closet and began throwing Naomi's clothes on the floor. He grabbed her red silk wedding dress and flung it across the bed. "Look at this whore's dress that ya go whorin' in. Yer nothin' but a whore. Yer not fit ta be anybody's wife," he screamed. Then he grabbed her wedding hat, the one that she had scrimped and saved to buy for her wedding.

"Ya don't deserve this hat," he yelled. "We're gonna git rid of it." He grabbed the hat and took it to the kitchen. Naomi followed.

"Come on. Take this hat! Take it n' burn it if it don't mean more to ya than that dead child in the next room!" Sam yelled at Naomi.

"Please Sam."

"Git over here n take this hat n' stick it in that fire in the stove. Otherwise, I'll tell everyone in town that this hat means more to ya than yer own kids."

"Sam, please don't make me do it."

"Ya do it or I leave n' tell everyone. I'll throw ya into that fire if ya don't. I'll kill ya!"

"Ya bastard! Those kids mean more to me than they ever did to you! If that's the way ya want it!"

Naomi grabbed the hat, walked over to the stove, opened up the grate, and threw it into the fire.

The feathers fizzled as the fire caught hold. The flames lashed out singeing the hair on her arm. She stared a moment as the fire consumed her last remembrance of love and romance in her marriage.

"Ya kin go ta hell!" Naomi screamed at Sam as she turned and ran into the bedroom.

November, 1997

Mamie

"*My* mom and dad separated numerous times while I was growing up," Mamie continued. "They'd have a fight. Horrible fights. She'd often accuse him of seeing another woman. He'd deny it. 'Well, I guess you don't need me!' I often heard my mom say that to him while I was growing up."

There were two fires in Iowa, Katherine remembered Mamie had said. She forgot to mention the hat.

Katherine took a deep look at Mamie and wondered what scars she kept hidden deep inside.

1916
Naomi

$\mathcal{I}$t was growing late when Naomi rang the shop to find out when Sam would be home.

"Who's the woman?" she asked when he answered the phone. She could hear the giggling in the background.

"It's a customer," Sam yelled.

"Really, Sam! Who is she really?"

"Just someone who's here helpin' me with the books."

"Fine then. Yer' covering up! And that's the same as lyin'! I'll be damned if I'm goin ta put up with my own husband lyin' to me! As I've said before, you don't need me." Naomi slammed down the phone and cried.

July 28, 1998
Chased

$\mathcal{M}$y heart is beating wildly as I pull onto a side street after leaving the restaurant parking lot. I want to be sure that he's not following me before I return to the Super 8 Motel. I can see the Main Street really well from here.

I see the red pickup. It must be the cowboy. I slouch down in the seat waiting for him to pass. Silence fills the dark night as I see his red taillights move down the street and turn about four blocks down.

I should go to the police. But, if the cowboy lives here, the police probably know him. I don't want to stir up trouble here in Brown Rock since I plan to do some digging around tomorrow to find out what happened to my grandmother. I don't want anything to get in the way.

My eyes watch the night and every car that passes on Main Street. Then I see another set of headlines coming up from behind. I hold my breath. When the lights reach the spot where my car is parked, I look over and see the cowboy looking at me smiling. Then he gives a wave and drives away.

My heart is pounding against my chest as I start the engine of my car and head back to the Super 8 Motel. I know I should call the police. But word gets around fast in these small towns. Tomorrow when I'm going to be searching for information, everyone in town would know about my run-in with the cowboy.

I stare off into the night as I hear the sound of crickets through the slight crack in my side window.

Something about the tree-lined street as I drive away reminds me of the street where Mama lived in Elk Mountain.

Back in my motel room, I make sure that all of the windows of the room are locked before I draw a bath.

* * *

My old love Robert used to cause my heart to beat like this, I remember as I lay my head back against the edge of the tub with my toes under the hot water coming out of the faucet. He also caused some problems in my life.

1984

Robert

"*W*hat beautiful roses! Who could have sent these," Katherine wondered. She opened the note and read: "*You are the only woman I want in my life. Love, Robert*"

The note and flowers stimulated a warm feeling inside. Then the phone rang.

"Hi. Did you get the roses?"

"Hi Robert. Yeah, I did. You didn't need to."

"I wanted to. You deserved them after what I did."

"What did you do?"

"I should have told you that I had a woman over to help me with my books last night."

"Oh. So why did you change your story?"

"It's not a story. It's the truth!"

"Well, then why didn't you tell me the truth last night?"

"Because you were upset and wouldn't let me talk."

"I asked you who the woman was when I heard her voice when I called, and you made up a story."

"Did you like the flowers," Robert changed the subject?

"They were nice. But I don't know that they resolved anything."

"Did you like the note?"

"Yes, but…"

"It's true. Every word of it. You're the only woman in my life."

So they fought awhile. Then he started calling every night. But she wouldn't see him.

Then one night when he called and invited her over for dinner, she finally agreed.

July 28, 1998

Winning

*H*e set out to win me back. And he did a pretty good job of it, I remember as I pull the spread down on the bed and slip under the covers.

Several months passed during which Robert and I seemed to be doing quite well together. So well, in fact, that I began to think, "This is it. He's the one." I stopped listening to the other message my mind was transmitting.

"Be careful," it kept telling me.

But I was too far gone to listen.

Then one night the phone rang and I picked up the receiver.

November, 1997

Mamie

"*My* family kept lots of secrets over the years," Mamie admitted.

"Like what?" Katherine asked remembering all of the fires that occurred in the Geislingen household while Papa was growing up.

"Well, I guess outside of how my mother died, my sister Ruth's pregnancy was one of the big secrets that most people in the family are still keeping."

"An unwanted pregnancy?"

"Yeah. But that's a whole other story."

1935

The cemetery

$\mathcal{B}$lack storm clouds loomed to the northwest. A breeze rustled across the cornfields that lay for miles across Iowa's green rolling hills. A black Ford coup pulled up next to the Pine Tree cemetery set out next to a white-steepled country church in central Iowa. A tall, willowy, dark-haired woman in a rose-colored coat got out.

"You kids stay in the car while I go tend the babies' graves," she told her children.

"What babies is mom going to see?" her daughter Tess wondered as she watched her mother walk through the black, cast iron gate to the graveyard and head immediately to two small white crosses between two large fir trees.

That's the question that Tess asked Mamie years later. But Mamie wouldn't tell her. She changed her mind about talking when Katherine finally came along and asked. But she would only tell her part of it. Katherine had to imagine the rest as she sat listening because Mamie would have been too embarrassed to talk about incest.

1923

Naomi

One day a week, Sam had Ruth come to the cabinetry shop on Main Street to help with his books. Often alone with his daughter, Sam had plenty of time to let his lustful eyes roam up and down her beautiful developing body. Plenty of time to let himself imagine.

At sixteen, Ruth made him feel good by the way she waited on him hand and foot and never questioned what he did. A contrast to her mother who continually demanded money to buy clothes for the children or interrogated him about his other women.

One Thursday afternoon, Sam pulled the front curtains and put the closed sign on the door of the store. He walked back to the office where Ruth was working and closed the door.

"Ruth, come over here and sit on your daddy's lap. I never get to hold my girl."

Hesitantly Ruth sidled over. She hadn't sat on her father's lap for years. He held out his arms and drew her down to him. She sat with her legs between his thighs and giggled. His hands caressed her hair, moved down her neck and found her breasts.

She pulled away as he began to undo the front buttons on her dress, but he held her tight with one arm.

"It's okay. I'm yer dad. You and I will have something special. We won't tell your mom or the rest of the kids."

Ruth relaxed as he pulled her dress down and let it fall to the floor.

His hand then moved up the inside of her legs between her thighs. "This is going to feel very good," he told her. "Spread your legs and sit down and face me."

She obeyed as he pulled her buttocks towards his hardened penis then ran his hands through her hair as he pulled her lips to his.

Sam and Ruth arrived home late for dinner that evening. "We had some extra work to do," he told Naomi. Ruth blushed and giggled nervously.

From then on, Sam closed the cabinetry shop early on Thursday afternoons when he could. On those days he told Naomi he and Ruth had to stay late because of extra work.

On those days Ruth wore her special dress, the one that buttoned down the front and clung to her body showing her thighs and breasts. It was Sam's favorite.

It was only towards the end that Naomi began to suspect as she watched her daughter preen herself before going to the cabinetry shop on Thursdays.

"Seein' anyone special today?" Naomi asked. "You act like yer goin' to the prom."

"I just wanna look nice when I'm workin' in the store," Ruth answered.

"I don't want Ruth workin' down in yer shop no more!" Naomi told Sam.

"Why the hell not?" he demanded.

"Cuz I don't like what she's becomin'."

"She's becomin' a woman is all," Sam stated.

"Yeah, an' somethin' more. Ya keep yer hands off her, ya hear!"

"Don't go tellin' me what I can n' can't do. She's my daughter!"

"Don't ya touch her or I'll call the sheriff!"

"Ya think he'll believe ya? He'll believe me first. I'm the one that runs this here house. Ya go causin' trouble, I'll kill ya!" Sam grabbed Naomi by the hair and shoved her up against the wall. "Ruth's goin' with me to the shop tomorrow and there's nothin' ya can do about it."

The next day when Ruth was dressed and ready to go, Naomi announced, "Yer dad ain't goin' to be needin' ya to work at the shop no more."

"We'll see about that," said Sam as he leaned over and put his lips to Ruth's ear.

"Yer comin' with me. Forget about her," Sam whispered. His lips lingered. Ruth reddened.

"Stay away from her, ya hear," Naomi yelled as she turned pancakes on the woodburning stove.

"We're goin'!" Sam stood up, got Ruth's coat and slipped it over her shoulders.

"Mom, do ya need my help?" Ruth turned back to Naomi and asked.

"She's okay. It's me that needs ya more." Sam kept his arm around Ruth's shoulders as he walked her out the door.

Naomi watched from the kitchen window. Then she ran to the door and yelled, "You bastard. Ruth, ya get back in here and help me!"

Ruth hesitated.

"You stay with me," Sam ordered under his breath. "We'll be comin' home late tonight," he yelled back at Naomi.

*   *   *

"It's time fer school. Ya gotta get up!" Naomi walked over to the window of the darkened room and pulled up the shade.

Ruth rolled over on the bed and moaned. "Mom, I'm not feelin' good. I need help."

"It's probably just the flu. Let me feel your head and see if ya got a fever."

Naomi stared dumbfounded at the red blood on the sheets and the baby lying next to Ruth's pillow.

"Mom, it's mine," Ruth cried. "I can't git it ta breathe. I don't know what ta do."

Naomi picked up the baby, held it upside down and gave it a swat on the rear end. Still no breath nor cry. The baby's flesh was turning blue.

"How long's the baby been lyin' there?"

"Maybe an hour. I didn't know what ta do."

"Was it alive when it came out?"

"It wasn't breathin' from the first. I did everything I could. I was too weak to do any more. So I went ta sleep."

"How long were you carryin' this child?"

"Eight months. She came early. Jim Carver's the father," Ruth quickly explained to Naomi.

"I got eyes. Don't think I don't know who this baby really belongs ta," Naomi exploded. "Don't think I didn't see ya dressin' up ta go down ta work at yer father's shop! Don't think I didn't notice that yer dad's lost interest in ya recently. Now I know why! He don't like big bellies! Didn't I bear and born ya? N' now ya bring me this. Ya thankless whore!"

"Mom, please I didn't want to. I didn't know what to do."

"Ya knew what you were doin' all right. And don't think yer dad's gonna stand by ya. He's not gonna let ya stay here when he finds out. I'm gonna call him."

Ruth's wail could be heard throughout the house. The younger children ran to the doorway and stared.

"Git to the table and eat yer breakfast!" Naomi screamed.

She stomped over to the telephone box hooked up on the wall next to the stove. She picked up the black receiver and began turning the crank to get the operator.

"Excuse me. I'm usin' the phone now," a neighbor's voice on the party line interrupted.

"Ya been on it long enough. I got an urgent call ta make," Naomi abruptly responded.

"Well, if it's that important." The line went dead. Naomi cranked the phone again.

"May I help you," the operator's voice came on the line.

"Sam's Cabinetry Shop."

"I'm ringin'."

"Hullo," her husband answered on the other end.

"Yer daughter Ruth had a baby this mornin'. It's all yer fault. The baby's dead. I want ya home right now ta take care of this thing."

The operator coughed on the other end.

Naomi hung up the phone, walked over to the wood-burning stove and continued fixing breakfast.

Ten minutes later Sam walked in.

* * *

"Git in there and take care of yer daughter! I wash my hands of it!" Naomi didn't even look up as he headed to the bedroom.

Naomi stabbed at the eggs as she pushed them around the pan. "How could I have let this happen," she asked herself over and over.

Five minutes later Sam walked out, sat down at the table. "Git me some breakfast, woman. I'm hungry. Didn't ya fix no coffee?"

"Ya talk to her?"

"She won't talk to me. And me her father. I oughta give her the thrashin' of her life and throw her out right now. She can crawl in the streets fer all I care. I don't care if it is snowin'."

Naomi swung around to face him, hands on her hips.

"Don't ya lay a hand on yer daughter! You've done enough already. Now git out and don't let me see yer face in that door again while yer daughter's here!"

"Yer not actin' logically, woman."

"Ya expect me ta act logically when my daughter's been knocked up? Ya expect me ta act logically when I know you was the one who did it! Do ya think a father puttin' his hands on his daughter is logical?"

"Don't go blamin' me for this. If it's anybody's fault, it's yer own fer lettin' yerself get knocked up and havin' so many children. A fine example you've made for yer daughter!"

Naomi grabbed his coat off the hook by the door and threw it at him. "You son of a bitch," she yelled at him as he walked out.

* * *

After Sam left, Naomi walked back into the bedroom with a pail of hot water and began washing Ruth's face and body.

"Mom, I'm real sick."

Naomi placed her hand on Ruth's forehead. "Yer burnin' up. I'm gonna send Mamie fer a doctor. Yer dad's gone. I'm not gonna let 'im ever bother ya again."

"But I thought you were mad at me."

"Yeah, I was. I'm more angry at myself for lettin' this happen to ya. I just wish I would have had more time to spend talkin' to ya. If ya could have talked to me, this might not have happened."

"It's okay ma. I know ya did yer best."

Naomi pulled her daughter to her and wept.

November, 1997

Mamie

"No one knew my sister Ruth was pregnant. She bound herself so tightly no one could see," Mamie explained thoughtfully.

"How did you know that. Did you see her doing it?" Katherine remembered the girdle she used to wear when she was trying to keep her pregnancy a secret from her mother.

"Sure I saw her. We shared a room. She didn't tell me she was pregnant. But I saw her putting that girdle on. I saw her gettin' sick in the mornings, but I kept my sister's secret from my mom. I'm no blabbermouth. My mom felt so guilty. 'How could I have let this thing happen ta ma daughter?' I heard her once say to a friend."

"So your mom had a good friend that she could talk to?"

"She had lots of friends but she didn't visit too much. But she was in a crisis over Ruth, so she and her friend sat in the living room one day talkin' and I listened in. 'I was just too busy with all the kids. Maybe Sam was right. I shouldn't have let myself have so many kids, but that's another thing I didn't know how to stop,' she said."

"What happened ta Ruth practically destroyed my mom! Maybe it did. She seemed to be dead ta feelin' from that point on. Looking back on it now, I think she should have left him then. But I guess she didn't know how to make a living strapped down with eleven kids and no education. So she stayed."

"What about Ruth? What happened to Ruth?"

"Things between my mom and Ruth was not right from then on. I could tell it watching them. Ruth used to always be by my mother's side in the kitchen. That stopped."

"How did the rest of your brothers and sisters feel? Did they know what was going on?"

"Yeah. I think they did. I think Ruth getting pregnant brought down the whole family in a way. The boys, being at impressionable ages, thought their dad's behavior was okay. I should have talked to 'em. But there was just no time. And my mom was too busy."

*   *   *

"There were two stories goin' around about Ruth's baby. Ruth said it belonged to a neighbor boy. I knew him; I used to watch Ruth go out to meet him. But the other story said the baby belonged to my father. They supposedly buried the baby in the ditch bank in back of our house in Greenville," Mamie continued.

"Which story do you believe? Do you think it was your dad's?"

"No! Don't go blaming my dad for that!"

"But I thought you said there were two stories."

"I told ya it belonged to the neighbor boy!"

"But you said your mom was upset. You just told me she talked to a friend about it."

"Well, I'm not talking about it anymore. It's done and gone."

And that was that.

But there was something going on between Ruth and her dad, Katherine was convinced of it.

*   *   *

"The betrayal my mom felt from both my dad and sister ultimately did her in," Mamie finally admitted.

"What do you mean, 'it did her in'?"

"Well, the light went out in my mom's eyes and never came back on again. She became troubled, couldn't sleep. I would hear her walkin' around the house at night. I'd get up and try to talk to her, but she wouldn't talk to me. She seemed to be constantly worrying about something and she took it out on my brothers and sisters. She just couldn't make herself leave my dad. I was fifteen at the time and kept hopin' that she'd get away and I would go with her; but her religion said she should forgive and move on. So that's what she did. I just wish she could have got it all out. I wanted to hear her wail and cry! But she held it all inside."

July 28, 1998
Secrets

$\mathcal{I}$ didn't see the light in Mama's eyes for several years after she divorced Papa, I recall as I lay in bed the next morning at the motel. The abuse and divorce seemed to eat her up inside. I found her diary after she died.

"I'm afraid," she wrote. "I'm afraid that what happened to his mother might also happen to me unless I divorce him and escape now."

What I read in Mama's journal prodded me to finally listen to Naomi's ghost and head to Wyoming to find out the truth. That's why I went to visit Mamie.

*   *   *

Incense and candles burned inside the Hindu temple in central Java in the mid 80s, I remember as I think about my mother and Mamie. The temple room had a funereal air. I let my eyes fall on the statute of the Hindu god Ganesha.

Suddenly, I could see the trace of a man standing there. He didn't tell me he was my grandfather. I just knew. I could feel him. He was briefly there then disappeared as I turned my back on Ganesha and walked out of the chamber.

Later that day at a shadow puppet play, I began to feel my grandfather's presence again from the spectator's side of the show traditionally reserved for Hindu women. The plays originated long ago as a way for the living to communicate with the dead, I remembered when I sensed him there.

Shadow and light flickered together in a type of dance as the unseen Dalang on the other side of the screen gave life to Sinta the good, Rawana the bad, and Jathaya the rescuer bird. The forms and forces whisked about the screen like Halloween witches. As I sat and watched entranced, my mind continued to open to the vision of my dead grandfather. The five-note beat of the gamelon at the shadow puppet play brought to life palm trees swaying in the ocean breeze, earth, flowers, fruit, the sea that lapped at the shores of Java.

When I got up and walked to the men's side where the puppeteer commandeered his puppets and scenery under bright lights, I wasn't able to observe anything more than a man moving figures around the screen and the gamelon orchestra that accompanied him. The man who played the puppeteer was the star of the show. Sinta and Rama were just pawns in his game. On the men's side, I wasn't aware of my grandfather's ghost like I had been when viewing the screen from the women's angle.

Similarly, in my search for Naomi, it's been easier to see her through a woman's eyes than from a man's vantage point. It was a woman who visited me in San Francisco. Since then, my father's sister Mamie has been the closest I've come to seeing my grandmother Naomi. My father has more than once slammed the door in my face.

1924

Naomi

"What ya want a new dress fer. Ya goin' to the prom?" Naomi stared at Mamie.

"I just wanna look nice when I'm workin' at the shop."

"Yer old dress'll do just fine. And ya don't need to be workin' at the shop no more." Naomi turned to Sam. "You'll just to have to find someone else to help ya."

"Fine," he said. "Connie can do it."

"I don't want Connie workin' there either. You can find someone out in the community."

"Hell! I can't afford to pay anyone to come in. I got two daughters here at home and one of 'em can help me."

Naomi didn't know what to do.

"Maybe Connie can take care of herself down there. She's stronger than Mamie and seems to lead her dad around by the nose," Naomi thought to herself. "Connie, yer dad wants ya to help out at the cabinetry shop."

"Really, Mom?" Connie loved the idea.

"I'm worried about what might happen to ya down there. You'll have to be real careful."

But Connie insisted she could take care of herself. Naomi let her go but worried as she saw her fourteen-year-old daughter go down to Sam's shop twice a week to help with the books.

Then one day a fire burned the shop down.

A small pan of gasoline placed on a bench ignited when Sam lit a match to light a cigarette.

"Jesus Christ almighty!" Sam tried to get out but the door was jammed. "Hell, I knew I should have gotten a new hinge on this!"

He finally threw the door open and staggered outside. The shop was lost.

"Thank the good lord there's one less thing to worry me," Naomi rejoiced when Sam came home and told her.

"What do ya mean, woman? How ya think I'm gonna make a livin'?"

"I'm more worried about my daughters than where the next penny's comin' from."

Though Sam tried to seem upset about the fire, the same day he went out and bought the whole family new clothes. He seemed like a man whose problems had been solved though the fire destroyed everything he had for making a living.

"But Sam, you know we can't afford new clothes."

"Hell, woman. Just take it while the gittins good."

* * *

"I'm movin' ta Wyoming," Sam told Naomi one day not long after the fire. "I'm takin' Connie and Mamie and the four oldest boys with me."

"Ya take the boys. But ya leave the girls with me," Naomi responded.

"I need em to do the cookin'," he told her. "They're goin'."

"Over my dead body," she answered back.

"Then I'll guess you'll be a dead un'," Sam responded as he slapped Naomi across the face. "I'll kill ya if I have to. But the girls is goin' to Wyomin' and that's that."

November, 1997

Mamie

"The day my dad and my four oldest brothers got into the car and drove away from our house in Greenville, Iowa, my sister Connie and I stayed behind," Mamie told Katherine. "The flu was goin' around at the time. And me and Connie got it. That's why we didn't go with him."

"Did you want to go?"

"I wanted to stay in Iowa and help my mom. Things between me and my dad, well, that's something I wouldn't talk about."

"What happened between you and your dad?"

"I didn't like what happened to my sister Ruth, but what's past is past and there's no sense in bringin' it up again now."

"Sometimes it helps to talk about the past."

"Sometimes. My mom and the younger children stood at the door and waved goodbye to my father and brothers. Then my mom went back inside, laid herself down on the bed and cried. I saw her because I was sleeping in that room."

"How did you feel about your dad leaving?"

"I was glad he went. It gave us some peace in the house."

"So you were glad that you didn't have to go to Wyoming with him."

"As I said, things between my dad and me was not as they should be."

"In what way?"

"Well, I was his daughter and all, and he should have treated me like a daughter."

"How did he treat you, if not as a daughter?"

"Well, my dad always made me feel like hidin' when he was around. Just the way he looked at me made me feel creepy."

"How did he look at you?"

"I don't want ta talk about that; but when my dad moved to Wyoming to find work, he practically abandoned my mom," Mamie said.

"Didn't he write?"

"Hardly at all. He never sent any money. I don't know what we would have done if it hadn't been for the garden and my mom's sister. My mom stayed back in Iowa a whole year with me and my sister Connie and the five youngest children until Iowa authorities told my dad it was about time he took responsibility for us," said Mamie. "My sister Ruth, well she left home not long after her pregnancy. But she sent us money from a waitress job she had taken in another town. My mom was forty years old in 1925 when she set out from the familiar world of Iowa where she was born and raised. My oldest brother Dan drove us out ta Wyoming in his new Chevrolet Coach," said Mamie.

"It must have taken you a long time to get there," Katherine said.

"Well, my niece told me that she drove from Greenville to Brown Rock last year in a 1996 GeoMetro and it took her about twelve hours. She was driving 75 miles per hour across Nebraska on Interstate 80. It took my mom and us kids three days back then because the road across Nebraska was unpaved."

"Ruth stayed behind in Iowa when the rest of us moved to Wyoming," Mamie said.

1925

Naomi

It was 10:00 at night by the time they got to Brown Rock. Sam was sitting at the kitchen table talking to a woman. Naomi and the children walked in and set their suitcases down on the linoleum floor.

The woman put out the cigarette she was smoking, then looked up at Naomi.

"Naomi, this is Laura Drew," Sam introduced her. "Laura, this is Naomi, my wife."

"Nice to meet ya," the woman stood up and held out her hand.

Naomi looked past the woman to Sam.

"I see ya been busy out here in Wyoming," she said as she pulled her children to her. "We're tired n' would like ta have some food n' git some sleep."

"Not much around. There's some eggs in the ice box. N' some bacon."

"Well Sam, guess I'd better be leavin'." Laura Drew got up and walked to the door.

Sam put his arm around her and walked her outside. An hour passed before he came back in again by which time Naomi and the children were sitting down at the kitchen table eating.

"Hell, wife. Do ya have to cause a scene?"

"I'm yer wife, ya know. N' who was she? The school marm?"

"It's none of yer damn business. After ya git those kids fed, ya kin take 'em into the bedroom there. Ya kin have my room. I'm spendin' the night out."

November, 1997

Mamie

"*My* father was through with my mother. And when a man is through with a woman, no one, not even the authorities, can keep him with her. My mother's once beautiful smile was gone a few months after she moved to Wyoming. She lost all of her teeth and my dad wouldn't get her false ones."

"So it was Wyoming that wore your mother out?"

"Yeah. That and my father. She told me that things were gitten worse and worse in her marriage, but there wasn't much I could do. I got married right after we moved to Wyoming. I was livin' out on a homestead and all and only saw her when I went to town."

"She must have felt very alone starting a new life in a strange place."

"Yeah, she did. Then two months after my mom arrived in Wyoming, my dad left the house one morning and returned with an envelope. He walked into the kitchen where she was sittin' at the table peelin' potatoes and laid the envelope in her lap."

1985

Robert

"*I*'m getting married," he told her.

Shocked silence as Katherine tried to get things straight.

"You're what?"

"I'm getting married."

"To whom?"

"A woman I met six months ago at the hardware store."

"You've been seeing her for the past six months while you were seeing me?"

"It just happened."

"I can't imagine you being married to anyone," she snapped.

A moment of silence. Then, "the reason I'm calling is, I wanted to invite you to the wedding."

What!? He had practically taken a knife and slashed it through her heart. Then he had enough nerve to invite her to his wedding?!

"I don't think so."

"I wish you would."

"No, I don't think it's a good idea."

"I'd like us to still be friends," he said.

"Friends? You want to be friends? I don't know whether that's possible. I thought we had something special, Robert."

"You're one of my best friends. I wish you would come."

Katherine hung up the phone and began to beat the pillow with her fists.

The next day when she woke up, she knew that she would not be going to his wedding.

*   *   *

She didn't see Robert again before she left Colorado Springs to live in Europe. When she decided to return to the U.S. five years later, she moved to the West Coast instead. Robert and his marriage were part of the reason.

1925

Naomi

"*W*hat's this?" Naomi asked Sam.

"It's a summons. They want ya to be at the courthouse tomorrow at two. They want to send ya to the loony bin cuz as far as I kin tell, yer crazy."

"So that's it. Yer gonna try to git rid of me that way."

"Woman, I'll git rid of ya any way I kin if I have to kill ya."

The day that Sam came home with the summons, Naomi waited for him to leave. Then she put on her coat and headed downtown.

"Joe Reese, Attorney at Law," the sign on the door said.

"I need to see a lawyer," Naomi told the secretary who ushered her in.

"You can go right in."

"I don't have much money to pay ya, but I need some legal advice," Naomi told the attorney who sat across from her at the large wooden desk. "My husband wants ta put me in the insane asylum. He claims I'm crazy. What kin I do?"

"Depends. How much money ya got?"

"$20."

"Kin ya pay me the rest, say $60 by April?"

"Yeah. I kin give ya what I take in fer ironin'."

"Okay. Are ya crazy?" the lawyer asked her.

"No, I'm not. Would I know enough to come n' talk to ya if I was?"

"Believe yer right there. So how far has this gone?"

"They've summoned me to the courthouse tomorrow."

"Okay, I'll go with ya. They're gonna test ya ta try to prove yer loony. Just be yerself like ya are now. If they git funny, I'll set them straight."

The lawyer spoke with a Wyoming drawl similar to people from Iowa, but with a little bit more of a twang, Naomi thought. All Wyomingites spoke the same no matter whether they went to school or not. His cowboy hat hanging on the door of the office added to the western flavor, though Naomi doubted that he'd ever wrestled a steer or spent much time on a horse out on the plains. "But I could be wrong," she thought as she sat facing him.

November, 1997
Mamie

"My mom turned up at the court hearing and they asked her a whole lot of questions. She left the courthouse that day a free woman," Mamie remembered. "They couldn't find anything wrong with her, but from then on, things got pretty bad in her marriage."

"How did you know? Did she talk to you about it?"

"She came to me and said she was afraid because she didn't know what he might do," said Mamie. "She told me that she had talked to a lawyer about a divorce."

Ω

1925

Naomi

Two nights after her appointment at the courthouse, Sam arrived home demanding that Naomi drop everything to get his supper ready.

"Ya kin fix yer own dinner tonight. I'm goin' ta church."

"What did ya say?" Sam demanded.

"I said I'm goin' out."

"Like hell ya are," Sam yelled as he grabbed Naomi by the hair and threw her across the room. Before she could get back on her feet, he was on top of her beating her with his fists.

"I"m gonna kill ya. I'm gonna kill ya this time!"

Dan, her oldest son, ran into the room with a piece of wood and held Sam off while Naomi put her coat on. "Don't ya touch my mother!"

"Git the hell out of ma way! If ya want ta fight, I'll fight!" Sam grabbed a butcher knife from the table and threatened his son.

Dan grabbed Sam by the wrist and forced him to drop it. He held him back until he was sure Naomi was safely out of the house. Only then did he let go.

"If ya ever touch my mother again, I'll kill ya!" he swore fiercely.

Sam grabbed the tablecloth off the table, then pulled the grate from the stove and threw it into the fire.

In 1932, when fireworks filled the air the year after "The Star-Spangled Banner" was designated as the national anthem, Naomi burned to death in the fire.

July 29, 1998

Passing the peace pipe

$\mathcal{A}$s I head north on Main Street towards the cemetery after a good night's sleep at the Super 8 Motel in Brown Rock, the Wyoming wind blows dust across the road. The light flashes, the barrier comes down, and the "ding ding ding" sound stops traffic as a train passes through town. I push down on the brake and wait.

There's something about trains that always makes me think of Mama.

The cancer ravaged her body in much the same way that Papa's physical abuse must have torn down her self-esteem during her first marriage. One day she had a light in her eyes. The next, she looked beaten and troubled. Every day of that marriage, like her bout with cancer, must have been a struggle.

She probably kept a mental calendar while she was married to Papa just as she did while she suffered the pain of lung cancer. I often saw her looking at the calendar that I sent her from San Francisco.

"What day is it?"

"It's May 1."

"Is that all? I thought it was much later."

No small coincidence, I believe, that Mama left this life on the day that would have marked her 61st wedding anniversary with Papa if she had stayed married to him.

I wonder if I will find some small glimpse of Naomi's mental calendar as I start to dig for clues here in Brown Rock. The light stops flashing, the barrier comes. I continue on down Main Street.

I ease my car into a spot in front of the City Funeral Home, a modern red brick building. A blonde, middle-aged, slightly overweight woman greets me enthusiastically as I walk in the door.

"I'm looking for a record of my grandmother's burial." I give her the name and the date. She heads to the back and returns a few minutes later with a copy of Naomi's record. I take a look then ask, "How much did it cost to bury my grandmother?"

"I'm sorry but we can't give that out."

"But that's historical information," I state. "Can't you give me an approximate? Was it $500? $400? $300?"

"All I can tell you is that her husband paid off the cost of burying his wife by making cabinets for the mortuary."

As I get back in my car and head up the street, I notice that it's already hot at 8:30. Far different from the cool early morning fog in San Francisco that I'm accustomed to in summer.

Not a soul in sight as I drive through the cemetery gate with my window down. A warm June breeze rustles the grass and my hair.

* * *

"Anybody here," I call through the screen door of the small white house just inside the gate of the cemetery. The caretaker doesn't seem to be around. I thump on the door and call out again.

Finally a tall overweight man appears from the shadows of the long hallway, his hand on his zipper.

"I'm looking for Naomi Geislingen's grave," I say.

"Wait there." He disappears into a side room and returns a moment later with a laptop computer. He plops
himself down on a large stone out front, opens the computer and, with a half-eaten piece of toast in one hand, he
types in the words "Geislingen" and "Naomi." I'm surprised to see such modern technology all the way out
here. I look over his shoulder at the computer screen and
see that he has made a database with each plot number
and name listed separately. He quickly scribbles a few
notes on a piece of paper.

"It's two blocks up there." He points up the hill.
"These are the names on the gravestones on either side of
hers. This here's the plot number."

"Thank you. That's just great."

"My pleasure," he says with his mouth full of toast.

I head up the hill and spot the grave immediately. An
unadorned gravestone a quarter of the way up marks the
spot where Naomi is buried.

"Naomi Geislingen, a Dutiful Wife and Loving
Mother." The words of the epitaph are worn but clear.
Naomi's grave had gone without a marker for many years
because the family couldn't afford a headstone, I remember from Mamie. She collected money from her brothers
and sisters to put one up fifteen years after the funeral.

I read the epitaph again and am caught by the word
"MOTHER". It stirs a gamut of emotions and memories
of my own mother, me, my daughter Cynthia. Intercon-
nected strings on the web of life that none of us has any
real control over. Always young is how I remember Mama
though I saw her disintegrate into old age before my eyes.

A small airplane buzzes above me, then swoops over
fields in the distance spraying some type of insecticide.

I check to see which way the breeze is blowing. I'm re-lieved that it's moving the spray away from the cemetery.

* * *

The wind blows dust across the hillside as I kneel at Naomi's graveside. As I let it ripple through my hair and across my face, I try to listen for the words of a red-headed ghost in a housedress.

"Naomi, are you there," I quietly cry into the air. A gentle breeze nudges me.

According to the story Sam told everyone, Naomi had spilled cleaning fluid while doing laundry; a spark from the stove caught her dress. I might have accepted that, but a dead woman asked me to help her. I wasn't going to close my ears to her.

I take one more look at Naomi's gravestone before heading downtown to the Western Square Cafe for breakfast.

* * *

"Don't cause a scene," Mama used to say. She was uncomfortable with me questioning the mechanic on how he fixed the car or sending the pancakes back in a restaurant because they were cold. "Don't hurt the family name," was the other thing she used to drill into me while I was growing up in Elk Mountain, where every-body kept up with the Joneses, where your secrets were everybody's business. I failed her on both accounts. Now I have more than a burning urge to know what really happened to my grandmother.

"Why are you doing this now?" a friend in San Francisco asked me before I headed to Wyoming.

"It's time," is all I could tell her. I could have added that unveiling the past is a freeing experience, as I learned when I found my daughter. Anything's possible—finding a person whose identity is locked tightly away in a bureaucratic vault, or coming face to face with a dead woman. I could also have told her about the muskmelon seeds my father helped me plant when I was four. Or, the white buffalo I saw on a visit home the year before my mother died. But I didn't.

*   *   *

The buffalo, according to Indian legend, signifies the unifying of all people from all races, I recall as I head towards the restaurant in Brown Rock for breakfast. That's what Mama wanted for her family before she died. She wanted us all together in one house getting along and liking each other. That didn't seem possible.

Talking about my grandmother's death is like passing the peace pipe. It ties together the pieces left dangling after Mama and Papa's divorce in the 50s. From time to time it brings up long suppressed emotions like how I felt when Papa drove away in his pickup that day, what I was left with after Mama died.

1996

Mama

"*I*'d like to have everybody get together for a dinner while you're here," Mama told her.

A dinner! With all the family together? With people who had been on the outs since god knows when and still weren't on speaking terms? Katherine had her doubts.

Nothing in the world could have been less appealing. A sit-down dinner with Mama, her sisters Sarah, Carol and Linda, and brother Jimmy would be anything but intimate. Forced conversation. Everybody on their guard to protect hurt feelings. The clank of silverware as people ate Mama's tender roast beef, fluffy mashed potatoes, pan gravy, jello and marshmallow salad, homemade rolls and apple pie. At that particular table with those particular people, food would probably not have much taste for her. But the oncologist had warned that the treatment worked best if the family worked together to create a positive, supportive environment. So Katherine agreed.

The first half-hour was the worst as each person tried to protect their own turf.

"If you want to find out what's happening in prisons, read *Twice Pardoned*," her brother Jimmy said halfway through the meal.

Katherine didn't need anyone to tell her what the book was about. Knowing Jimmy, she realized that any talk about the book would lead to a religious discussion.

"So some guy was pardoned twice?" her brother-in-law asked.

"Yep. The first time he was pardoned by the warden," Jimmy said. "The second time by Jesus Christ."

Stunned silence at the table except for the clank of silverware. Her sister Linda jumped up from the table and began to clear dishes. Katherine moved to help her. Soon her other sister Carol appeared in the kitchen also fleeing evangelism in the dining room. All of a sudden Katherine felt like laughing. She couldn't help but see the comedy there.

Jimmy, a fundamentalist Christian, was at it again. He had always considered his family as his mission field and liked to proselytize at the drop of a hat. If healing were to come, he would probably take the credit.

"Number one," was what her sister Linda called her stepfather Clark's only child. He had always been Mama's favorite; the girls always took second place to him. No wonder sibling rivalry and tension cut off any real communication at that dinner table. Jimmy's religious arrogance didn't help.

July 29, 1998

Breakfast in Brown Rock

A group of old-timers sitting at a table over by the counter looks up as I walk in the door of the restaurant for breakfast. I nod my head as I head for a table and sit down.

"The breakfast special," I tell the waitress. "Bacon. Scramble the eggs. I'll take the pancakes. And bring me some coffee and water."

I take out my little book and glance through the neat handwritten notes as the waitress sets down a cup of coffee in front of me.

I never returned to Elk Mountain for anything more than short visits and my stepfather Clark's funeral after I left in the 60s until the summer of 1996 when I stood in front of a mike at my 29th high school class reunion, I remember as I drink my coffee.

Standing in front of 150 people, none of whom I had been close to in high school, is something I wouldn't choose to do again, but I'm a woman used to expressing my opinion. Reading a poem I had written formulating my view of the "Equality State" seemed like a good idea at the time.

"The poem is very revealing," a friend cautioned me when I read it to her before the reunion.

"Yes, I know; but the time is here and I have to seize it," I told her. I did.

I look up when the waitress brings my breakfast. There at the next table sits the cowboy.

"Does he have business here?" I wonder as I look into the smiling brown eyes of the man slowly sipping a cup of coffee. I'm not sure whether to be irritated or pleased as I dab butter on the pancakes, cover them with syrup and take a bite. Then my thoughts drift as the cowboy walks over to the jukebox and puts a coin in.

I force myself to continue writing.

1996
Flashback

Katherine would rather have been a fly on the wall watching the performance than being the one who actually got up and read at the high school reunion that night. She had forgotten how uncomfortable small town meddling made her feel. Doing the gutsy thing took her a little too close to something she once left behind. It took her awhile afterwards to leave it behind her again.

"My voice sounds like a broken pipe organ," Katherine thought that night as she blundered her way through the reading in front of an audience of husbands and wives who had lived all of their lives in Wyoming.

"They never said that Nellie Tayloe Ross was governor just because her husband died and left her.

Nor in the name of people like Joseph Smith, Jesus Christ, and even John Birch,

Some women have worn the scarlet letter in Wyoming."

Shocked silence filled the room when Katherine finished reading.

July 29, 1998
Covering my breasts

$\mathcal{A}$s I lift my cup of coffee to my lips, I notice the cowboy staring. With a half smile, he gives me a wink. Then his eyes travel down to my breasts. Quickly, I look to make sure the front of my blouse is buttoned. While living in Spain in the late eighties, I didn't think twice about walking on the beach with my breasts exposed or expressing my sexuality in more sensually designed Spanish clothes. Here, a woman has to be more careful.

When I first returned from Spain, I ran into an old friend on the street in downtown San Francisco. I took his hand and kissed him on both cheeks, the usual Spanish greeting; but the man mistook it for something else. He pulled me to him, grinding his pelvis against mine, similar to what Robert did in Colorado Springs in the 80s. But I had been away and forgotten. Shocked, I pulled away. A lot of men in the U.S. have a one-track mind about sex. They also have a lot of suppressed rage towards women. That's why I'm careful about what I wear in the United States. Violence against women—rape, physical abuse, and murder—slam us in the face on a regular basis in the headlines of local papers. I felt safer living in Madrid, a city of almost six million than I did anywhere in the U.S. after my return.

1996

Flashback

"Sounds like you felt stifled growing up in Wyoming." A woman came up to Katherine after the reading.

"It certainly took a lot of courage to get up there and do that," said another.

Everybody else milled around not knowing what to say or do. A lot of people stared. Some avoided Katherine. Only one came up, gave her a hug, and said what a good job she had done.

"Genni Hass comes to these reunions every year. Whenever she comes, she brings that woman. Nobody's ever seen her husband," another male classmate informed Katherine later as people stood around drinking.

"Oh really?" Katherine turned away when she realized he was telling her he thought she was a lesbian. She thought he was wrong.

"Katherine really likes men," another male classmate commented as Katherine sat smiling and listening to the country and western band that played that night.

"What makes you say that?" she asked him.

"Oh, just the way you're looking at those men in the band."

He didn't use the word "slut" nor "lesbian," but Katherine knew more than one person was trying to figure out which one she was. They couldn't decide what to do with her because she wasn't married.

July 29, 1998
My pleasure Ma'am

$\mathcal{I}$ look up from my notebook at the café in Brown Rock and notice the cowboy still looking my way. I close my notebook and get ready to leave. The cowboy puts on his hat, gives me a smile and a nod and walks out the door. He gets in his red pickup and drives away.

I let out a sigh of relief and pay my bill. Time to return to the motel.

I pull to a stop on the north side of the tracks as the signal alerts drivers to an oncoming train. There must be 20 trains a day that pass along the tracks that dissect Brown Rock. They head west through town empty, then head back east again brimming full of coal from the boom town of Gillette in northeast Wyoming.

A train full of coal passes through, the red light stops blinking, the barrier lifts, I begin to pull across the tracks. Just as my car straddles both rails, it dies.

"What do I do now?" There's nothing but a click when I turn the ignition key. There's a line of traffic behind me. And I think I just heard the sound of another train whistle coming this way. "Yes, a train is very definitely coming!" I keep turning the key as my heart beats faster and faster.

I'll have to leave the car on the tracks and make a run for it.

"Oh god! Oh god! What do I do?"

"Put it in neutral," I hear a man's voice yell from behind.

Wouldn't you know it. That's one thing about Wyoming. People here are always willing to help you when you need it. "God! I hope he's right!"

"Okay! Okay! It's in neutral," I yell out the window! My car lurches forward across the tracks.

"Whew!"

The train passes. We just barely get across the tracks in time. I sit gasping for breath.

I finally get the car door opened and get out to thank the person who helped me. I look straight into the eyes of the man in the cowboy hat.

"Oh god! Not him again!" I want to turn around and make another run for it. Instead, I quickly mumble, "Thank you for helping."

"My pleasure, ma'am," he smiles as he tips his hat then reaches out and touches my hand. "Any time."

I feel my face redden.

"Pull the hood."

"What?"

"Pull the hood and let me take a look at the engine."

"Oh. Okay."

I pop the hood and the cowboy sticks his head in.

"Turn the key in the ignition."

I turn the key and hear nothing but a click.

"Okay. It must be ya got a bad solenoid. I can give ya a push to the gas station down the street. They can look at it and see what needs done."

"Okay."

"Now ya need ta put the car in neutral. When I start pushin', turn the ignition, pop it in first gear and push down on the gas pedal. The car might start on its own. If it does, you can drive it to the fillin' station and ask them to look at it."

"Okay."

I put the car in neutral as he positions his truck behind my rear bumper. I'm still a little light-headed from the confrontation as I feel a bump and my car begin to move. I put the car in gear and turn the ignition and push down on the gas pedal. The engine starts. I give him a wave as I head down the street to the gas station.

*   *   *

Still flustered by coming face to face with the cowboy and feeling his hand brush against mine at the railroad tracks, I lie on my bed at the Super 8 Motel trying to rest up after returning from the gas station. The man there said it was nothing more than a loose wire that caused my car to stall. I'll lie here a few minutes before heading downtown to the library.

What is it about the cowboy that makes me think of Robert?

I must be careful. The emotions that started to come up when the cowboy touched my hand make me feel out of control, the same way that I used to feel with Robert.

I seem to have a knack for attracting and getting attracted to the wrong guys. I read somewhere that one keeps repeating bad relationships until the mind works out some unresolved issue. So evidently, I still have some lessons to learn.

That's what Mama would have said, I think as I stare at the curtains.

I saw a light flicker on the curtains in my bedroom in Elk Mountain the night after we buried Mama. I lay and watched it awhile as it blinked, then disappeared. It made me think Mama hovered somewhere near. Maybe she had come back from the dead to ask how I was doing with men or whether there might be someone special in my life.

She used to ask that question whenever I went home. I either had nothing to tell her, or I was trying to keep it hidden. After I turned forty, she quit asking. That's why I guess she never asked about Robert, though he called her the year before she died trying to get my San Francisco number.

1996

Robert

$\mathcal{K}$atherine was home alone on New Year's Eve writing on her computer when the phone rang.

She waited to pick it up. Sometimes she didn't answer the phone at all. Usually not at night which was the high time for telemarketers. Never when she was writing. But it was New Year's Eve when usually only family called.

"Hello."

"Katherine. This is Robert Smith. How are you?"

"Robert! How are you? God, how long has it been? Twelve years?"

"Yeah. Something like that."

"I've changed a lot since then," she thought.

Even so, Katherine felt herself being sucked back through time and space. As soon as she heard his voice, she felt the same gentle wind that brushed her face the time he walked by in the Colorado Springs restaurant. It had been several years since she had last seen him. She felt her heart begin to sing.

"I'm divorced. My wife left and I moved to Utah," he told her.

Immediately Katherine's spirit soared. She tried to calm down as she said, "That's too bad." But her heart said that it was one of the best things she had heard in years.

Twelve years had passed since the fateful phone call telling her that he planned to marry. She hadn't seen him since. But he still knew how to draw her like a fly. He made her feel alive again.

Then in soft lulling tones, like a phantom calling her back a millennium of years, he drew Katherine's heart into his life again. Her mind had little time to say "Stop!"

"I had just taken some tissue from a woman's cervix for a pap smear when the nurse knocked on the door and told me the sheriff wanted to see me," Robert told Katherine. "I went out to meet him and he handed me a divorce summons. My whole life fell apart."

"Oh. When did this happen?"

"A year ago."

"How are you doing with it?"

"Hell! She took almost everything. Then the next week, there was a fire. I lost everything."

"How did that happen?"

"I don't want to talk about it."

"Okay."

"You haven't been with a man for six years," Katherine told herself as she listened to the soft tones and the neediness in his voice. "You're vulnerable," her mind said.

But life sometimes gives us second chances, she had read somewhere, and she really wanted a second chance.

July 29, 1998
Marlboro man

A good man definitely knows how to treat a woman, I think, as I drive around the block looking for a parking space at the library. I haven't met too many men who did. Maybe they were around and I just hadn't let myself get hooked up with them.

Robert was the only man that I really fell hard for. That happened before I came face to face with his other women. My mind tried to make me see him as a villain, but my heart beat too strongly when he was around and I couldn't control myself. I was crazy about him. Then he got married. Eleven years later when he called on New Year's Eve, I was watching my mother die, the relationship with my daughter change, my body enter menopause, my youth fly away. I needed something familiar to hold onto. And he had a familiar spirit.

Crazy Horse, a courageous and fierce warrior, represented what was good in the Indian culture. White men looked on him as barbarian and annihilated him and his race. They replaced him with the European archetype for manliness, what they saw as a more civilized form of brave.

Owen Wister's *Virginian*, chivalric, muscular and heroic, helped establish the American model of a good man and paved the way for the box office success of the western movie and John Wayne. Aha! There it is on the shelf.

The tough-skinned Marlboro man who played in the ads on T.V. in the sixties and seventies was a carryover of the Wister model. A lot of Wyoming men still pattern themselves after that type.

My stepfather Clark wore a cowboy hat at an angle, just like the guy walking into the library. What? Oh god. Not again, I think as I see the cowboy walking over to the librarian. I hide behind the history stacks.

The cigarette hanging out of my stepfather Clark's mouth gave him the air of being tough, though underneath he was soft and sensitive. But that's what finally killed him and perhaps my mother, too.

"Who knows what you kids have to look forward to," Mama told me and my sisters after the oncologist diagnosed her condition.

Mama sounded like she was blaming Clark. I understood that he used tobacco as a crutch to help him deal with the emotions he stuffed inside when he came back from the war and found he had no one to talk to. A lot of those World War II men started dying in the seventies and eighties. Most of them are gone now, like my stepfather Clark.

*   *   *

"Naomi Geislingen badly burned by gas explosion."

The headline screams at me from the front page of the January 10, 1932 paper as I wind the tape through the machine at the library.

January 17 — "Local Cabinet Builder Questioned in Death of Wife."

That's my grandfather they're talking about! Proof of what I've long suspected. I read on. I take a deep breath as I stick a quarter into the slot and push the copy button. I spend two hours at the library. Then my stomach starts growling. So I decide to go eat and come back later to look for more information.

*   *   *

As I get ready to leave, the cowboy walks up to the desk to check out some books.

"Hi, Tim," the woman smiles as he puts a stack of books in front of the woman.

All the librarians make a big fuss over him. That's how women used to treat my stepfather Clark, I remember. They always acted like they were just crazy about him. It was because he liked to flirt.

Big Rock Candy Mountain by Wallace Stegner lies on top of the stack of books that the cowboy has handed to the librarian, I notice.

So he's a reader. Is he a good man or bad? Maybe he's one of those western types who never seems to be able to settle down.

He certainly likes to flirt with women. A womanizer? Can't prove it from one encounter. Women used to also fall over backwards for Robert, I think. What is it about men like that that makes women lose their minds and hearts to them? Women think that they can't live without them. They give everything they have to them and seldom get anything in return.

As I walk out of the library, I realize I left my keys locked inside my car. I walk back into the library. The cowboy looks my way as one of the librarians gives me a coat hanger. I walk back out and begin to pry it through the top of the window. As I'm trying to break in, the cowboy shows up.

"Can I give you a hand with that?"

"Thanks, but I think I can take care of it myself," I tell him smugly.

This is going to work, I tell myself as I unwind the hanger.

The cowboy stands back and watches as I pry the hanger through the crack in the window. Up comes the lock and the door opens.

I glance over my shoulder at the cowboy as I get in, start the car, and back out. I give him a wave as I drive away.

*   *   *

"Lemon chicken and a large glass of water," I tell the owner of the only Chinese restaurant in town. The owner is a Chinese man. He and his hired Chinese waiter are the only two in town, besides the Mexicans, who aren't white.

He sets a glass of water down in front of me. I take a sip. Then I notice the cowboy sitting in a booth across the restaurant talking to the woman I saw him with in the parking lot of the Super 8 Motel the day I arrived in Brown Rock. I take a look at the woman's face again. There's no doubt about it. She's the spitting image of Naomi. The cowboy glances over. Our eyes meet.

I observe the Chinese waiter taking orders from customers. Then I look at the man in the cowboy hat, who fits right in.

I wonder how the Chinese men are managing in this small Wyoming community where the Klu Klux Klan used to be strong. How have the people of Wyoming responded to their presence?

The white waitress runs into the Chinese waiter. She spills two glasses of water that she was carrying.

"You idiot," I hear her scream. "You should go back to your country!"

Why is she blaming him, I wonder? She ran into him. She must be stressed and unsure of herself, I think. People who are sure of themselves don't usually need scapegoats. Good thing he isn't the owner.

The cowboy jumps up and helps the girl with the spilled water. Then he turns and talks to the Chinese waiter. I overhear him say, "You're very welcome in this country no matter what anybody might say."

My view of the cowboy begins to change.

I finish eating my lunch. Then I head back to my motel room to get some rest before I return to the library.

1993
Stepfather Clark

"You know I love you, don't you," Katherine's stepfather Clark asked her a few months before he died.

"I don't know." Katherine couldn't lie to him. She couldn't let him go without telling him how deeply it hurt that he had not been there for her while she was growing up. He had been too busy working.

"What do you need from me?"

"I'd like you to call me on the phone just one time to say hi," Katherine told him.

What she didn't say was that she wanted him to be the same man who used to pretend like he was calling her on the phone as he sang "Hello my honey" to her just after he married Mama when she was five. She wanted to start over from there and try again, but she couldn't tell him because he was too ill. Clark had been unable to make that call before he died. She suspected Mama helped keep him from it.

"Just look at all Clark has done for you. The reason that we have this house and you have all of your clothes is because of Clark. You need to treat him better."

Mama's constant harping on the subject caused Katherine and her sisters to resent him. He must have felt their resentment. Maybe that's why he stayed away and spent all of his time working. Maybe that's why after her brother Jimmy was born she practically became non-existent.

"Clark's home! Jimmy, come on in so you can take a bath and visit with your dad while he's shaving."

Katherine lay on her bed in the next room listening to what transpired as Clark came in and began running water in the bathroom sink as he cleaned up and shaved.

"Hey dad, guess what I did today?"

"What?"

"I went over to the lake fishing. And I caught a big fish."

"You did? I can't wait to see it."

"What about me?" Katherine wondered. "I guess I'm not as important as the fish. He walked by my bedroom door on the way to the kitchen and didn't even stop to ask what I had done today. He didn't even ask about me."

July 29, 1998
History lesson

"*P*apa never made the effort either to let me know he loved me," I remember as I return to the library an hour later. I continue to turn the wheel on the microfiche machine and read about my grandmother.

Violence in the U.S. appeared to be running rampant in 1932, the year my grandmother died, I note as I read through back issues of the local newspaper. Gangsters were killing each other in Detroit and Chicago. A wife shot her policeman husband in Denver because she said he was beating her. A girl was strangled in San Diego. A Cheyenne, Wyoming woman filed for divorce charging that her husband beat her with a hammer.

In the 30s in India, Ghandi was promoting women's equality. Throughout most of the U.S., women had been able to vote since 1920. In Wyoming, women gained the right in 1869.

Television was not accessible to the American public in the 1930s; but for the first time in history, the pope presented a message of peace via the Vatican's new radio station built for Pope Plus XI by Marconi. Radio was the current high technology. Still, much of the world gained its information via word of mouth or newspapers.

In 1932, many people in Wyoming were isolated by distances. It was 60 to 100 miles between some towns. Many people still did not have telephones. If you lived on a ranch or homestead, you likely did not know what was going on in town.

But, if you lived in a small community like Brown Rock, Wyoming, you likely knew everybody else's business.

You probably knew who was bootlegging and who was not. You knew who was having an affair with whom, what people were on the rampage, what judge was not doing right, who had murdered whom, who had committed suicide.

By the time the January 10, 1932 headline of my grandmother's burning hit the front page of the local newspaper, most probably already knew the details.

*   *   *

Local people had probably already been discussing the issue extensively by the time they read on the front page of the January 24 paper "Husband charged with murder of wife." In small towns, tongues like to flap. Few talked about anything except the Geislingen's.

The Brown Rock district attorney John Smedley filed charges of first degree murder against Sam Geislingen. The state accused Sam of murdering his wife Naomi. His case—the *State of Wyoming vs. Samuel Geislingen*—went to trial.

"At 1 p.m. on Friday January 30, 1932, crowds began to fill the Brown Rock courtroom for the trial," I read in the newspaper. "By 2 p.m. when the judge arrived, the courtroom was crowded to standing room only. The hallways and stairways of the district courthouse were filled with people. The overflow stood on the courthouse lawn."

Edward Thompson, Sam Geislingen's attorney, asked that the case be dismissed. The judge denied the motion. "Sam was bound over to the district court. His bond was set at $9,000 and he was returned to jail," I read.

During Sam's trial in Brown Rock in 1932, "public opinion was emotional and mixed." I continue to read. Before she died, Naomi Geislingen accused her husband of throwing cleaning solvent on her then lighting a match. Sam pleaded not guilty, claiming that Naomi was hallucinating when she accused him. She accidentally spilled cleaning fluid on her dress while she was doing the laundry, he said. Then she leaned over a burning fire in the stove. Town opinion was divided.

Wyoming newspapers in the 1930s labeled my grandfather as the "torch murderer." Front-page headlines in local papers blared the story of his court case for weeks. The Geislingen family was ostracized.

* * *

I sit back on my chair at the Brown Rock library and let the wheels of my mind turn out a picture of the times during which my grandmother died.

Victorian attitudes that attributed every problem between a husband and wife to hysteria or mental weakness on the woman's part were very strong in 1932 in Wyoming as they were in many places, I have discovered from my extensive reading.

Awareness of women's rights was beginning to rise in eastern urban environments like New York City, but in Wyoming, known as "the equality state," women suffragists were few and far between. When Naomi accused Sam of killing her, the do-gooders probably thought she should have gone quietly to a good Christian woman's grave. Others may have felt she was strange and possibly insane because, after all, she was a poor housekeeper and had spoken out about her husband before. And there were probably others who just couldn't believe that a good church-going man and father like Sam, the town cabinet-maker, could do such a thing even though he had a reputation as a womanizer. But for whatever reason, most of the town rose up against my grandfather. The case was transferred to Wheatland, Wyoming on February 22. A jury was selected and the trial began on April 14.

"Defendant seems to be confident of acquittal," the headline in the Brown Rock paper said that day.

1932

The trial

"*My* wife suffered hallucinations. She was under the illusion I wished to kill her but her fears were ungrounded." At the trial Sam told about problems at home.

Dr. Jerry Hanson, the family physician who treated Naomi's burns, testified that when he was called to the Geislingen residence at 6:20 a.m. "She was burned from her knees to her head with her chest and back burned to a crisp."

"How strong was the morphine you gave Mrs. Geislingen?" Sam's attorney asked the doctor.

"Maximum strength," Dr. Hanson told him.

"Do you think she might have been suffering from a mental delusion?" Thompson asked.

"Objection! Mrs. Geislingen was badly burned and still had some wits about her!"

"Your honor, it's relevant here because she accused her husband of killing her."

"Your honor, anyone who was burned as badly as Mrs. Geislingen would be under serious physical strain, but I don't think we can call it a mental delusion."

"The question is dismissed."

"But your honor…"

"Question dismissed. Next witness."

"One of the Geislingen boys called me to the house around 8:00 a.m.," county sheriff Dawson testified. "The first thing Mrs. Geislingen told me when I arrived was 'he threw cleaning solvent on me and set it afire with a match.' On the way to the hospital, she kept repeating what had happened," he said.

* * *

"I was in bed when I heard Mrs. Geislingen scream-ing. I raised up and saw her through the glass in the door and she was in flames," Mrs. Paxton, Naomi's black next door neighbor stated at the trial. "I grabbed a quilt and ran out the door. She fell just before she reached me. I smothered the blaze with my blanket. Mrs. Geislingen cried, 'Don't carry me back there!' So I took her into my house and placed her on the bed. She then told me 'Go git the kids.'"

John Smith, another neighbor, said, "I heard screams and saw Mrs. Geislingen in flames. When Mr. Geislingen asked me to go into his home about three minutes later, I didn't notice any warmth in the house. I don't think there was any fire in the stove. I was within eighteen inches of it but didn't feel any heat. It was early in the morning and it was too dark to see plainly," he said.

Naomi's sixteen-year old daughter Dana said that "me and all my brothers n' sisters was in bed when I heard the call for help. I rushed over to the Paxton's. My mother said, 'he did this to me. I can't live. I'm cooked.'"

Dana went back home that night and got out the shotgun, according to her sister Mamie. She and her other sister sat up all night waiting for her dad to come home and kill them, too.

But according to the newspaper article, after being advised by Dr. Hanson, sixteen-year old Dana changed her testimony from "My mother said he did it" one day to "He didn't do it" the next.

"Do you think your mother was delirious?" Sam's attorney Thompson asked Dana according to the newspaper article.

"Yes. She was hallucinating," Dana responded.

* ✦ ✦

July 29, 1998
From the mouth of God

*H*ow could someone persuade her to change her testimony, have it reported in the newspaper—therefore public knowledge—and have it stand up in court, I wonder as I read the account in the newspaper. So I ask the librarian.

"Back then, like today, small town politics influenced most people. The town doctor had a lot of clout," the librarian said. "So no one was going to question him tampering with evidence or persuading a witness to change a story. They would listen to her changed story because it was almost like it came directly from the lips of God."

1932

Love triangle

"*M*y husband abandoned me. So I rented out some rooms in the house. I rented one of the rooms to Sam Geislingen," Mrs. Laura Drew told the court.

"Were you and Sam Geislingen having an affair?"

"I've known Mr. Geislingen a long time. My husband left me. Mr. Geislingen was separated from his wife at the time. We had talked about getting married."

"You were going to get married?"

"We talked about it."

"But you knew that Sam Geislingen was already married, didn't you?"

"Yes. But he said he planned to divorce her."

"But he was a married man. Mrs. Drew, you should have known better."

"Objection."

"Okay. Mrs. Drew. How long had this affair between you and Mr. Geislingen been going on."

"Mr. Geislingen and I had been seeing each other for about seven years. His wife was living in Iowa when I met him. I thought he was a widower at first. Then his wife moved out to Wyoming. And that was the first time I knew that he was married."

"So Mrs. Geislingen showed up. And you stayed in the relationship."

"Mr. Geislingen and I were talking about him leaving her and getting married. He said that his wife was crazy. I believed him."

"So Mrs. Drew, you stayed in the relationship even when he stayed with his wife?"

"I believed that he would leave her and that he and I would marry."

"So on the morning of January 10 when his wife was burned, were you and Mr. Geislingen still seeing each other."

"Yes."

"When was the last time that you saw him?"

"I saw him the night before. He left my house late."

"How late?"

"It was about 2 a.m."

"And what were you doing until the wee hours of the morning?"

"Objection."

"Okay. So did Mr. Geislingen talk to you about killing his wife?"

"No."

"Did you and he plan together to get rid of his wife so that you two could marry?"

"No."

"Objection."

"Did you not conspire together on how to get rid of her so you could be together?"

Someone in the courtroom whistled. Then the whole room applauded the prosecuting attorney's last comment. The majority thought that if Sam were guilty of killing his wife, Mrs. Drew was the reason.

July 29, 1998
Burns

I put the newspaper down and sit back in my chair. I rub my forehead as I absorb what I've just read. I'm tired. Time to rest.

Naomi died from third degree burns, according to the newspaper. With third degree burns, the nerve endings are totally exposed, a woman at the burn center in San Francisco told me before I made the trip to Wyoming. Naomi's pain must have been excruciating.

As painful as childbirth? I wonder. I don't know. I can't remember the pain I felt when I gave birth to my daughter. At the time, though, I remember feeling I hadn't experienced anything worse. People talk about physical pain but they don't often talk about the emotional scars. It's been years and I still haven't fully pardoned Papa for driving away in his pickup and never coming back when I was four. The way I feel about Papa tends to be the way I feel every time I get close to a man and he disappoints me.

But even if I didn't have issues with my father, it wouldn't be hard to see that a lot of men in this culture don't know how to treat women. Take the American medical profession, for example. They're the ones who treated my grandmother's third degree burns. A male doctor arrived that day, ripped her clothes off and applied ointment, according to Mamie. Her mother was in incredible pain, she told me.

"Oh please, slowly. It hurts!"

The doctor seemed not to hear her cries but continued slapping the ointment on, Mamie said.

"Oh god! Let me die!" Naomi moaned.

Doctors don't use ointment today for burns because it's not water-soluble. But that's how they treated burns in the thirties.

In the 1990s, the white male doctor rolled his eyes as he told my sisters and me that, "It would be a waste of time to have a C-scan done on your mother."

It was a waste of time, I felt he was saying, because she was a woman and over sixty-five.

I recently walked into the examining room of a highly reputed local orthopedic surgeon to have him look at my shoulder. He was standing there with another man staring at me. They looked up surprised when I came in.

"What seems to be the problem?" the orthopedist asked.

"I have a lot of pain in my shoulder and neck," I began to tell him.

As I talked, he rolled his eyes at the other man and laughed.

"Is there some reason why you prefer to laugh instead of listen to me?"

The two men looked surprised as I picked up my bag and walked out.

Doctors are trained to make people question themselves. That way patients will lose their power. They usually do it more with women so they will look to the doctor as an authority. God on a throne is how many doctors in the American medical system like to be treated.

Like a human being is how I prefer to be treated. That's why I prefer Chinese medicine to Western. The American medical profession looks down on the mental aspect of human beings. Chinese medicine treats the whole person.

1997
Robert

*A*nother burn of a different type festered at 6:15 one morning as Katherine's plane took off from San Francisco. She sat in her seat on the way to see Mama a few months before she died. She kept wondering how things might have been different with Robert. She had wanted to cast all care to the wind and do something wild and free. But he began to change after their New Year's Eve phone conversation.

He came back into her life after the phone call and began to take over every conscious thought.

Countless phone calls and e-mail messages later, she began to notice something different in his voice.

"You seem different. I can't pinpoint it. Just a change in the way you talk. Is something different," she asked him after they had been talking on the phone and communicating by e-mail every day for six months?

"No, nothing's different," he wrote back.

"You must be very honest with me," she replied. "Before I move ahead with you I need to know, do you have anything going on with anyone else?"

Since he had previously told her that there was no other woman in his life, she expected him to say "no" when she asked.

Instead, "I do have a somewhat thing going on. We are best of friends and there is a sexual relationship."

"Stunned and hurt that you would do this to me," she wrote back.

"I'm very sorry for anything I have said or done that hurts you," his response.

The past suddenly came tumbling down around her. She remembered his phone call out of the blue 12 years earlier announcing his marriage. This was history repeating itself.

"I need to change my ticket. I have reservations to go round-trip from San Francisco to Wyoming with a one-day stop in Salt Lake. I need to cancel the Salt Lake part of that ticket."

"You're in luck. We haven't sent your reservation in," the airline sales agent told her. "All we need to do is credit your Visa."

When Robert called her later that day, she caught her breath as she picked up the receiver.

"Robert, I'm not going to be stopping in Salt Lake on my way to Wyoming. I think it's best that we end this now. I can't go through with you again what I went through with you twelve years ago."

"What was that?"

"You told me there was another woman like it was no big deal. I can't believe that you would do that to me again. I can't believe I let you. It's best we cut the thing off now. Nip it in the bud. I'm sorry, Robert."

"I'm sorry, too. The other woman means nothing to me. I will end it if it bothers you that much."

"No, it's best that we stop all communication."

"But, the woman meant nothing to me. That's your own paranoia."

"That may or may not be. But I've got to go with how I feel on this. I'm sorry. But I guess this is goodbye."

"Oh."

"I've got to go now."

"Okay."

"Goodbye."

"Bye."

Her hands were shaking as she put the receiver down. She laid her head down on her pillow and cried.

When the plane landed in Salt Lake on the way to Wyoming and she got off to change planes, she looked at the faces at the gate thinking that he might have come to make some last effort. But he never came.

July 29, 1998
A lifetime

$\mathcal{I}$ look at the streets of this small Wyoming town as I head back to the Super 8 Motel. It's just like most Wyoming towns, but a lot has changed since I lived in Wyoming.

During Mama's lifetime, she saw development of the automobile and America's super highways, first JC Penney then Walmart, transcontinental travel by airplane, television, computers, the Internet, women developing careers and working outside the home, her own marriage and divorce, and forty years with my stepfather Clark. Mama's life spanned most of the 20th century.

During the few short years that my grandmother Naomi lived in Wyoming in the twenties and early thirties, Prohibition was in effect. Men with stills were being arrested. Women had the right to vote in Wyoming, but other than that they stayed home and slaved away.

During my life, I've seen young men in uniforms heading off to war in some strange place that most had never heard of. Women burning bras, people protesting the Vietnam war, the majority of my generation using marijuana, a big move back to the land in the early 70s. Then came yuppies with money. Bill Gates introduced PC software. Silicon Valley began to grow. I'm a bit of the 1960s, Spain, San Francisco and Silicon Valley all mixed up together. But most of all, I am Wyoming.

Cynthia Jane

1994
Close encounter

*K*atherine saw the west—the red brown hills, the dusty feel of men wearing cowboy hats, women being kind and children looking after their elders—through the windows at the Denver Airport. It looked just fine. That was three years before Mama died.

A rosy glow, translucent blues as far as the eye could see, filled the sky early one morning as Katherine flew into the sunrise leaving home and San Francisco behind her. Later that morning, she drove north in a rental car from the Denver Airport into Wyoming to meet her daughter Cynthia.

That afternoon the sky over the Big Horn Mountains in northern Wyoming looked totally black as she headed towards the mountains to join Cynthia and her grandchildren for the weekend.

The storm clouds made her uneasy. Were they a warning of things to come? she wondered as she drove towards her destination.

"I have sometimes thought that you might have anger towards me for giving you up for adoption. Do you?" she remembered asking Cynthia a year or two before her husband Kenneth died.

"I need to think about it." Then a few months later, Katherine got the letter. *Dear Katherine, "I thought about what you said—me holding anger towards you. You are right. I know I have had anger towards you. The reasons why, I'm not sure. Cynthia"*

Katherine felt relieved when she got the letter. "Now that's out in the open, we can deal with it," she thought.

But, then cancer grabbed hold of Kenneth. He died and his ashes were scattered over the Big Horn Mountains. Six months later, Katherine received another letter from Cynthia. *"Dear Katherine, I've discussed this with my mom and dad. And I'm not angry. You can ask my mother and my father. And they'll tell you that I'm not angry."*

"What? So she had discussed this with her adoptive parents and they told her she had no anger to deal with," Katherine thought. She felt something like a door slam shut. *"But Cynthia, you told me earlier that you were angry. Why did you change?"*

Cynthia wrote back. *"Dear Katherine, I'm very angry with you about your letter. It's almost like you feel I'm this naïve little girl who doesn't know how the world works."*

Do I think that? Katherine asked herself as she drove towards the Big Horns. Am I expecting too much from her like Mama did from me? She looked off across the plains towards the mountains and sensed Kenneth's presence as she drove to meet his wife and children. The dark-haired, dark-eyed man of Spanish descent who had been married to her daughter, had believed in family first, blood family, and had supported the relationship between Cynthia and her birthmother.

Now he's gone. But "I feel him somewhere near watching over what happens here." As she approached Buffalo, Wyoming, she saw a tornado. "An indication of things to come?" she wondered as she remembered Cynthia's anger in the letter. Why did her anger tear at her heart so hard? "Maybe I'm to blame for expecting too much from the relationship," she thought as she pulled into the Amoco quick stop in Buffalo to take a closer look at the tornado.

Within half an hour the tornado was gone and Katherine headed on down the road.

Up close, the Big Horn Mountains didn't seem quite so big. When Katherine was at a distance they seemed high and rugged, almost frightening. Desolate and jagged, there was something about them that made her feel that if she drove up into them, she might disappear. She felt a similar fear about Cynthia's anger. "What little thing might I say to upset her?" The road curved towards the mountains.

Katherine drove up and up and up as she headed over the mountains towards Ten Sleep. Then she turned north on a dirt road headed towards Hyattville. Katherine crossed a cattle guard and saw another sign that said "Big Horn National Forest." On the dirt road, she slowed down to 40.

Katherine looked around and felt she was out in the middle of nowhere. She just hoped she was on the right road and that she was going to find her daughter up there. Once she arrived at the campground, it wouldn't be long before it got dark. A sign said 17 miles to Hyattville.

It was the kind of road that once you were on it you didn't turn back after it had been raining. Once a birthmother enters a relationship with a birth daughter, one doesn't turn back either no matter how hard the going, she thought. The black clouds must have dumped heavy rain there. Katherine hit a bunch of mud.

As she fishtailed back and forth, she hoped she wouldn't slide off. She wanted to turn around at a cattle guard, but she couldn't back up. Katherine knew if she went forward she would get stuck in some deep muddy water covering the next maybe tenth of a mile. But she kept going forward.

The black clouds looked like they had more heavy rain to dump soon. "Will Cynthia also have some anger to dump when I see her?" She struggled to hold the car on the road. She brought the car under control at last and eased her way forward. It was 5:25 and she still had about seven miles to go. It was very slow going.

She came to some really bad mud and pulled to the right as two four-wheel drive vehicles crept past in the opposite direction. The first one had its windows down and three young guys in baseball caps. Katherine yelled, "Is it muddy all the way to Hayattville?"

The driver stopped and yelled back, "Well, it's muddy, but it's not this snotty kind of stuff here."

Katherine let out a sigh of relief as she kept pushing forward in her two-cylinder GeoMetro.

*   *   *

As Katherine turned a corner and saw some peaks set in the sky ahead, she felt something mystical. A similar feeling to how she felt the day of the reunion with her daughter in 1984. She took one look at Cynthia and felt something like God's love reach down and touch her.

She turned another corner and looked at the vista in front of her—pine covered mountains and a creek. She took a deep breath and let the beauty of the surroundings help her forget all of her fears and doubts. The perfect spot to get away from it all. No wonder Kenneth wanted his ashes scattered there.

Katherine reached the camp spot. She got out of the car and started walking. Then she saw her.

"Cynthia! Over here!"

Cynthia's long black hair blew in the wind as she walked up the hill towards Katherine. Suddenly the clouds disappeared and sunlight poured down through the trees touching Cynthia's hair as Katherine went to embrace her.

"When did you get here?"

"Just now. How did you like that mud?"

"It was pretty bad. We were in the four-wheel drive. But we did weave back and forth a lot."

Cynthia led the way to her camp spot. She had everything set up. She had a clothesline strung between two trees. A cooler sat next to a barbecue. Boxes of food sat on top of the wooden picnic table.

So this was Cynthia's place. Clearly, Katherine thought, she had done this before. She looked at her daughter with new eyes. She saw a tall young woman with long black hair, tanned arms and legs who moved about the campsite like she knew exactly who she was and what she was doing.

"Did you and Kenneth go camping a lot?" Katherine asked her.

"Yes. We used to go hiking up in the Tetons."

Katherine and Cynthia started gathering dry wood and kindling. Pretty soon they had a big fire going.

The next few days were like a vision quest in which Katherine learned a new meaning of relationship between mother and daughter. The days were filled with blue skies and sunshine. No sign of Cynthia's anger as they chopped wood, built fires, and cooked dinner over burning coals together.

Katherine looked up at the tall lodgepole pine trees. A slight breeze moved them. Bumblebees buzzed around columbine. The air was still. Katherine absorbed as much of paradise as she could. She tried not to think of how things might quickly change. She tried not to think that anything could cause her to lose these special moments with Cynthia.

"Hey, Jeff and Ben, would you help me carry this log over to the fire?" Katherine called to her grandsons.

The boys, already ten—how could they have grown so quickly?—hauled it over then used an ax to chop it into small pieces. As Katherine helped them stack the wood, add kindling, then watched Jeff light a match, she felt strongly connected to her grandsons. They sat together and watched the fire grow.

Though it had been over twenty years since Katherine had lived on the farm in South Dakota, she felt the connection to the land stir deep inside her. She looked across at Cynthia frisking the dog and thought "I need this connection to my daughter." She took a deep breath of the mountain air, smelled pinesap and wood burning. It felt good to be alive up there. She missed that living in the city so far away from Cynthia and the boys.

The next day, Cynthia, Katherine, Jeff, and Ben took the trail that led up towards Medicine Lodge Creek where

Kenneth's ashes were scattered. They walked through some timber and sat on a rock by the creek and ate their lunch as they dipped their toes in the water.

Cynthia and Katherine looked for the stone cross that Kenneth's dad had made and planted under a tree when they scattered Kenneth's ashes a year earlier. It had disappeared. Cynthia looked as if she would burst into tears.

"Who would do that?"

"I don't know. Maybe a wild animal or man knocked it down and dragged it off somewhere."

"But why?"

Katherine had no answers for her.

"I can't believe that you're not concerned about it." Cynthia sounded upset.

"I am concerned about it. But I don't need the cross to remind me of Kenneth. I can feel him in just the way the sunlight touches the water of the creek, the way the trees gently sway. Isn't that where his spirit is?"

Cynthia calmed down and looked up at the trees as a breeze blew through her hair. "You're right. This place is alive," she said in an almost whisper. They talked about life and death. A year had passed since Kenneth died, but in that place he still felt near.

"Kenneth still visits me at night," Cynthia admitted as she looked out across the creek at the petroglyphs on the red sandstone cliff wall. Then she leaned back on the rock and dipped her tanned feet over the edge into the icy cold stream on the hot July day. "I wake up and he's there in my room. He's real. He's definitely there."

"So you're still going through the grieving process with Kenneth, having dreams and personal encounters with him during the night while Charles is sleeping in the same room on the other side of the bed? How does he feel about it? You've been seeing him for almost a year now, haven't you?"

"Yeah. Hey Jeff, do you have that chapstick I gave you?"

"Yeah Mom. It's in my pocket."

"Give it to me. I need it for my lips."

"Does Charles feel secure enough in the relationship that it doesn't bother him?" Katherine asked her.

"Yeah. I've talked to Charles about it. He understands." Cynthia's voice had an edge to it when she answered, Katherine immediately noted. Am I making her feel like she's a little girl by asking these questions, she wondered.

Cynthia reached over and picked up a stick and began stirring the water. "Yeah. He understands." The tension had gone out of her voice.

Katherine changed the subject. "You must tan easily. Your legs and arms are really dark. I've never been able to tan that way."

"Really?" Cynthia's ears perked up just like they always did when Katherine brought up anything related to genetics like how much longer Katherine's second toe was compared to her big one. Or her chiropractor having found a hollow place where one of her lumbar vertebrae should have been. Or any illnesses that run in the family.

"Yeah. You are really lucky that you tan so easily."

Cynthia seemed pleased that Katherine had noticed.

Katherine then thought back to Charles hoping the subject might be safe now. "So things are going well with you and Charles?"

"Oh yeah. Really well. He understands my grieving process."

Katherine remembered her last visit to Cynthia's house in Idaho. Every nook and cranny was filled with photos and memories of Kenneth. Not much room for a new man to find his own space in there. Not much room for a birthmother either, she remembered feeling when she looked at all of the faces that lined Cynthia's hallway walls.

Then the last time she went out to visit, Katherine saw an old black felt cowboy hat turned upside down with silk flowers in it setting on the floor near the fireplace.

"Where did you get this," she asked Cynthia?

"Oh, Charles gave it to me for Valentine's Day."

Katherine smiled as she looked at the hat and thought about the man who gave it to her daughter. Though Katherine liked the man who seemed to have captured her daughter's heart, at first she had been somewhat skeptical about Cynthia getting involved with someone new so quickly after Kenneth died. But when she tried to talk to Cynthia about it, Cynthia responded that *"I'm angry that you are putting a time limit on my grief! Everyone works through grief at different times. Don't assume that mine is the same as yours."* Katherine backed off. Maybe I do put too many expectations on her, she thought. Maybe I do to Cynthia what Mama did to me.

Katherine and Cynthia watched the stream tumble over the rocks. Light touched the water. A gentle breeze rustled the tops of the tall lodgepole pines. They moved and swayed in a majestic dance. The air was alive with subtle whispers.

That night, back at camp, Cynthia and Katherine and Jeff and Ben built a fire and cooked hamburgers, potatoes and carrots, and green beans in aluminum foil.

Later, they sat around the campfire and listened to coyotes howl from somewhere up in the hills at the full moon hanging over the mountains above the camp.

Cynthia and Katherine sat beside the fire and talked and laughed together. This was how Katherine had always wanted their relationship to be. Mother and daughter sharing the simple things in life, not preoccupied with the fact that Cynthia had a set of adoptive parents somewhere else that she must be loyal to. Even without the adoptive parents there, Katherine sensed that they would probably still have mother-daughter things to work through. Cynthia, though, seemed more relaxed and willing to get close to Katherine up in the mountains away from it all. Katherine was very aware, though, of how fragile the path upon which mother and daughter groped their way.

*   *   *

On Katherine's final night, she suggested roasting marshmallows over the fire. "We should do something special since I'm leaving in the morning."

"Okay," Cynthia looked across the campground a moment with a troubled look in her eyes.

"Is that okay? Do you want to do marshmallows?"

"Yeah. But the boys and I are going to take the dog for a walk first. We'll be right back."

Katherine sat alone by the fire for the rest of the evening listening to the sound of a twig snapping now and then and rustling near the trash barrel, remembering the warning sign she had seen for bears earlier that day. She waited for two hours for Cynthia and the boys to return. She was just feeling like nodding off when she finally heard the bark of the dog and laughter from the boys as they walked back up the hill at bedtime. "Too late to roast marshmallows now," she thought. Was this Cynthia's way of saying she didn't need her? she wondered. It definitely felt like Cynthia was making a statement by disappearing the night before she was supposed to leave. Was she? "Maybe I'm making too much of it," Katherine thought. "Maybe Cynthia just lost track of time."

The next morning, Katherine gave Cynthia a hug and prepared to leave. Cynthia seemed tense.

"Are you leavin' so soon?"

"Yeah. I want to get on the road before more rain hits." Katherine felt pain ebbing up out of her throat. "God! Why is it so hard to say goodbye? Maybe Cynthia feels it, too. Maybe that's why she took off with the kids and dogs last night. Maybe saying goodbye is hard for her, too."

As Katherine turned the key in the ignition of her car, she glanced at her daughter who was staring at her intently from her seat at the picnic table. Was it anger or something else that Katherine saw in her eyes?

The road was dry. The drive was easy. Clouds came in and heavy rain began just as Katherine turned onto the paved road with the yellow line in the middle at Ten Sleep. As the needle on her speedometer reached 65 again, she looked back to what she left behind.

"My history is deeply mixed with Cynthia's," Katherine thought as she drove away. "One quick glimpse, one moment in time would have been enough to bind the connection. Eight years of knowing her helped shape and mold it. Even if I never saw my daughter again, the connection would hold us together through time."

Katherine carried the memory of Kenneth and the vision quest with her daughter—black skies and tornadoes, rustling pines and coyotes, the full moon over the mountains and light shining on water at Medicine Lodge Creek in the Big Horns—as she headed back down the road towards the Denver airport. As she drove she thought, "This is one of the best times that Cynthia and I have ever had together." She also recalled the look in Cynthia's eyes as she drove away and remembered that some things were still unresolved between her and her daughter.

1987

Seven years earlier

"*I*'ll pick you up at the airport," Cynthia said when Katherine called to tell her she was coming.

When she landed in Boise, Cynthia wasn't there. Perhaps she got hooked up in traffic. She waited. Then she picked up the phone and dialed Cynthia's number.

"Hello, Cynthia. I'm at the airport. What happened?"

"Our pickup won't start," she answered. Katherine sensed anger behind the terse words. Anger at her? Or simple frustration over the situation?

"Okay. How should I get over to your house?"

"You'll have to catch the bus."

Katherine had just traveled six hundred miles to see her. And she was left stranded at the airport! She wasn't sure what to make of it all. She hauled her suitcase to a bus stop and caught a bus to downtown Boise. There she caught another bus that took her south across town.

When she finally arrived at Cynthia's house, anger and tension cut the air, but Cynthia refused to say what was wrong. Instead, she busied herself at the sink doing dishes. She never looked at Katherine.

"You kids get in her and pick up your toys. And I mean now."

"It's hard to have a pickup break down on you."

"It's been broken down all week." Cynthia continued on with her dishes without looking at Katherine.

"Oh. If you had let me know ahead of time, I could have arranged a different way to get here."

"I don't like to make long-distance calls on the phone." Cynthia walked out to the patio with a broom and started sweeping. Katherine followed and watched.

"I hope my coming out to visit isn't too much. You've probably got lots of things to do."

Cynthia didn't answer. Katherine looked at her thoughtfully. She sensed that her coming had stirred up some anger in Cynthia. But Cynthia wouldn't talk to her about it.

"Do you want me to help you with anything? Why don't I finish doing up your dishes for you."

"You don't have to. I can do them." Cynthia kept sweeping.

"That's okay. No problem at all." Katherine cleared the dirty dishes off the table and put them in the sink. As she washed, Cynthia came into the kitchen and let out a sigh of relief. Katherine sensed a big weight had been lifted.

"Thanks for doing those dishes."

"It's okay. There are just a few."

"Maybe Cynthia just has too much to do," Katherine thought as she noticed her daughter relaxing and beginning to make eye contact with her. Maybe it was just inconvenient for her to have company with two boys and a house to take care of. Maybe it was also inconvenient for a birthmother to show up at this stage of her life when Cynthia was still acting out her adolescence. "Cynthia is trying to become an adult and is ready to stretch her wings and fly," Katherine thought. "She doesn't want anyone holding her back."

1940

Mama

"*I* made a mistake," she told him just before the wedding.

"What da ya mean?"

"I can't go through with this wedding. We're just not right for each other."

"I think yer scared."

"No. I just shouldn't have let it get this far."

"We're gonna hafta git married now. Yer mom spent all the money preparin' for the weddin'. Ya should have thought of this sooner. I'm sure yer mom had these same feelin's the day she got married. And her mom before her and so forth. You'll be okay once the weddin's over."

Evelyn Duran stifled her doubts and walked down the aisle to meet Leonard Geislingen, her husband-to-be.

1997

Cynthia's wedding

"*I*'d really like you to come to the wedding," Cynthia told Katherine on the phone when she called to tell her she was going to marry Charles. The wedding was still several months away but Cynthia was excited by all the preparations. That was three years after their encounter at Medicine Lodge Creek.

Katherine remembered the doubts Mama said she felt the day she married Papa and hoped Cynthia knew what she was doing. "I guess these kinds of fears go through the minds of most mothers when their daughters tell them they're getting married," she thought as she tried to let go of her fears and listen to Cynthia. "Are you sure you want me there?" Katherine asked her.

"Oh yes! I definitely want you to come."

"Do you need something borrowed or something blue to wear?"

"I already have everything I need," Cynthia answered. Katherine noticed an edge in her voice.

"Are you sure?"

"Yes," Cynthia answered very curtly before she changed the subject.

"Was that anger I heard in her voice?" Katherine wondered. In the past, Cynthia would have jumped at the chance to wear something of hers, she thought.

Their relationship had changed. Cynthia had even written Katherine in a letter after she met Charles that *"Our relationship is different now."* Katherine had panicked when she read it. Just words said in anger or did she mean it? Am I losing her again? Cynthia never told her what she meant and later when Katherine noticed the change she couldn't pinpoint exactly how or why things were different; she just knew they were. Cynthia seemed changed after she began the relationship with Charles.

She changed again after her adoptive mother Phyllis passed away in 1996, a year before Mama died. Death has a way of shifting people around, deciding who will be close to whom, she thought. Maybe I just need to accept the changes instead of panicking each time I feel Cynthia pull away.

Phyllis was the one Cynthia did the mother-daughter bonding thing with. Then she died and Cynthia seemed to change. Katherine wondered if perhaps Phyllis was the link that kept her and Cynthia together, if Cynthia's interest in her had been a subtle rebellion against Phyllis, her adoptive mom.

Katherine thought about all of the changes the day before Cynthia walked down the aisle. Then, she went through all of the emotions any mother would feel with a daughter getting married. She was surprised by the depth of loss she felt at losing her daughter again.

* * *

Cynthia's new husband Charles seemed to know how to treat a woman. He had been on his own, knew how to cook and do the dishes. So when Katherine lamented the distance that seemed to have developed between Cynthia and her, she wasn't trying to fault him.

"Sir, I'd like to ask for your daughter's hand in marriage." Charles phoned her adoptive father John before they decided to marry.

John immediately replied "Yes."

As though Cynthia were still a child and needed an adult's permission, Katherine thought as she remembered her daughter's strong presence at Medicine Lodge Creek in the Big Horn Mountains.

Charles left the house the night before the wedding. "It's bad luck for the groom to see the bride on her wedding day," he insisted.

"What culture does that come out of?" Katherine asked Charles when he told her.

"I don't know."

"It sounds Arabic," she mused. She hadn't meant it as a criticism. But she noticed that Charles started to apologize as soon as she said it.

Still, Katherine feared his old-fashioned thinking might have made him decide that there would be no place for a birthmother in Cynthia's life after the marriage.

Cynthia would be part of Charles' family now. She would be one of his people just as she had been part of her adoptive father's clan, then of her first husband Kenneth's. She had never been part of Katherine's.

*　　*　　*

"I don't want to see her. Yes, I do. Maybe I'll just stay in Reno," Katherine thought when she woke up in the middle of the night in a motel room on the way out to Cynthia's wedding.

Katherine dragged herself out of bed early the morning after she flew into Reno from San Francisco. She picked up a rental car. Then she drove alone across the god-forsaken landscape of the west.

She saw clouds and mountain tops with snow as she drove across Nevada towards Idaho. They looked like craters of the moon. Miles and miles and miles to a town. It gave her time to think and unwind.

"Cynthia's life has been very similar to Mama's," Katherine reflected. "Both married at seventeen. Mama had a bad marriage. Cynthia's marriage to Kenneth was good but there were problems, of course. They both lost husbands at a young age, Mama to divorce, Cynthia to death. Both remarried quickly, to men they thought would be good fathers to their children."

Thinking about the similarities helped keep the fear at bay. "I'm not ready for another change," she thought. "Not enough time to be her mother. Now she's getting married." Katherine didn't want to think about what might await her when she got to her daughter's. She hadn't forgotten the look in her daughter's eyes as she drove away from the camping spot on Medicine Lodge Creek in the Big Horns. She knew that she and Cynthia still had things to work through. Would they?

*   *   *

"Don't sit in the font row. That's reserved for family," Cynthia's new stepmother ran up to Katherine as she was getting ready to sit down. "You can sit in the second row."

Katherine felt like she had been slapped in the face as she got up and sat down in the second row pew. She glared at the back of the head of the woman who had married Cynthia's adoptive father John two months before.

"Who in the hell does that woman think she is," Katherine thought angrily; then she remembered

Cynthia's deep layer of anger, the anger that she no longer talked about. "Did Cynthia set this up? Or was this the doing of the new stepmother?" She was tempted to walk out, but her desire to see her daughter married kept her in her seat.

The wedding march began. Cynthia walked down the aisle in an off-white satin dress carrying a bouquet of red roses.

Katherine's heart leapt when she saw her. "This is my daughter. No matter what," she thought proudly. She watched Charles put the ring on Cynthia's finger.

But her feelings about having to take second place were not so easily allayed. "Will I always have to stand back and watch other women mother my daughter?" she wondered. "Will I have to stifle my feelings and allow this woman who has just married into the family and hasn't the slightest clue about what it means to be a birthmother take my place? The culture, of course, would always recognize an adoptive mother or stepmother before it would acknowledge the real birthmother. That old stigma still lingers," she thought.

*   *   *

Katherine headed back to Reno to catch a plane after her daughter's wedding.

As she approached Winemucca, there were white covered mountains to the right, blue sky.

Katherine never did get to see Cynthia crawl; her feet had taken her many miles by the time Katherine found her. But Katherine remembered the mystical feeling she had when she approached the camping spot near Medicine Lodge Creek. It was the same feeling she had as she looked out over the Idaho plains near Cynthia's house on the way to the wedding, the same feeling she had as she watched Charles place the ring on her daughter's finger.

The same feeling she always had when the plane took a turn to circumvent Indian Mountain on approach to a landing in Elk Mountain when she went to visit Mama before she died. Every time the wheels touched down on Wyoming soil, tears came to Katherine's eyes.

He Did It

July 29, 1998
Papa has a change of heart

"*M*y brothers and sisters and I were sleeping on a closed-in porch just off the kitchen. Ten minutes before it happened, I went out to the kitchen for a drink of water. Mom and Dad were out there talking. There was no fire in the stove then," he said.

Papa had obviously calmed down after their fight and seemed willing to talk now when Katherine rang him from Brown Rock to ask him for directions to the house where his mother Naomi died.

"Whatever happened after that, only the good lord will ever know for sure," he added.

If there were no fire in the stove, no spark from it could have caught her grandmother's dress, Katherine thought. The fire would have to have come from the match Naomi said her husband lit after he threw the solvent on her.

Katherine knew Papa would never go so far as to say he thought his mother was murdered, but this was a different twist from the accident story he told her earlier.

1932

Naomi

Sam came in late after Naomi had already gone to sleep. He moved quietly across the room slipping his shirt and pants off as he went. He got in beside her then he turned his back on her and went to sleep.

Early the next morning Naomi got up and walked into the kitchen to wash her face.

Sam was sitting at the table cleaning an old pair of trousers with cleaning solvent. Ten minutes later, Naomi went running out of the house with her clothes on fire.

"I'm sorry, Naomi," Sam said when he followed her out.

Naomi frightened began to scream, "He did it! He did it! Don't let him near me! Don't let him take me back into that house. I don't know what he will do!"

So Mrs. Paxton carried her into her living room and laid her down on the couch.

November, 1997

Mamie

"They had my mom's funeral three days later. It took place at the local Baptist church in Brown Rock though the Baptist minister refused to preach at it," Mamie told Katherine.

"Why would a preacher refuse to preach at a funeral?" Katherine asked.

"Local preachers thought they might lose parishioners if they preached at my mom's funeral since there was so much controversy in the community over how she died," Mamie said. "I couldn't find a preacher in town who would do it."

"So what did you do?"

"'My mother wasn't to blame for the way she died' was what I told the Presbyterian minister when he said he couldn't preach at her funeral."

"That's right." Katherine thought back to the 60s and the minister of the Christian church in Elk Mountain, the one who told Mama that her daughter was no longer welcome there after the word got out that she was pregnant with an out-of-wedlock child. The same type of thinking, she thought as she listened.

"But your mother was such a horrible housekeeper," the Presbyterian preacher's wife answered critically.

"And that warrants burying her without a service?" Katherine demanded in outrage. Then she remembered how she, too, had been ostracized by her small-town community in the 60s.

"I couldn't believe the small-minded things I heard from people after my mother died. I was very hurt by all of it," said Mamie. "Finally, a revival minister, the kind who travels from town to town holding prayer meetings, agreed to give the sermon at the funeral. He lived in Brown Rock, but didn't have a church there so he wasn't as afraid of what people would say."

July 29, 1998
Roles

$\mathcal{S}$he comes to me at night. I feel her as a presence hovering near to my shoulders and neck. She feels close, too close. Sometimes I think she wants to kill me. Other times I feel that she has something to tell me, something that she really wants me to hear.

"What will people think?"

"When are you going to get over that?"

"Stop that crying!"

These were just a few of the phrases I heard Mama tell me while I was growing up when I tried to express the grief I felt over some kind of loss, I remember as I sit back down before the microfiche machine at the library.

Pretend that you're happy. Don't let anyone know that you aren't, I learned. There were so many hurts to keep hidden.

Papa left.

I lost Mama—the woman who used to laugh and sing while she did the dishes. She became inaccessible to me when she stuffed her emotions deep inside and never dealt with what happened to her during her marriage to Papa. She never talked to anyone about her divorce. She was hiding from herself so how could she help me deal with my pain?

I lost my sisters — Carol, Sarah, and Linda — one by one as they each began to take on the parts assigned to them.

In order to cope with loss and to find a safe place, my oldest sister Carol — down to earth, perceptive, and sometimes so off the mark that one had to recognize some

form of truth in what she was saying — ran away to
Canada in the 60s. She hid there. She called once every
three or four years, but she gave no one an address or
phone number. When she finally returned, the best word
to describe her was "needy."

Sarah got away early by getting married. That marriage provided her with what she lost when Papa left us,
I observed. She flaunted that marriage as a perfect one
just as she learned from Mama. "Don't let anyone know
that something is wrong," I could almost hear Mama's
voice telling us each time I walked in the door of Sarah's
house and saw a cushion placed just so on the sofa or a
plaque next to Sarah's kitchen sink professing the sanc-
tity of home and kitchen. She presented a picture to the
world of the perfect life. I knew that nothing or nobody
was going to make Sarah believe her world wasn't real. I
tried a couple of times.

"We've got a perfect relationship," she used to respond in defense of her marriage to her first husband. She
told me how much he liked her pies and cakes. But, she
finally divorced him after pretending for twenty years that
she was happy.

"Well, if it were me, I'd do it this way," Linda often
told me.

"Oh. You would?"

"I'd never do it the way you're doing it."

"Why not."

"Just because I wouldn't."

I backed away from Linda who became the family role
model. While growing up, I was supposed to look at her
and know how to get good grades, how to deal with boys
and have a lot of boyfriends. I was supposed to have a date
for every formal and prom like Linda did. I was supposed

to meet a man and get married young like she did. Linda had a lot of things to live up to. She became rigid and bitter as she tried to protect her role of perfection. I knew she judged me because of my out-of-wedlock pregnancy and because I wasn't married. I quit talking to her because I didn't seem to measure up to her expectations.

"Jimmy is Clark's son and remember how hard Clark worked to keep this family together," Mama continually harped at us. Perhaps that's what drove my brother Jimmy to become a religious fanatic.

And me? For awhile I was the family scapegoat. But I rebelled early and tried to leave that role behind me. I later became the one who tried to get the family to change and face things. But they wouldn't. Then I decided to let them go and take care of myself, though I longed for a human hand, a kindred spirit, a place to go where I could just be me. I seldom found it at Mama's house though we drew closer just before she died.

I glance out across the plains as I drive around the periphery of Brown Rock and remember that the earth and sky were the only places I found solace out here.

* * *

I lost Papa.

I lost Joe, my first love.

I lost my daughter Cynthia.

I lost Mama.

I never recognized how all of the losses were connected until Mama died. Then all of a sudden, my whole life came tumbling down.

I lost my energy and drive. I isolated myself from people because no one could understand what I was going through. Not only did I lose Mama, but I was losing everyone who was special to me—especially my daughter Cynthia.

While finally facing my losses, I was getting older and my body was breaking down on me. I was losing my youth, my vitality, my appeal to men. My hair was getting gray, my bones fragile, my muscles weak. My youth was gone!

That's why the soft tones of Robert's voice stirred something deep inside of me when he called me on the phone on the New Year's Eve before Mama died.

I wanted to jump back in time to my thirties when I still had my whole life before me.

But all of that was behind me. Life had gone on after I turned forty. Mama was gone and death loomed before me.

*   *   *

It has come as a shadow, a shiver, a repulsive hand, wanting to caress my neck and arms. It has come as a voice while going to sleep, a gentle yet urgent nudging. "You…go…Wyoming." Death has already spoken to me several times, I remember as I wind up the film in the microfiche machine.

A voice from beyond the brink was riding with me in my car on the way to Brown Rock. It has seemed that I've been communicating more with the dead than those alive and vital.

Earthbound. Unable to move on to the next level. That's when the dead try to make contact with the living, I read somewhere. Maybe Mama and Naomi have been needing my prayers to move on. Maybe my grandfather

Sam, in the form of Robert and the cowboy, has been trying to make me see things his way. And what way might that be I wonder as I continue reading in the library?

The cowboy walks in as I sit at the microfiche machine. He leans over next to me to pick up a book; I feel warm breath on the back of my neck. He leaves after I move away. Something about him makes me feel alive again. Just like Robert made me feel when he called me on the phone that night the year before Mama died. I must be careful.

I have read that one should not make major decisions or break off important relationships during the first year after the loss of someone important, whether by death or divorce; but just after Mama died, I was too tired to keep giving. Robert's old patterns had come back to haunt me just at the point when I needed some nurturing in my life. So I said goodbye to Robert.

*   *   *

"It's past! Why do you have to dig up the past?"

Papa couldn't understand my need to know the truth, that it was part of my process of leaving it behind me. There are five stages, they say, to the grieving process.

I was in stage two, anger, when I said goodbye to Robert once and for all.

I finally moved into the fourth stage of letting go. I realized the record had gotten stuck many years back when Papa drove away in his pickup. What happened between Joe and me and every other man I have ever loved including Robert was just a replay of what transpired after Papa left. I was angry that he left me. All I could do was sit and wait.

I knew after Mama died that I had to let Robert go; but as soon as I walked away from him, deep pain began to enfold me. All I wanted to do was sleep. Then I sat down to write him a letter. But all I could think about were his last words in the e-mail message: *"I do have a somewhat thing going on. We are best of friends and there is a sexual relationship.* I never wrote him the letter.

After more than forty years of waiting for a pickup that never came, it was time to stop waiting.

What is it they say? The first time you have a run-in with someone else's stuff, it's the other person's fault. If it happens a second time, it's yours. I guess that's what some people call addiction.

That doesn't mean you need to carry guilt over it, though our puritan culture tries to label everything as good and bad. We don't really learn unless there's repetition.

1997

Flashback to Mama's house

*T*wo days after the funeral, Katherine sorted through Mama's clothes. Her sisters didn't want any. Katherine suspected they didn't like what the clothes represented— the way Mama tore down their self-esteem while they were growing up—but for Katherine, the clothes were a link to the something she had lost somewhere in the past.

She stood alone in front of the mirror in Mama's bedroom. She pulled her shirt off over her head and slipped on a red silk blouse that used to belong to Mama. As she buttoned it, she looked at herself in the mirror. She liked the way Mama's clothes looked on her. The reds, lavenders, pastel pinks, and blues made her feel like a woman again.

She hadn't really felt like a female since she returned to the U.S. after living in Spain. She had to cover up her breasts and womanhood in America, she felt. But, most of the time she didn't have time to think about clothes and how certain colors made her feel. Mama, a totally feminine woman, thought about them a lot.

Katherine unbuttoned the blouse and picked up a turquoise blue v-neck sweater. She pulled it down over her breasts and noticed that the cut of Mama's clothes fit her body well.

As Katherine stood alone looking into the mirror in Mama's room, she saw a shadow move across the hallway outside the door. Someone was there, she felt, watching her as she undressed. She shivered.

She walked out into the hallway to see if anyone was in the house. She looked in every closet. She even opened the door to the garage and looked out. No one was there.

As she walked back towards Mama's bedroom, the lights flickered in the hallway.

It was a spirit watching her, she thought.

Katherine put her own clothes back on and went into the kitchen to make some coffee.

July 29, 1998
Naomi's house

A white frame house with green shutters sits one house down from the corner two blocks south of the Super 8 Motel where in 1932, Barker's Motel used to sit. I take my camera out to take a picture.

Just as I push the button, the cowboy walks out the front door.

"What are you doing here," he asks. He has his shirt off revealing a chest full of black hair.

"Taking pictures. This is where my father's family used to live, I think. Do you live here now," I ask as he pulls a T-shirt down over his head, covering up his chest hair.

"My mother does. My family has owned the house for sixty years."

The woman I had seen with the cowboy at the Super 8 Motel and at the Chinese restaurant walks out the door.

"Ma'am, my name is Tim. I'd like you to meet my mom. I don't think I got your name."

"It's Katherine."

"Nice meetin ya'. Ya say yer family used ta live here?" the cowboy's mother asks. "What's their name?"

"Geislingen."

"Yeah, I remember them. I used ta go ta school with their daughter. Their mother died, I remember."

"Yeah. She got burned here."

"Oh yeah. There used ta be a wood burnin' stove in the kitchen when we moved in. I used ta watch my mother light it in the mornin'. My parents gave me the house when they died. My husband put in an electric range in the 50s. That's what we've got in there now.

Would ya like to come in and look around?" the cowboy's mother asks.

"Yes! If it's no problem, that is."

"No problem at all. Come on in."

Once inside the house, I notice the closed-in sleeping porch where Papa said he and his brothers and sisters were sleeping the morning that Naomi got burned.

"This here's the kitchen." His mother shows me through the door at the back.

An electric range stands in the kitchen where the wood burning stove had probably been.

The phone rings in the next room.

"Hullo." The cowboy's voice booms. "Yeah, just a minute. Mom. Could ya come here a minute?"

The cowboy and his mother leave me alone in the kitchen.

I glance out the window across the yard. I see a woman standing there talking to a black woman. I open the screen door for a closer look.

Red-haired with the look of "almost hillbilly," the white woman looks back at me. The black woman leans down and picks something up off the ground. Then she says something to the white woman. The two glance over to where I stand in the doorway and smile.

I wonder what they're talking about. They seem to be looking at me so intently.

I start to walk out into the yard towards them. But just then the cowboy and his mother saunter into the kitchen and I'm distracted. When I look back across the yard, the two women have disappeared.

"Is there a black woman living next door?" I ask the cowboy's mother.

"No, no black people livin' in Brown Rock now as far as I know. When my father first bought the house, though, there were some livin' next door."

"I just saw a black woman standing in your backyard talking to a white woman with red hair," I tell her.

"We have ghosts here." The cowboy's mother looks at me peculiarly. "I don't pay them too much mind. They're pretty harmless. The only time I get concerned is maybe once a year, I think in January. That's when I see the black woman standin' out there leanin' over the white woman helpin' her like she's hurt or somethin'."

"Are you sure?"

"Never been surer of anything in my life. I know it sounds a little far-fetched. But those two women are definitely out there."

I go to the door again and look outside. Nothing there now except a gentle breeze blowing through the cottonwood trees. I shiver.

"I want to thank you so much for letting me come in here. I can't begin to tell you what this has meant to me."

"No problem. Yer welcome any time. Ya in town doin' family research?"

"Yeah."

"Well, any time ya want to come back, feel free."

"Thank you so much." I take her hand and shake it. The cowboy walks me to the front door.

"If ya need anything, I'll be glad to help ya."

I cross over to the other side of the street and look back at the house where my grandmother used to live. Then I glance at the one next door where the black woman Mrs. Paxton lived. It looks empty and very innocent now.

A heavy breeze stirs up dust in the street as I head back to the Super 8 Motel.

* * *

Cowboy music blares from the jukebox as I walk into the restaurant that night to eat dinner. I look across the dining room and see the cowboy. He looks up. Our eyes meet. I feel my face getting warm.

He jumps up from his seat and walks towards me.

"Come on over and sit down."

"Okay."

What do I have to lose, I ask myself, except an hour at dinner? But I must be careful.

He pulls out a chair and I sit down opposite him.

"Good evenin', folks. What'll ya have fer dinner tonight?"

"Give me a medium rare T-bone. And I'll take a beer. What about you?"

"I'll have the shrimp. Give me a glass of wine. Chardonnay."

I look into the cowboy's eyes and remember how respectfully he treated the Chinese man in the restaurant at lunch.

"Yer welcome here no matter what anybody tells ya."

"I heard what you said to the Chinese waiter today at the restaurant. I felt you handled that well."

"Well, those two Chinese men have been livin' here for about a year now. And I've gotten ta know them pretty well. They're friends of mine."

My grandfather Sam always sided with the underdog, according to my aunt Mamie. He was good friends with a lot of the Shoshoni and Arapaho Indians living on the

Wind River reservation at a time and place when most white men treated them like trash. The hair on my arms stands on end as the thought crosses my mind that I could be sitting across the table from my grandfather.

"Have you always lived in Brown Rock?" I ask the cowboy.

He shakes his head. "My parents moved out here from Omaha just after they got married. I was born in the house where yer grandma died. I grew up here and married. Then I left for awhile."

"Does your wife live here?"

"She died."

"Oh, I'm sorry."

"That's okay. She's been gone for five years. So I guess it's okay to talk about it."

"How did she die?"

"Car accident."

"Oh."

"My wife looked a lot like you, ya know. That's the first thing I noticed. She was strong, too. Like you. Maybe a little too strongly feminist fer this state. She was an activist for abused women."

"How did you feel about your wife being a feminist?" I catch my breath before I ask.

"Hell, I don't know." He cuts his steak. "It was kind of hard sometimes because she wouldn't let me take care of her. And she didn't really want ta rush into havin' children. She was definitely someone who was goin' ta do things her way and not somebody else's."

"So what happened?"

"She had a meetin' one night in a little place west of here. She didn't come home. Around midnight, I called the sheriff. They went out lookin' for her. Found her car in the river over by Fort Windpeak." He turns his attention to his steak.

I take a sip of wine as I look at the cowboy. He looks back at me with his dark brown eyes that seem to penetrate mine. I blush. His hand reaches out and touches mine. I pull my hand back and continue eating.

"Does that bother you? My touchin' your hand?"

"A little."

"I'm sorry. I've wanted to do that ever since I saw ya in here yesterday. I'll try not to do that if it bothers ya."

"Thank you."

"Where ya from?"

"San Francisco."

"Ya like it out there?"

"Yeah. You know, I grew up here."

"So ya got away from the wild west and became a city girl?"

"Not exactly. A lot of my heart is still here."

"Oh yeah. Do ya miss it?"

"The beauty and the wide open spaces, the quiet, sure."

"But the rest ya could do without?"

"It's hard living in small towns."

"Small minds?"

I ignore his question.

* * *

"I planted muskmelon here when I was four," I tell him with a little laugh. "Everybody laughed and told me I'd never get it to grow because the growing seasons were too short. My dad, though, told me that it never hurt to try. So that's what I did."

"Did yer muskmelon come up?"

"I don't know. My mother divorced my father and we moved away before I had a chance to see. Just the same, my dad planted in me the idea that it doesn't hurt to try the impossible."

"I think yer dad did a good thing there."

"Me, too."

"Ya know, I like you."

"Thank you." I pull back. I feel differently about him now, especially since learning he was born in my grandmother's house; but I can't quite forget my fear as he followed me on the road to Brown Rock. And I can't forget how much he makes me think of Robert and my grandfather.

"Can I see ya again sometime?"

"I don't know. I'm only going to be here for a little while, you know."

"Yer grandma meant a lot to ya, didn't she?"

"Well, that's why I'm here. I've been trying to find out what happened to her. My dad has one story, my mother and his sister another. It's always made me wonder."

"Another stab at the impossible?"

"I don't know."

"So what's their stories?"

"My dad said my grandmother's death was an accident. My mother used to side with him. Then she changed her story. My aunt says my grandmother was murdered by my grandfather."

"So what do you think?"

"I thought murder—it probably was murder—but then at some point while I was doing some reading in the newspaper, it hit me that I'm so intent on proving that he killed her that maybe I haven't been listening to his side of the story. Whatever the truth, it would answer some questions about the way my father was."

"Well, you listen ta what yer heart tells ya. And let yer head guide ya. And I hope ya find out the truth."

"Thanks."

I smile at him and he smiles back at me.

"So how about it. Ya gonna let me see ya some time?"

"I'm leaving tomorrow."

"For Frisco?"

"Yeah."

"Drivin'?"

Do I want to tell him? "I'm flying out of Cheyenne," I lie. I'm really driving across Wyoming to Salt Lake and flying out of there. But, Cheyenne is the closest city with a major airport.

"Well, that's too bad. I wish ya were stayin' longer."

I look at him thoughtfully. He stretches his legs out as he leans back on his chair.

"Do ya want some coffee and dessert?"

"I don't think so. I've got to go."

"Are ya sure?"

"Yes. I have some work I need to do. It was good talking to you."

"Ya might as well at least let me walk ya to yer car."

"Okay. Let me just stop and pay the cashier on the way out."

"No. I'm paying."

"No. I insist." I hand the money to the cashier on the way out.

He watches as I fumble for my keys. Just as I open the door, he leans over and kisses me. His arm pulls me to him. Our bodies meet. His tongue probes deep.

"Where ya stayin'?" he whispers in my ear. "Let's go back to yer place."

"I'm sorry. I can't. I'm not ready for this. I'd better go."

"I'm so attracted to you."

"I can't."

With pounding heart I get in the car and put the keys in the ignition and start the motor.

As I back out and drive down the street, I notice headlights following me. I pull into a filling station. The lights pass. I recognize his red pickup with the gun racks on top. I wait awhile before I head back to the Super 8 Motel.

My heart beats quickly as I drive. Perhaps I made a mistake by having dinner with him. He's still following me even though I said no. "Why did I talk to him?" I ask myself. He may be a key, I feel, to help me unlock the truth about my grandmother. That's the reason and I'm not going to let my own fears stop me. He knows something that I don't because he grew up in the same rooms that my grandmother lived in just before she died.

Naomi's Ghost

July 30, 1998
1:00 a.m.

Being chased

*R*un! Run! Quick! Quick! I've got to get away from here! Footsteps slap the ground at my heels! I can feel his hot breath on my neck just before two hands reach out and grab me! They shove me down to the ground and hold me there! I try to scream but can't. I try to project it out into a high-pitched scream. But my voice is choked and blocked as if two hands are bearing down on my windpipe.

"Oh-o-o-o-oooh." A low groan like that of a half-dead man suddenly awakened in his crypt comes forth from my lips. The eerie drone of my own voice wakes me out of a deep sleep.

I lie in bed trying to get my bearings straight. A light flickers around the window frame of my garden level window. It hovers there. Then it stops.

"Scrape. Scra-a-a-atch." When I hear the sound, I sit bolt upright. Something or someone is jiggling my window. Thank god I checked the lock before I went to sleep.

I sit in silence with my eyes glued to the curtains hanging in front of the windowpane.

A fuzzy numbness envelops my mind as I wait. Death and darkness are the topics oozing out of every pore and crevice of my memory.

"Who was the man holding me down just before I woke up?" Was it my grandfather? I try to remember, but a veil descends down between my waking mind and that of sleep. The dream is now lost to me.

*　　*　　*

The night is long as I think back over other rude awakenings I have had in the wee hours when shadow and light come to play their ominous game.

Naomi's nocturnal visit is what prompted me to come to Wyoming and why I'm lying here at night in the Super 8 Motel in Brown Rock.

When the floor creaked outside my third floor apartment in San Francisco, and I saw the red-headed woman in a housedress sitting in the yellow overstuffed chair by my bed, I tried to ask her one question.

"Is my grandfather the reason why you're here? Is he still walking the earth wanting to leave but can't?"

The woman didn't give an answer. Her eyes, though, spoke a thousand words. If only I knew the language of the dead, I could have interpreted and set my mind at rest.

Aunt Mamie said she was out in the kitchen talking to a friend when her dad, whom she was caring for during a lengthy illness, got up and walked to the bathroom to relieve his bladder. Then he went back in the bedroom and got in bed. A half an hour later she went to check on him. He was dead.

When someone started knocking on Mamie's door in the middle of the night a week later, Mamie said, "I'm not worried. It's probably something supernatural."

She and her daughter Ann assumed it was her father Sam with some unfinished business to take care of. They thought it would probably soon end. But it didn't.

All is silent but the wind as I sit and listen in my room at the Super 8 Motel in Brown Rock. The light at my window that had gone away for awhile returns again. I keep my eyes focused, ready for action.

*   *   *

A strong wind rattles around the motel. The light flickers in the window and I hear what sounds like gravel crunching under someone's feet. Still I lie in bed not moving an inch. I make sure the telephone is within reach.

The night that free speech movement leader Mario Savio died, the phone rang and I picked up the receiver.

"Hi Katherine. This is Kenneth."

"Kenneth? Where are you?" I asked not surprised to receive a call from my daughter Cynthia's husband even though he'd been dead four months.

"I'm here with Cynthia," he said as he laughed. He was in high spirits that night.

"Is she okay?" I asked him since I had been desperately worried about her.

"There's something I need to tell you. It's about Cynthia."

"What is it?"

He started to tell me. But I couldn't hear him. A curtain came down between us, and his words faded away. Fear came in and blocked me from receiving a message from a dead man, the same way it did the night the dead woman came to visit me in San Francisco. When he finally hung up that night, his call intensified rather than relieved my concerns about my daughter. Her husband had only been dead for three short months when she told me about the man who had spent the previous night in her bed.

"Take your time. Experiment. Find out about a lot of men before you get involved again," I wrote back to her.

"I can't believe you aren't supporting me in this!"

I backed off.

What did Cynthia's dead husband Kenneth want to tell me? Was everything really okay with my daughter and grandchildren. Or were my fears valid?

The dead have the right to communicate with the living if they like. The living, though, are often too afraid to hear what they have to say. Where has my grandfather Sam been while I've been hearing from the ghost of my dead grandmother Naomi? I sit bolt upright as a shiver moves up my spine and into my shoulders. Maybe he's outside my motel window trying to get in!

*   *   *

I hear the crunching gravel again and the flickering light outside my window. This time I hear the sound of something being pried as if with a screwdriver. I sit motionless, almost paralyzed.

The night the dead woman visited me in San Francisco, I began to shake. A cold chill took hold of my body. My teeth began to chatter as she stared at me intently as she moved her mouth. No sound came, though I craned my ears trying to hear. Fear took control of my body and my mind closed off.

Does she want me to go with her or what, I asked myself as the blind descended down between me and her. Just before it did, I heard her say something.

"Don't be afraid," the red-headed woman was saying. "I won't hurt you."

The lights of a car pass across my Brown Rock motel window. I see a man's shadow there. I sit up wondering if I should call the police. I don't. I sit and wait.

Thinking back to my apartment in San Francisco, I remember that I turned and looked the dead woman full in the eye. I talked to her about something important. Then fear took over my mind again.

"You're dead. And I'm afraid to cross that boundary between living and dying," I wanted to tell her. But my tongue was paralyzed. Similar to how I feel now as some man or ghost pries at my window.

* * *

She must have been dead awhile, I thought. Women don't wear housedresses in the 1990s. Mama used to wear a cotton housedress in the fifties. They also wore them in the twenties when Naomi was alive.

I think back to another time and place. In another dream in the dead of night in Europe during the 1980s, I became one of the casualties of the age of scientific rediscovery that began around the time that Columbus discovered America.

"Let me go. Oh, please let me go," I cried as I fumbled to release the bars of the tightly closed in cell where they had put me.

"Don't worry," they told me. "We'll just lock you up for a few minutes as an experiment. Then we'll let you go free." But the moment they had me locked away, they threw away the key.

"Let me out! Please let me out of here," I cried as I shook and rattled and pounded on the locked and barred door.

On another night at my friends' house in Paris at Christmas time in 1987, a cool breeze blew through my hair, and I shivered as I stood at the open second floor window in their guestroom. The dream had come again to wake me. It was the third time in two months that I woke up in a panic trying to free myself from sealed up boxes, locked up cells, chains or bars that held me. This time I was trying to get out the window.

Suddenly, the open yard before me and the trees blowing in the cold December breeze in Paris that night shocked me to my senses. My heart was pounding wildly.

Where had I been just seconds before I awoke that night? Locked up in a barred cell in the prison at the Isle de la Cite in Paris in 1510. My name was Ann Bolyn.

Back in Madrid later that year, another dream awoke me.

"Why have you done this to me?" I cried in anguish. The year was 1431 and flames lapped at the hem of my skirt when I woke up in a sweat trying to free myself from the stake where they had tied me. I think I was Joan of Arc that night. Though, adjust the clock just a bit and I could have been any of the thousands of women burned at the stake during the European witch purges of the Renaissance. I could have been a Jewess burned alive during the Spanish Inquisition. I could have been an American at Salem.

Four months after I arrived in Madrid, I woke up in the night in the middle of another dream.

"Let me go! Let me go! Oh please let me go free," I cried as I wore the American flag and tried to dance across the floor with the same abandon as the bare breasted woman in the painting "Victoire de Liberacion". When my feet got tangled up in the stars and stripes and I stumbled, they locked me in a box and threw it into the sea.

A year later, after a two-month visit to the United States, I awoke to find myself trying desperately to push the screen out of the window of my fifth floor apartment. The voices of the two Russian women in the next room distracted me from pressing further out the window to the pavement five floors below.

When I woke up that night, I was me. That was the last time that I dreamt of being tied up and locked away in Europe.

When Naomi visited me in San Francisco, I tried to hear what she was saying as she sat in the chair by my bed. Her voice was nothing more than chatter. My mind grew fuzzy as I listened.

* * *

I hear the sound of a car passing the Super 8 Motel, then the sound of gravel again like someone walking away from my window. I have been sitting and watching for almost an hour. I glance at my watch. It's now 2:00 a.m. I stay put.

Level-headed Americans don't believe in ghosts. When they encounter them, they turn up their noses at them. They chase them out of haunted houses. Most run away and hide from them.

When Shakespeare encountered the dead, he quizzed them.

The Tibetan Book of the Dead says to talk to them and pray.

Elizabeth Kuebler Ross says she's spoken to the dead.

The Arapaho Indians in Wyoming believe you have to give a person a proper burial. When you don't, their ghost wanders the earth causing trouble.

1932

Naomi

The night that Naomi died in 1932, a strong Wyoming wind blew heavy drifts of snow across the town of Brown Rock.

Family members passed in and out of her room in the twilight hours just prior to her passing.

"Be a good boy," she told her four-year-old son when he was brought to stand at her bedside.

"Don't let my husband near me," she cried when the nurse came to announce he wanted to see her.

As Naomi drifted in and out of morphine-induced semi-consciousness, the pain became so great she couldn't bear it. After fighting for her life for twelve hours, she was too weak to go on.

The doctors and nurses who stood at her bedside didn't believe her when she told them her husband killed her. Family members called her insane. Her daughter Mamie was the only one who refused to take her father's side. She stood by Naomi to the end and continued to do so after she died.

July 30, 1998
2:20 a.m.

Face of the dead woman

*A*gain I hear the sound of scraping at my window. A light flickers up and down around the edge like the flame that killed my grandmother. Then it settles at a spot in the middle near the lock. My eyes stay focused on the window lock as once again I hear something that sounds like the prying of a screwdriver.

Again I see the face of the dead woman who visited me in San Francisco almost as if she is sitting right in the motel room with me.

The red-headed woman took my hand and whispered something I could not hear. Whatever it was, it calmed me.

I'm not into ghost chasing. Nor am I involved in any new age religion. But the first time that I became aware that the dead might be around in some other dimension was in the mid-1980s in a Hindu temple in Indonesia. Though I didn't start believing it until after I had the visit from Naomi.

*　　*　　*

Though the shadow of the man at my motel window is no longer there, a light still moves and searches for something out there. It reminds me of the fire that killed my grandmother Naomi. It keeps me from drifting off into a sleep I would gladly welcome.

The dead woman who sat in the yellow overstuffed chair by my bed in San Francisco seemed to be in no hurry to leave my bedside the night she visited me there. I would have gladly drifted off, but I was frightened. She tried to tell me what she wanted me to hear. I proved not to be a good listener. Did she want to tell me something about the innocence or guilt of my grandfather? Had something been left unsaid during the final moments as death came quickly to claim her. What words would she have me say, what message would she have me convey?

★

November 1997
Flashback to Mamie

"*I* was the only one who took my mother's side when she died," Mamie remembered. "Everyone else sided with dad. They wouldn't talk to me for awhile after mom died. They thought I was just causing trouble when I asked for an inquest."

As Katherine looked at Mamie sitting in the overstuffed chair in her living room in Utah, she remembered the dead woman who sat in the chair by her bedside in San Francisco. A striking resemblance!

"Yes! That's it!" she thought. "They were both sitting in the same pose, looking at me in the same way, telling me the same thing. 'My father killed my mother,' Mamie said more than once. Those were the words Naomi wanted me to hear."

July 30, 1998
2:40 a.m.

A candle

*T*houghts of death envelop me.

"I want to light a candle," I told the mortician in the mortuary where my stepfather Clark's body lay in an open casket.

"We only have catholic candles here," he said.

"That's okay," I told him.

"No, it's not. Clark wasn't a Catholic. You have to get permission from your mother if you want us to light the catholic candle for you." The mortician belonged to Mama's Christian church.

"A candle is a candle," I thought. I lit them in Spanish cathedrals when tragedies were taking place throughout the world in the 1980s. Thousands of people lit them in St. Stephen's in Vienna in 1989 when Rumania was in revolt. When a policeman died on the street in Copenhagen in 1988, people laid flowers and lit candles there. Now this guy is telling me I have to have my mother's permission to light a candle? Still, I went to Mama for permission. I didn't tell her I wanted to light a catholic candle—People in her church think the Catholics are going to rot in hell—so Mama said it was okay to light one.

The white votive candle burning inside the red glass holder provided a warm atmosphere for the room in the mortuary where my stepfather Clark lay. It didn't look like a catholic one, I observed when we went to visit the open coffin.

The light flickered as the candle burned providing, I hoped, protection and a clear path to wherever souls go when they depart the body.

*   *   *

One more time a light passes across my window. This time it's a car passing. When I hear the sound of rattling at my window, I recognize it as the Wyoming wind.

I get up out of bed, turn on the light and pick up a newspaper lying on the table.

"The Brown Rock Courier," the masthead reads. A photo on the front page catches my eye. It's a picture of the cowboy.

"Local Man Returns to Brown Rock" shouts the headline. The story states that the cowboy has been on a rodeo circuit of the western states. At the bottom is a picture of a woman. I sit in utter surprise as I look at the photo. It could have been my picture in the paper. His wife could have been my twin. The last sentences of the story catch my eye.

"His thirty-five year old wife died in an auto accident five years ago. Though local authorities at the time suspected that the woman's car had been forced off the road into the river, they've never been able to prove her death was more than an accident. An eyewitness from out of state saw a pickup truck tailing the woman's car earlier that night. They didn't get a license number so no identification could be made."

How does one explain this likeness? I wonder as I put the newspaper down.

Am I a ghost? Or am I a real person? I pinch myself to be sure. Sometimes when I have these contacts with the dead, I begin to wonder what reality actually is.

Am I going crazy? Or is it normal to be able to talk to a dead person? And why are all of these dead people flocking to me? Maybe it's because I'm one of the few that they feel they can actually talk to, I think as I sit at the table staring at the newspaper.

Whatever the reason, I am dumfounded by the likeness between the cowboy's ex-wife and me. He surely couldn't have seen the resemblance while he was following me in his pickup on the way to Brown Rock. He was too far away.

It must be coincidence, but I have ceased to believe in coincidence on this trip to Wyoming. It's as if someone set up my itinerary ahead of time. It was all planned. And I'm just a pawn in the game.

For the time being, I will continue on with my life as if I'm still me.

Epilogue

July 30, 1998
10:00 a.m.

Saying goodbye

"*C*oo-ah, coo, coo, coo."

The mourning dove greets me as I drive my car through the cemetery gate. I park the car in the spot just opposite Naomi's grave. I walk over and look at her gravestone.

Naomi Geislingen, a dutiful wife and loving mother. January 1, 1885 to January 10, 1932.

A breeze blows through the trees. A black bird sings on top of a nearby gravestone.

"Naomi, I'm leaving now. I think I've found all I'm going to find here. I know what you wanted to tell me. And I believe you."

A gentle breeze touches my cheek in response.

I think back over the events of the past few days—the newspaper articles, the ghosts, the cowboy, my grandfather. And me?

The sins of the fathers will pass down to the seventh generation, Papa told me. "You're the third or fourth generation as far as I can tell." Three more generations to go. But I'm hoping the sins have stopped with me. Perhaps now we can all move on.

The trip I took with Cynthia to visit her birthfather's parents in Wyoming has started the healing of our relationship. I hope that at some point she will come to terms with how she feels about me. She has her route to follow. At this point, her route resembles that of her adoptive mother's more than mine. I hope she doesn't forget her genetic past and the cord that connects her life to mine. I hope she keeps her power no matter what route she takes.

Cynthia is now a devoted wife and mother, just like Mama and my grandmother before me.

I have grieved for Cynthia just as I grieve for Mama. Whenever Christmas or mother's day or her birthday come around, I feel a great emptiness inside me. The rest of the time, I feel Mama near me, egging me on to do what she had always wanted to do before she married Papa. Write.

1932

The verdict

"*W*hoever purposely and with premeditated malice kills any human being is guilty of murder in the first degree," wrote the judge who presided over Sam's trial in 1932. "Whoever purposely and maliciously, but without premeditation, kills any human being is guilty of murder in the second degree. Whoever kills without malice, expressed or implied, either voluntary or upon a sudden heat of passion is guilty of manslaughter."

The judge instructed the jurors to include all degrees of unlawful homicide in their verdict.

The jury found Sam Geislingen guilty of manslaughter in connection with the fatal burning of his wife. The jury also recommended leniency in his case. The jury deliberated for sixty hours to reach that verdict. Sam was sent to the Wyoming State Penitentiary for a minimum of twelve years.

"Sam Geislingen's face was lined with mental pain, his eyes red-rimmed with unshed tears," a reporter from a Wyoming newspaper wrote after the verdict was announced. "In appearance he was far different from the man the world would associate with murderers—the gorilla type."

July 30, 1998
Questions

So if he was convicted of my grandmother's murder, why has everyone in Papa's family been pretending that it was an accident?

I believe that they all got together after their mother died and decided to stick with one story to tell their children. Basically, they made a plan to deny any wrongdoing on their father's part. Emotionally, denial took its toll on all of them. Lying about how their mother died has never eased the pain. I have wondered how many of them lived in post-traumatic stress like Papa, bombs waiting to explode whenever the topic of their mother's death came up.

One sometimes has to live a lie to appease the small town minds that judge so quickly. I know that so well from my experience growing up here in Wyoming. So I understand why Papa's family felt a need to hide.

Their being in denial, though, left things unresolved. Denial helped keep their mother Naomi and father Sam earthbound in their minds at least. Three generations after Naomi, I feel I must release them.

1932
Sam Geislingen

The man who came slowly walking out of the courtroom that day had aged considerably. A receding hairline, a bulging belly, eyes cast down, mouth set in a frown, the middle-aged man looked like he had been beaten, according to one newspaper story.

When asked if he would appeal, Sam Geislingen said: "What's the use? I wouldn't mind serving the time if only it wasn't for the little kids I'm leaving at home." Then tears came to his eyes.

Sam's trial was one of the most sensational in Wyoming during the 1930s. As a model prisoner, his prison sentence was commuted to six years. Then he was released to parole.

He continued his pre-prison womanizing and married two more times before he died.

July 30, 1998
Forgiven

$\mathcal{T}$he courts tried my grandfather. They found him guilty not of first degree murder, but of manslaughter. A fair verdict? Maybe not, if he planned out her killing.

But as Papa said, "only the good lord will ever know for sure."

*　　*　　*

I hear the sound of a truck as I stand at my grandmother's gravestone. I look up and see the cowboy's pickup pulling up behind my car.

"Oh god! What should I do now?"

The cowboy gets out and walks towards me.

"Hello there."

"Hi."

"I thought I'd stop by to be sure I didn't miss ya before ya left."

"Thanks."

"So is today the day?"

"Yeah."

"Too bad. I was hopin' ya'd be here at least one more day."

"I have to get back to San Francisco."

"Well, I brought somethin' for ya ta remember me by."

"You did?" I look nervously at the bag he's holding. I remember how many times he has followed me and I think of the newspaper article about his wife.

"Yeah. It's nothin' big. Just a little somethin' ta make ya think."

"Make me think? What's he talking about," I wonder as I look at the bag.

He hands it to me. "Ya don't have ta open it now. It'll last fer awhile."

"Thank you. That's nice." I eye the bag doubtfully.

"Ya take care of yerself and drive carefully." He reaches out and pulls me to him.

I feel his arms around me. Oh god! That feels so good. But I can't forget that he tailed me to Brown Rock. Then when I got here, he followed me around town. He may have been at my window at the Super 8 Motel last night. Now he's here giving me a present and a hug. And to boot, I'm the spitting image of his dead wife!

"Take care."

"You, too." I stifle my feelings hoping to make a quick getaway.

He leans over and places a gentle kiss on my lips. Then he turns around and walks towards his pickup.

I watch him leave. His truck approaches the cemetery gate, then turns and disappears down the street. My mind moves back forty-four years to the day Papa got in his pickup and drove away.

Tears begin to stream down my cheeks, falling like a river onto Naomi's tombstone, washing away years of unresolved grief. I take out a tissue and blow my nose. I feel like a weight has been lifted off me. Still, I don't know what lies before me on the road as I leave Brown Rock. Will he follow me?

The mourning dove coos. A breeze rustles as I look at Naomi's gravestone one last time then open the door of my car and get in.

Before starting my car, I look inside the bag the cowboy gave me.

I pull out a muskmelon and a package of muskmelon seeds. No note. I already know the message, "It doesn't hurt to try."

"Did he force his wife's car off the road and into the river?" I wonder as I put the muskmelon back in the bag. Perhaps I can find something at the library. Surely there's some evidence. Hmmm. Let me think.

I turn the keys in the ignition and start the engine of my car. As I drive away from the cemetery, I know that not everything is impossible. Sometimes, though, one has to move on. As I head my car back out on the highway, a wispy slip of a cloud passes over the land.

Margaret Benshoof-Holler grew up in Wyoming in the 1960s. She is a journalist and a writer of fiction and poetry. She has worked as a freelance writer and op ed columnist for various newspapers and magazines writing about U.S. culture, women's issues, life in Wyoming, and California community college education. She has also written abut post-traumatic stress disorder, race and domestic violence. She lived and taught in Boulder, Colorado, Jakarta, Indonesia, Malmo, Sweden, and Madrid, Spain before moving to San Francisco in 1990 where she currently writes and teaches at City College of San Francisco. *Burning of the Marriage Hat* is her first book.

Acknowledgements

My thanks go to Shelley Buck, Kristen Jensen and Judith Rosenberg for support during the writing process. I also want to thank Adrianne Fitzpatrick for editing, George Foster for the book cover, Val Sherer for layout design, and Jill Lublin for promotional guidance. I'd also like to thank Audrey Ferber and John Kremer.

Thank you to all of the California, Wyoming, and Iowa libraries and museums that helped me while I was digging. Thanks to Joe Soll for his knowledge of the adoption industry. Thank you to all of the writers whose books were a great support to me as I pushed forward.

I would also like to recognize Allen Ginsberg who helped instill in me the idea that a writer must come to the table with all of one's cards and be willing to lay all of them out on the table. His spirit gave me courage and helped me write this book.

Recommended Reading

Women Writers of the West
Daughter of Earth by Agnes Smedley, 1973.
Solace of Open Spaces by Gretel Ehrlich, 1985.
Dakota, A Spiritual Biography by Kathleen Norris, 1993.
Windbreak: a woman rancher on the northern plains by Linda Hasselstrom, 1987.
Old Jules by Marie Sandoz, 1935.

Pregnancy and Adoption
Wake Up Little Suzie: single pregnancy and race before Roe v. Wade by Rickie Solinger, 1992.
The Abortionist: a woman against the law by Rickie Solinger, 1994.
The Other Mother: a woman's love for the child she gave up for adoption by Carol Schaefer, 1991.
Adoption Healing...A Path to Recovery by Joe Soll, 2000.

Death/Loss and Grieving
Death in the Family by James Agee, 1957.
I Heard the Owl Call my Name by Margaret Craven, 1967.
Final Gifts: understanding the special awareness, needs, and communications of the dying by Maggie Callanan and Patricia Kelley, 1992.
The Grief Recovery Handbook: The Action Program for Moving Beyond Death, Divorce, and other Losses by John W. James and Russell Friedman, 1998.
On Death and Dying by Elizabeth Kuebler Ross, 1969.

The Tibetan Book of the Dead by Francesca Freemantle
and Chogyam Trunpa, 1975.
The American Way of Death by Jessica Mitford, 1963.

Domestic Violence
The Burning Bed by Faith McNulty, 1980.
*The Violent Home: A study of Physical Aggression between
Husbands and Wives*, by Richard Gelles, 1974.
The Battered Woman by Leonore E. Walker, 1979.

Family
*The Way We Never Were: American families and the
nostalgia trap* by Stephanie Coontz, 1992.
Worlds of Pain: life in the working-class family by Lillian
Rubin, 1976.
Delta Wedding by Eudora Welty, 1946.
One-Hundred Years of Solitude by Gabriel Marquez, 1970.
Bastard out of Carolina by Dorothy Allison, 1992.
The Shadow Man by Mary Gordon, 1996.

The West
Crazy Horse, the strange man of the Oglalas by Mari
Sandoz, 1942.
The Virginian by Owen Wister, 1925.
Angle of Repose by Wallace Stegner, 1971.
Big Rock Candy Mountain by Wallace Stegner, 1978.
The American West as Living Space by Wallace Stegner,
1987.
The Nine Nations of North America by Joel Garreau,
1981.
Wyoming: A Bicentennial History by T.A. Larson, 1977.

Women

How I Grew by Mary McCarthy, 1987.

Intellectual Memoirs by Mary McCarthy, 1992.

Between Friends: the correspondence of Hannah Arendt and Mary McCarthy, 1995.

Margaret Sanger, An Autobiography, 1938.

Nobody said not to go: the life, loves, and adventures of Emily Hahn by Ken Cuthbertson, 1998.

Times and Places by Emily Hahn, 1970.

Women Who Run With the Wolves by Clarissa Pinkola Estes, 1992.

An Unfinished Woman by Lillian Hellman, 1965.

Scoundrel Time by Lillian Hellman, 1976.

Memoirs of a Dutiful Daughter by Simone de Beauvoir, 1958.

The Second Sex by Simone de Beauvoir, 1952.

Birth

The American Way of Birth by Jessica Mitford, 1992.

A Midwife's Tale: the life of Martha Ballard, based on her diary by Laurel Thatcher Ulrich, 1990.

U.S. History

A People's History of the U.S. by Howard Zinn, 2001.

The People's Almanac edited by David Wallechinsky and Irving Wallace, 1981.

Middletown by Robert S. and Helen Lynd of Columbia University who surveyed the town of Muncie, Indiana and substantiated the tendencies toward conformity in U.S. society, 1929.

Only Yesterday, an informal history of the 1920s by Frederick Lewis Allen, 1931.

Burning of the Marriage Hat
Order Form

Fax orders:	415-661-4542
E-mail orders:	orders@burningofthemarriagehat.com
Telephone orders:	1-866-WindWomen (1-866-946-3966)
Postal orders:	Wind Women Press
	P.O. Box 1918P12
	San Francisco, CA 94119 USA
Online orders:	www.burningofthemarriagehat.com

First name: _____

Last name: _____

Company name: _____

Street address: _____

City:_____State:_____Zip: _____

Telephone: (____) _____

e-mail address: _____

Shipping address: _____

City:_____State:_____Zip: _____

Total books ordered: _____@$14.95 each $ _____
Sales tax: $ _____
   8.50% to California addresses $ _____
Shipping & Handling (per location): $ _____
   $4.75 for the first book
   $2.00 each additional book
TOTAL enclosed: $ _____

PAYMENT:
___Check or money order payable to: Wind Women Press
___Credit Card: ____Visa ____MasterCard

Card number: _____

Name on card: _____

Signature:_____ Exp. Date ___/___